# Praise for Marci Blackman and *Tradition*

The very best of writing transports through vividly drawn characters and an attention to detail that renders every scene not only believable, but compelling. *Tradition* is such writing. The author, Marci Blackman, is invisible here: there is only the story and we are seized by it and its voices soon after we have heard the very first word, "Dead." Arresting, *Tradition* deftly conveys us through space, memory and meaning. This is a novel to be savored and remembered, much as we do *Their Eyes Were Watching God*. Brilliant.

—G. Winston James, author of *Shaming the Devil*

"Grit. Red earth. Southern spices. Tight like a shot gun house/filled with characters that live full, and hard. Flava permeates every bit of this story. Beautifully crafted. *Tradition*."

—Sharon Bridgforth, Lambda Literary Award winning Author of *the bull-jean stories*, RedBone Press

Tradition

Fiction

Marci Blackman

Published by Water Street Press
Healdsburg, California

Water Street Press paperback edition published May 2013

Cover art by Sally Eckhoff
Interior design by Typeflow

Produced in the USA

ISBN-13: 978-1-62134-110-9

# tradition

## marci blackman

Water
street
press

For the sisters:

Martha, Leah, Ruth, Cora, Patty
Virginia, Georgia, Maryland and Lanthe

**tra·di·tion:**

the force exerted by the
past upon the present.

*Webster's Third New*
*International Dictionary*

# book one

# may 6, 2007

"Dead," is all he can get out of her.

"Finest still around?" he asks.

"Finest Coon's dead. Been dead."

Thunder rolls after the haze in the lazy gray sky. Bulldozers plow through the walls of the house next door. Through the walls. Through the floorboards. The probated tables and chairs. It feels like they're plowing through his head.

He stands with his back to her. Stooped. Head bent. Staring at the light. Pale and flickering in an otherwise empty refrigerator, save the half stick of butter and the moldy loaf of bread hiding the stale box of baking soda in the back. The same hungry position he assumed sixty years before, the morning he left.

It had been full then. The refrigerator. No light nor state-of-the-art cooling system. Just a box and a block of ice. Melting on a tray on the bottom. And he was scared. Rummaging through the dark as if he were robbing the place.

He is still scared, and you *were* robbing the place, he thinks.

While the others slept he stuffed into a gunny sack a left-over quarter of ham, two thick wedges of banana cream pie, a can of beer and a handful of dinner rolls. This morning he'll be lucky if he can find a still-good center in a long-since-turned loaf of bread. Wonder Bread. White bread.

He removes the loaf and butter from the fridge then opens and closes the drawers and cabinets until he locates a knife.

"Since when?" he asks, slicing off the molded crusts.

"Nineteen ninety."

He searches the shelves in the pantry for a forgotten jar of jam. Or, even better, a forsaken bottle of maple syrup tucked back in a corner in the dark somewhere, turned to sugar no doubt by now. Instead, among the old yellowed newspapers and screwdrivers and boxes of nails, plastic and paper bags, heating pads, he finds a dust-covered box of matches and an old tin cookie sheet.

"Nineteen ninety?" he says, kneeling down to light the oven. His knees crack and pop as he rises. Dust and paint chips from the ceiling sprinkle the stovetop. He glances through the window at the bulldozers, then places the bread-centers on the cookie sheet and slides it into the oven.

"Ninety-five. Ninety-nine," she answers. "What difference do it make? He's dead."

Her hands shake as she nurses a long slow sip from her coffee mug.

He pulls out a chair and sits across from her at the table.

Grease cakes the wall, yellowed behind her head. Her hands hold tight to the coffee mug. Her eyes are distant.

He watches her.

"How?" he asks.

"How what?"

"How did he die?"

She licks and gums her lips before answering. "Rotted to the quick," she says. "Most likely." Then sips from her mug and swallows. "Just like that big ol' house he was livin' in."

"What big ol' house?"

"Whutchacallit's."

"Whutchacallit's?"

"You know, whosit's, over on North Hill."

"The *Simler* place?"

"Mmm hmm. What's-his-name give it to him."

"Who?"

"Or maybe it was the widow."

"Beatrice?"

"Mmm hmm."

He raises his voice to compete with the bulldozers. "What you mean, give it to him?"

"What?"

"I say what you mean, give it to him?"

"Willed it to him!" she hollers. "From her deathbed!"

It was a Sunday, she remembers. Nineteen seventy-three. She knows it was a Sunday because she was coming out of Caleb's market and she only ever went to Caleb's on Sundays. She knows it was nineteen seventy-three because it was the year before the big tornado and all that Watergate madness was going on and all week long they interrupted her stories on the television. "I was coming out of Caleb's," she says. Arms spilling over with grocery bags, when all of a sudden white folks started scrambling everywhere. Ducking in and out of doorways to spread the news like they were running for cover. As though Negroes had suddenly donned bed sheets and taken to burning crosses. It was bad enough the widow of the richest man in the county called a colored man to her deathbed instead of her two grieving sons. But for that colored man to turn out to be Finest Coon was worse than blasphemy. "Must be true what they say," she says, eyes lighting up over the rim of her coffee mug as she laughs. "Craziness runs in the blood."

*Finest Coon.*

She spits out his name as if he is some kind of monster. Turns it on her tongue and pushes it through her partial the way she might an evil upon which she is disgusted to look. A predator. Or child molester. Some other kind of vermin little kids are warned to avoid, instead of the orphan boy she took into her home.

Sixty years gone and little has changed between them. Her drinking is new. As are the bulldozers. The lines in both their faces more pronounced. The silver in their hair. And words are searched for a little longer now. But everything

else—including her deep-seated hatred of Finest Coon—
has been engraved and fossilized in stone, and what he has
never understood, not as a boy, nor in all the years since, was
if she hated Finest so much, why she ever bothered to save
his life?

"When'd you get the Edsel?" he says to her. He nods his
head toward the window at the car parked on the side of the
house.

"Sojourner bought it for me. 'Fore she went to California."

He whistles and shakes his head. "California, huh?"

She nods.

"She married?"

She stares through the window and drinks.

Images of his years in the Bay shuffle before his eyes like
decks of Polaroids with handwritten captions locating each
in place and time. "The Shipyards, 1942." "Dizzy at Jimbo's,
1950." He shakes his head again.

"Is it still runnin'?" he says, finally.

"What?"

"The Edsel."

"Last time I drove it, it was." She sips from her mug.

"When was that?"

"Nineteen ninety-two."

"Shit!"

He looks at her and laughs.

"Ninety-two? How the hell you know it's still runnin'
then?"

"Watch your mouth!" she says to him then sniffs at the
air and coughs, suddenly. Glances at the stove, smoking and

rattling from the vibration of the bulldozers, and waves her hand back and forth in front of her face like a wilted fan.

"You tryin' to eat that crustless bread?" she hollers. "Or just seein' how black you can burn it?"

Smoke sweeps into the room as he rescues the cookie sheet from the oven. The smell of something charred.

"Sojourner drives it," she says, as he scrapes the blackened bread-tops into the sink.

"And when was So here last?"

"Christmas, maybe. Thanksgiving. One a them two."

He places the salvaged centers on a plate and sits at the table to butter them.

"Got gas in it?" he says.

She looks at him. The first time all morning.

"Why you so concerned about my car?"

"I need to borrow it a minute."

"Ha!" she says.

"Just for a minute," he says.

"That what you come back here for? Steal my car like you stole my food?"

"Be back in an hour," he says.

"For what?"

He looks at her. "Grocery store," he lies. Burnt cardboard toast sticks to the roof of his mouth as he chews. "Put some-thing in your icebox 'sides a broken light and a bad loaf of bread."

"Can you drive?"

"'Course I can drive."

"Can you see?"

He picks up another center of toast and bites into it then looks away from her toward the window. Chews, swallows then looks back at her without answering.

"You got a license?" she says.

"Can I borrow the car or not?"

She stares at him awhile then drinks again. A limp drunken hand waves him toward the kitchen door.

"Key's on the rack," she says.

He stands and slips into his jacket and reaches for the keys. The chimes ring as he turns the knob and pulls it toward him.

"Wait," she hollers as he steps outside.

The bulldozers are quiet.

He stops.

She puts down the coffee mug and pushes back from the table. Struggles into her walker and maneuvers it over to the silverware drawer and turns her back to him. When she faces him again she has twenty-five dollars gripped between her hand and the walker. She drops it on the table and sits back down in her chair.

"Bring me a bottle," she says without looking at him. "The big one. Number seven. And a lottery ticket. A Pick Three. Six ways. Backed up."


"BONE DRY," SAYS the man who stopped to help him. "No pun intended," he adds. His stomach rolls and gurgles like it's filled with water as he laughs and explains himself. "*Bone dry?*" he says. "Git it?" The middles of his words stretching on for miles before easing into the finish like cars into drive-ways at the end of a long Sunday drive, lurching them back into the good ol' boy time he remembers. Slow time. Deliberately slow. Just so everybody knows what's what time, with vast expanses of silence between like sleeping landscapes. Not quite southern, but southern enough. "It's what they call this road runs through here," he says. "The Bone? The Devil's Backbone? 'Counta all the treacherous curves it's got?"

He looks at the man and nods his head and laughs a little to be polite, not sure which is making him more uncomfortable: the fact that the man is helping him, or how easily, after just one day home, he has slipped back into place.

"You know right back there, 'cross from that clearing, there used to be a grist mill?" the man says.

He does not answer that he used to work there.

The man points to a patch of earth backed up against a gorge in the middle of a stand of river birches and oak trees and a red leaf maple outlined by the remnants of a stone foundation that once supported a building. "County condemned it a few years back and finally got around to tearing it down."

He watches as the man turns and labors to the back of his truck.

"Soon as the new development's finished," he hollers, breathless, over his shoulder, "all along through here gonna be prime real estate. 'Course, we're gonna have to clear it first, but it'll be worth it," he says. "Specially if we can get a decent price on the lumber."

The man returns to the Edsel holding a gas can cradled against his belly like a baby. "Don't believe I caught your name," he says. He balances the can against the grill of the Edsel and extends his hand, his fingers stretched and bloated like sausages. The smell of gasoline turning the air.

"Gus," he says to the man.

The man wraps his fingers around his hand and holds it there while he looks at him. "Dixon," he says in turn. "But everybody 'round here calls me Dix."

Gus nods and pulls his hand away.

"Hell of a place to run out of gas, Gus. Take a wrong turn or somethin'?"

"Used to live here," he says. "Came back to visit my sister."

Dix stops and looks at him then turns his back to him and pulls up the spout on the gas can and inserts the nozzle into the Edsel's tank then stops again and smiles. "This is that Weesfree woman's car. Mabel, isn't it?"

Gus nods.

"Well, I'll be damned! I didn't know she had a brother. Didn't know she had anybody, 'cept that lady comes by from time to time." He pauses for a minute and looks toward the clearing. "White lady," he says, then turns back to the car and tilts the butt of the gas can high in the air and shakes it.

"My niece," says Gus.

"Your niece?"

Dix looks at him then back at the gas can. "Well, I'll be damned. Thought she was a social worker," he says.

Gus stands there and watches him. The trees creaking and swaying around them in the wind, the urge to run rushing at him like waves crashing.

Dix replaces the nozzle and recaps the tank and the gas can.

"Careful if I was you. Drivin' this road," he says. "Last accident out this way they had to bring out the Jaws o' Life."

Gus looks at him. "How much do I owe you?" he says and reaches in his pocket for the twenty-five dollars Mabel gave him.

"Save it for the station," says Dix. "If ya make it that far. Didn't give ya but a couple dollars worth. Hell," he drops the hood of the Edsel and presses it down with the balls of his hands until it clicks. "This hog?" he says. "Use that up 'fore you get there. Maybe if you're lucky you can coast the last couple of blocks."


IF HE SQUINTS he can just make out the house. An old man's squint, fuzzy, not so reliable. But the fact that he can see any part of it at all from here tells him that the whole place lies in ruin. That and the high grass swallowing the fields and most of the lane. He is parked in front of the gate, facing the farm. What's left of it. The barn is gone altogether. As are the trees. He sits there and squints awhile longer and thinks he might see something moving alongside the house and soon he can hear him. Laughing. That wheezy guttural laugh that pained the listener almost as much as it did Finest and now there are other people about. A handful or so.

Their backs to him. Huddled in front of the gate, the "S" at the top shining like new in the rain and the trees are back. The Great Wall of them the property line around. Sycamore and oak, walnut and pine, spruce and dogwood. Shielding the house like a fortress. He closes his eyes and rubs them a bit and wipes his hand over his face and stretches his neck side to side and when he opens them again Finest is still laughing but the people—onlookers, they called them—have gone and the sky is gray and lazy again. Thunder lolling after the haze. The Simler farm and gate returned to ruin.

He steps from the car and leans against the grill and fingers the length of rope in his pocket, tying it into a slip knot as he searches for a path through the towering grass. He's no longer sure what's real anymore. Hasn't been for years. The woman sitting next to him on the bus or the Ellington tune suddenly stuck in his head. They've been stalking him like this since he left. Because that's what old memories do. They stalk. Especially those we've neglected to bury. Like film trailers, whether we want to or not, the talented ones prod and tease us into going to see the movie. Out of nowhere they appear as people, shadows, a whiff of something. A taste we can't quite place and though he's no longer surprised when they sneak up on him, and has ceased trying to outrun them or hide, when he was younger, at least he could tell them apart from what was happening in the moment.

Aches and pains ain't shit, he thinks, the real bitch about growing old is losing the ability to distinguish.

*They are racing. They are always racing. Or at least Finest is always running and Gus is always trying to keep from being left behind.*

*"How come we can't walk sometimes?" he hollers up ahead.*

*Finest keeps running. Wheezing and running. The wheezing discordant to his smooth powerful strides.*

*This morning they race because Mabel kicked them out of the house.*

*Finest hasn't bathed in nearly a year. Not since Mabel removed the last of the bandages. After that time, the first she was able to dunk his head under the water, he flat out refused. By the time July rolled around and the temperatures soared to triple digits, the air wet and thick as molasses, his funk had been baked and steamed into every porous surface in the house.*

*"You stink!" Mabel finally yelled at him when he strolled into the kitchen in his wife-beater this morning.*

*Finest stopped in front of her and raised his arms in the air then blew the stink from his armpits back into her face like he was stoking a fire.*

*Next thing Gus knew they were running and for awhile Mabel was running after them with a carving knife in her hand hollering something they were too far ahead to hear. They dropped her when they reached the turn-off to The Bone.*

*Bees and horseflies blind and drunk on humidity bounce off their chests and faces as they run. The length of The Bone to Oak Street. Oak Street to Birchwood. Birchwood to The Hill, and the onlookers clustered outside the gate.*

*Finest reaches the top first and almost collapses as they hang their heads over their knees, hacking and wheezing and sucking up air together, and some of the onlookers turn to stare at them awhile then back through the trees toward the farm.*

*"They always out here?" he asks Finest.*

*Finest wheezes and nods.*

*"What for?"*

*Finest looks at them. "Tryin' to see crazy," he says after catching his breath.*

*After awhile he turns away from them and stands up and starts laughing.*

*Gus starts laughing, too, though he doesn't know why.*

# 1930

She opens the cabinet in the Hoosier with the cups and saucers in it and takes down a drinking glass. From the icebox she removes a pitcher of water and fills the glass to the halfway point then returns the pitcher to the icebox and sets the glass on the counter next to the sink. The bottle Doc Agee handed her when she left is in the pocket of her housedress. Milk jug shaped, but miniature. The size of her hand. She reaches into her pocket, rummaging past the rags and lists and cleaning tags stuffed inside, and grasps the bottle by the neck and studies it in the rain-soaked midday light washing through the window. The pills are white and pea-shaped and remind her of the little mint candies Sister Tremble carries around in her pocketbook. She unscrews the cap and shakes a couple onto the counter next to the glass then looks through the window and dumps out the rest. From the drawer she digs out a knife. The good knife, her mother used to say, with the flat silver handle.

*When? she asked Doc Agee.*

*When it's close to the end.*

*How would she know?*

*You'll know.*

Rain. Insistent and steady as a thousand faucets. Pours onto the roof and blurs the grime caked on the outsides of the windows. The house is still and quiet save the rain and the tapping of the knife handle against the counter as she grinds the pills into powder. She does not hear Sister Tremble enter. The sodden complaint of her shoes over the loose boards in the floor as she passes through the living room. Only the disgust ebbing and flowing in the current of her voice, trailed by a plume of Prince Matchabelli and Sweet Georgia Brown, as she blows into the kitchen hollering, "Lord have mercy!" The righteous rebuke of the faithful in the presence of true evil.

Hurrying. Shielding her hands with her body. Using the blade now instead of the handle, she scrapes the pills and powder back into the bottle, leaving two tablets on the table. Screws on the cap and stuffs the bottle back into her pocket.

"Did you fix it?" says The Sister.

Mabel turns to face her.

"Ma'am?"

"Thought I heard pounding. Sounded like you were mending something."

Mabel shakes her head.

"No. Just fixin' Daddy's medicine."

Sister Tremble nods. "I swear," she says, winded slightly as she removes her bonnet and unloads her belongings onto the table. "I will never cease to be amazed at the schemes white people come up with."

She whispers the words *white people* as if they are a dreaded or fatal disease like *consumption* or *cancer. Syphilis.* Sister Tremble always whispers the words *white people,* even in passing. What Mabel has never figured out is whether she whispers them out of fear, believing that the hand of God will strike her down just for thinking on them. Or out of spite, judging the words unworthy to bear the full weight of her vocal cords.

"Mint?" she offers, sliding a small cardboard box across the table after rifling through her pocketbook.

Mabel shakes her head.

Spewing with outrage, like sinners gyrating at a revival, caught up in the Ghost and speaking in tongues, Sister Tremble mumbles to herself as she peels off the wet newspaper wrapped around the soup pot she brought over.

Mabel watches her.

Standing there. Mumbling to herself. Make-up running. Smelling like perfume and grease. She looks like something out of a vampire movie. Her milk-chocolate skin pale and pasty. Her dress clinging to her breasts and her thighs, dripping water onto the floor. The front of it stained with ham hock juice and tiny specs of fatback stuck to her sleeves and the lapel on her collar.

"A child, no less," she says, as she kicks off her shoes and dances to the stove in stockinged feet as if she is walking on hot coals. She washes her hands in the warm water basin then glances around for a towel.

Mabel hands her a rag from one of her pockets.

A white lady in Pennsylvania murdered her stepdaughter, Sister Tremble tells her. Set her on fire while she was sleeping. She had been nicknamed the Torch Killer.

"While she was sleeping!" seethes The Sister, wrenching the towel through her hands as she dances back across the floor to the table. "Did it for the money," she adds, disgusted. "Six thousand dollars. Six thousand dollars!"

Mabel watches as The Sister hurls herself around the kitchen snatching bowls and saucers from the cabinets. Spoons and hand towels from the drawers. Familiar. As if she is at home still, talking to no one and everyone in particular. Moving so fast from one injustice to the next she barely has time to take in air. As if her husband, The Pastor, is still within earshot in his private study off the church house kitchen, scribbling in his sermon book mumbling *uh huh* now and again to keep her from wondering what he's up to.

"It isn't much," she says as she lifts the lid on the soup pot. The sharp smell of vinegar cutting into the odors of hair grease and perfume. "Just greens," she adds. "From the garden. And a leftover ham hock to help 'em taste like something. A child!" she says again and bites her lip and shakes her head.

The curls she spent an hour hot-combing into her hair for this morning's service are gone. Rain-kinked and flattened, they stick to the sides of her face like the coarse wet strands of a mop. Hair grease dews the creases in her forehead and slides through the fuzz on her cheeks to her chin. Her eyes blink and widen as if she is caught between the verge of tears and the edge of wonder at the difficulty of living. She fills the bowls with greens, setting each on a saucer in the middle of the table, then collapses into the chair beside her and pushes the hair from her face. With the rag Mabel gave her to dry her hands she clears some of the fatback from her sleeves.

"Whew!" she says. "Come up out of nowhere, didn't it?"

Mabel nods.

"Practically ran the entire way." She looks through the window then down at her dress. "Lot of good it did me. You'd think," she adds, waving the rag back and forth in front of her face like a fan," with a rain like this, it would cool off some. But it seems hotter now than it was before it started."

Mabel sits at the table across from her.

The wrist on the hand fanning her face is wrapped in muslin. Every Sunday the bandage is in a different place. Sunday last it was wrapped around her knee. The Sunday before, her elbow. "Clumsy," she explained then. "Always falling down or twisting something. Pastor Tremble says I can't hold my balance to save my life."

She turns and stares for a long while down the hall. At the door closed at the end of it.

"How is he?" she says, finally.

Mabel shrugs her shoulders. "Doc Agee say it won't be much longer," she says.

Sister Tremble stares at the door. "Did I tell you The Pastor's taking up a collection?" She turns to Mabel and smiles. "To purchase a radio," she says. "Thinks a little hymn music might soothe some of the pain."

Sister Tremble studies her.

"When," she says, "are you going to cut out wearing that smock dress, child? And do something about that hair? Young girl like you. How do you ever expect to find a man? Someone to take care of you after he's gone? You and Gus Junior? You've got to fix yourself up some, honey. Make an effort. Give the young men something to look at. You know, I promised your mother…"

"Don't need no man to take care of me," says Mabel. "Been taking care of myself since Mama died."

"Don't be silly, child! Of course you do! And it's *I don't need* a *man*, *not* no *man*," she says and glances back down the hall. "How do you expect to live? Who's going to pay for it?"

Until today, she has never asked about him. Never mentioned his pain. Acknowledged that he is dying. Most days she comes and goes as if the door at the end of the hall doesn't exist. And when Mabel starts to tell her that in the last eight years the man dying in the bed behind it hasn't paid for a thing save the still whiskey Doc Agee says is killing him, Sister Tremble waves her quiet.

"I know you've been taking in wash," she says. "Cleaning here and there in some of your mother's old houses, rest her soul. But just scraping by is not the same as living. Not the same at all.

"If you don't want to think about yourself think of Gus Junior. Boy his age needs a firm hand. Someone to make him mind and go to school. Teach him how to be a man. A good man." She turns and speaks to the window. "You think you can handle him now," she says. "Now that he's small. But come a few years when he's standing here looking down on you, you'll want him to be a good man."

The rain has stopped. Sunlight peeks through the breaks in the clouds beginning to drift south. A rainbow the pale wax of crayons colors the sky.

"Well," she says after a time, "I'd better get back and get The Pastor's supper on. Put myself back together before he finishes with the Bible study. Probably scare him straight to Hades, he saw me looking like I do now."

Mabel gets up from the table and reaches into the cupboard beneath the silverware drawer and hands her the pot she brought over last week, then walks Sister Tremble to the door.

"I don't outstay my welcome, do I?" The Sister asks her.

Mabel holds the door and looks at her. "Ma'am?"

"My welcome. The Pastor hates it when I outstay my welcome."

"No, ma'am," says Mabel.


GUS STEPS UP on the milk crate and peers through the corner of the window into the kitchen. Sister Tremble is standing at the table stirring something in a pot. Mabel is watching her. Her back to him. The door at the end of the hall is closed still. These days it only opens when Mabel goes in to check on him. He steps down and tiptoes onto the porch and reaches for the bucket then tiptoes back. Checks in the window again then steals across the yard into the cemetery. Head ducked as if he is dodging bullets. From the cemetery he sprints through the woods toward the clearing. The earth is soaked with the rain. Almost mud. It collects between his toes as he runs. When he reaches the tree line he stops. Looks around and waits a few seconds before entering then crosses to the well. The pump squeaks as he works the handle and after awhile water begins to spurt into the bucket.

He is covered in house paint. When the bucket is full, as soon as he dunks his hands into it the water turns wood moss green and darkens as he rubs them together and scrubs them with dogwood leaves. The backs, the sides. His arms. Raw in spots, though in most the paint is stubborn and will only come off with turpentine.

*How come you never fight back? Mabel will ask when she sees him. It's the same question she always asks.*

*He does fight back.*

*Maybe next time then you should run.*

*That's what he did this time after hurling a rock at the back of Tommy Pettiford's head for saying that Mama killed herself because Daddy did it with a white woman and that both he and Mabel were running around with half-white blood in their veins.*

*Mama didn't kill herself. She got sick.*

*Like Daddy?*

*No.*

*What's "did it" mean?*

*Makin' a baby. And ain't nobody round here walkin' round with half-white anything.*

He refills the bucket and washes his feet, then sits there awhile letting them dry. The top half of his shirt stiff with house paint. He takes it off.

The little he remembers of her passes through his mind in seconds. The rise and fall of a body lying unconscious in a bed. The sound of her breathing. Like pigs squealing only muted. Men in white coats. The window. And even though he's still alive, of *him* he remembers even less. Always with a bottle in his hand and sitting down somewhere away from them. His chair. The back porch steps, drinking and staring off into the cemetery. Ordering him to *go on and git someplace else* whenever he sat next to him or tried to run alongside him the few times he went walking. Then he went behind the door at the end of the hall and never came out.

*Doc Agee say Daddy's dyin'*, says Mabel.

*When?*

*She shrugs her shoulders.*

*He looks at her.*

*All gotta die sometime, she says to him. Some never live past kids.*

*We goin' to a orphanage?*

*Who?*

*Cyrena Matthews went to a orphanage when her daddy died.*

*We ain't Cyrena Matthews.*

*She looks at him.*

*What? You wanna go live with a bunch a people you don't know nothin' about? You can if you want to.*

*He shakes his head and stares down the hall.*

He rinses and refills the bucket and listens to the crows caw, chasing each other through the dogwood circling the clearing. The sun, released from a veil of clouds and rain, hangs low above the tree line, casting a blood red pall on the half-light winding down the day. He picks up his shirt, walks back toward the house. Bat shadows swoop and dive in front of him, snatching insects from the sky.

SHE GRINDS UP the rest of the tablets and pours the powder into the glass. From the top of the Hoosier she reaches an unmarked bottle and adds four fingers of whiskey to the water then stirs it around with the knife. The moaning has started. It's all he does anymore. Cry out. The medicine quiets him some, but only for an hour or two.

She had not planned this. When she woke this morning she had not planned on doing anything different with her day than she had done yesterday or the day before. But when she was preparing his pain pills this afternoon just before The Sister came in and told her about the *Torch Killer*, she looked at the rain coming down outside and those two little tablets there all alone on the counter and thought *why not?* Why not make this day and all that come after different? For all of them. For Daddy. What was the sense in making him lie around in pain and excrement day to day until he finally stopped breathing? In her trying to provide some kind of comfort through it? Around the clock? In Junior living and fighting like he was already orphaned? When the outcome would be exactly the same whether it happened today or in a hundred todays? What was the point in wasting all that time?

She checks on the number of rags in her pocket and drains the last of the water from the warming basin into a bucket, then reminds herself as she carries everything down the hall to send Gus Junior for well water when he gets back.

She calls to him before she enters. "Daddy," she says. "Time for your bath."

She opens the door and enters and sets the bucket on the floor next to the bed. The glass on the floor beside the bucket, and reaches over and turns up the lamp burning on the night table. The smell of sickness and death choking the room. She pulls a rag from her pocket and submerges it into the water.

His breath is heavy and raspy. Sour. He opens his eyes and looks at her. The whites are yellow.

"Hi, Daddy."

The yellow eyes blink at her.

"Bad today?"

They blink again.

She unbuttons his nightshirt and climbs onto the bed with him and straddles his waist with her kneecaps, sliding her hands under his armpits, and she grabs hold of the bones pushing through the yellowed and pockmarked skin on the back of his shoulders and pulls him to her. To her chest and eases him into sitting.

Knees still straddled around his waist, she pulls her hands back through his armpits and around to his collarbone, working the unbuttoned nightshirt over his shoulders down the length of his arms and over his hands. Easy, she lowers him back onto the bed and fluffs his pillow.

Climbing down off the bed, she unfastens the safety pin on his diaper. Rolls him onto his side. Frees up the diaper and nightshirt. Then rolls him back as he moans, tossing the nightshirt and the diaper onto the floor next to the bucket.

Slowly then, ringing the rag over the water, starting with his face, she begins to wash. She washes his forehead and his temples. The sleep from the corners of his eyes. She washes his mouth and the crust from around his nose. His ears. Inside and behind. She washes his neck and his collarbone and his shoulders. The nappy and brittle hair on his armpits. His arms. His hands. His fingers. Underneath the nails. She washes his chest. Sunken and pockmarked. His belly and the rise in his hips. The nest of hair around his privates. The misshapen and shriveled privates themselves.

She washes his legs and the insides of his thighs. The sores on his knees and the dead flaking skin on the heels and balls of his feet, and she picks with her fingers the scabs peeling off between his toes. When she has finished washing the front side of him, she rolls him onto his stomach and washes the back.

From the drawer in his bureau she removes a clean diaper and nightshirt. Then rolls him onto his side to fasten the diaper and, easing him once more into sitting, she works the nightshirt over his arms and shoulders and buttons it.

Finally, after fluffing the pillow and making him comfortable again, she reaches for the glass of whiskey and water.

"Time for your medicine," she says to him.

He tastes the whiskey and blinks his eyes at her.

"Doc Agee say it's okay this one time," she tells him.

He looks at her and blinks.

"It's okay, Daddy," she says. "It's okay." Then presses the glass to his lips.

After he is finished she sits on the edge of the bed and waits awhile for his eyes to close and his breathing to slow. For the sleep that is not sleep to begin to take him away. When she gathers up the glass and the night shirt, the diaper and bucket, and dims the lamp and turns to leave, Gus is standing there watching her from the doorway. She looks at him awhile then rises to open the window. Outside crickets chirp and katydids sing and tree frogs call out to would-be mates across the river and somewhere in the nearby distance an owl hoots. When she turns back to face him he is gone.

# may 6, 2007

*He falls back against the headboard and pulls her down beside him so that her head rests in the crook of his armpit and he reaches for her hair. His neck burns from the scratches she left. He winces and wonders if she drew blood this time.*

*Gonna have to cut those nails, he says to her.*

*She laughs.*

*He stares at the stars painted on the ceiling. Gold against a deep purple sky. And picks out the constellations. The Dippers. Orion. The only ones he knows.*

*Knew a cat in the Bay, he tells her, used to tell time by the stars. Man, we called him.*

*Man?*

*You know, how when you greet a brother, you say, "Hey Man?" Just stuck after awhile. Never knew his real name.*

*Had tattoos all over his arms. Sleeves of them. A collar inked around his neck. Ask him what time it was and he'd drop whatever he was doing, look up at the sky awhile then go back to what he was doing again and casually mutter ten forty-seven, or thirteen past two. Cat must've been a savant or something. Always got it right within half a minute. You could bet money on it.*

*Did you?*

*You kidding? I was his barker.*

*What did he do when the sun came up?*

*Slept.*

*We had a good run going 'til he OD'd on me and landed in the morgue.*

*They lie there awhile. Silent. He looks out the window.*

*Gus?*

*Mmm hmm.*

*I've been thinking.*

*Uh oh. So early in the morning?*

*She traces the wounds on his neck with her fingers.*

*I think you should go back, she says.*

*Back? To San Francisco?*

*He sits up and looks at her. Wait a minute! You kicking me out?*

*Home, she says. I think you should go back home. To Tradition.*

*Pigeons coo on the telephone lines outside her window. Car engines rev in the street below. The workday starting. Funny how fast things change, he thinks. He hadn't even left yet and already he was calling it* her *window, when just a few minutes before it existed without ownership. He smiles.*

*What's in Tradition? he says.*

*She gets up and puts on her robe and lights a cigarette.*

*I don't know, she says to him. You never say her name. But whoever she is, she's haunting you. You were dreaming again last night.*

It wasn't so much that they didn't make it. He never truly believed he could make it with anybody. But she was the first who'd made him think, *maybe*. Maybe it was time to try. What stayed with him, what he could never relinquish, was the fact that she beat him to it. That she was the one to end it, even if she was right. There was no place for them to go, she told him. Not as long as he was tethered so taut to the past. He never saw her again after that. He thought about her. Every hour of the day at first until little by little, like all the others, time and distance distilled her to memory.

He wonders where she is now. What her life looks like now that she's nearing the end of it. The movie of it that plays on repeat in her mind. She was right about his. It took thirty more years and a whole lot of going nowhere before he could admit it. But here he is, finally. Home. At least he can say that much. Hoping to rewrite the ending.

He sticks the rope back in his pocket and walks up to the remains of the gate. The latch lies rusted through on the ground. The hinges groan and frighten a deer concealed in the grass as he opens it. A doe. He can just see the white on the underside of her tail bounding above the crest of the stalks and vanishing as she runs away. Listening for the sound of car engines accelerating up the hill behind him, when he hears none he turns and checks on the Edsel then slips off his jacket and makes his way after the doe.

No way he could just sit there and take Mabel's word for it. Not after coming this far. The Finest Coon he knew couldn't die. He would never agree to it, for one. Not unless God suddenly recalled to heaven all the cute little girls with big tight asses. And even then he wouldn't just sit there and rot away in some borrowed mansion on a hill. He would have a hand in it at least. At the very least a hand in the planning.

The deer trail follows what's left of the lane. Crumbs of gravel sprinkle the ground beneath his feet. He walks slowly, his arm out in front with his suit jacket wrapped around it up to his elbow, pushing aside obstinate spears of grass and nettles.

*Finest? he whispers in the dark. Finest? You asleep?*

*He waits.*

*Finest? he whispers again.*

*Finest stirs and clears the mucous from his throat.*

*What? he answers.*

*You asleep?*

*Not no more I ain't?*

*You ever been to Xenia?*

*Where?*

*Xenia?*

*Maybe, why?*

*Tommy Pettiford says there's this lady down there. If you give her a quarter, she'll let you do things to her.*

*What kind a things?*

*You know, touch her and stuff. Tommy says she's a friend of his daddy's. Says Lucky takes him with him sometimes when he goes to see her.*

*Finest wheezes and clears his throat.*

*You think he's tellin' the truth? says Gus.*

*No, answers Finest.*

*Can we go to Xenia sometime?*

*No, says Finest.*

*Why not?*

*You too young for that stuff.*

*No, I'm not.*

*Go back to sleep, he wheezes.*

Toward the end of the trail, the lane reappears and the house, rising up from the embers of another time, suddenly looms in front of him. Honeysuckle blankets the crumbling brick façade like a bad shag carpet. Plywood, cracked and weather-beaten, covers the doors and windows and the dormers in the roof. "Keep Out" signs plaster the plywood. On the other side of the lane a bare patch of earth and weeds lie in place of the barn.

He looks back to the house. If he's in there, he thinks, won't be much left to him.

He follows the lane around to the back to search for a way inside. Silly, he knows. Old man's folly, but he has to be sure. Plus, he needs him.

A bicycle. Ten speed. Wheels missing. Leans against the wall of the house. Cinder blocks litter and flatten the grass in the yard. Along with a toilet seat and an old television set. An empty clothesline sags between two broken pulleys attached by a pair of oxidized eyehooks to a rotting oak beam at the edge of the yard and a crumbling brick in the honeysuckled façade. He steps over the clothesline and works his way around the perimeter. Every opening is sealed with plywood. The stairwell to the cellar cobwebbed and fleeced with barbed wire. The front porch stairs gone the way of the barn and the Great Wall of trees.

He returns to the back.

"Guess you're on your own, old man," he whispers to himself. "Even if he ain't dead, he's long gone from this place."

He looks at the house.

"I sure as hell would be."

Thunder grumbles again across the darkening sky. Soft, like hunger. A hawk sails on the current as the wind picks up. Banded tail. Wings spread. The clouds have returned. It smells like rain and the grass sways back and forth like the raised hands of a Baptist choir promising to see him again "In The Sweet By and By."

He turns away from the house toward the trail to beat the rain back to the Edsel, then stops and turns back. A makeshift staircase of cinderblocks leads to the plywood covering one of the windows beside the back door. He'd missed it the first time. He climbs the steps and examines the window. The plywood is loose. He works at it until it slides off in his hands.

The glass panes in the window behind it have been kicked out. Must and mildew escape through the opening like steam from a pot, the lid just removed. He sets the board on the ground then cups his nose and mouth with his handkerchief and crawls inside.

*Hurry, whispers Finest. This way!*

*They slip in through the back while Sara's down in the cellar and run through the kitchen into the back stairwell.*

*What if somebody comes?*

*Nobody gonna come.*

*Finest leaps the stairs two at a time and hisses at him from the upper stairwell. Come on, Schoolboy!*

*Gus follows.*

*What about the doctor?*

*Been here already.*

*What about Sara? What if she brings supper up?*

*Ate already.*

*They stop at the second floor landing. Finest puts his hand on Gus's chest to quiet him, then listens awhile before scaling the rest of the stairs to the attic.*

*When they enter, Beatrice is sleeping.*

*Gus stares at her.*

*What if she wakes up?*

*Ain't gonna.*

*But what if she does?*

*Doctor give her a shot. Ol' girl be lucky if she wake up tomorrow afternoon. He stands there and stares at her a minute, then points to the nightstand and a glass of water. If she do, pills is in the drawer. Give her one and she go right back to sleep.*

*She's gonna know I'm not you.*

*Finest shakes his head and stuffs a change of clothes and flashlight into a duffle bag. One ugly colored boy same as the*

*other 'round here, he says. Only thing you got to worry about*
*is stayin' awake 'til I get back. He heads for the door then turns*
*back to face him. You feel sleep comin' on, Sara leaves a pot a cof-*
*fee on the table. Be back before sunup, he says, then disappears*
*through the door.*

He was always running off somewhere. Finest. Playing out
some scheme to pocket a little side money. Convince some
girl to look past his face and scars. His smell. And though
it never worked out the way he had hoped or planned, the
outcome, no matter how disastrous, never stopped him from
dreaming up something new to change his lot.

That was the difference between them, thinks Gus as
he feels his way through the dark into the violated kitchen.
Finest never gave up trying, whereas Gus, observing how
stacked the odds were, never saw the point in trying to
begin with.

Streams of daylight trickle through the cracks in the plywood and wash the room in shadow. Glass crunches under
his feet as he steps. Raped is the only word that comes to
him. The place has been raped. Walls gutted. Brick exposed.
Cabinets and plaster piled into mounds in the middle of
the floor like funeral pyres ready for burning. As if someone
were searching for something. A getaway stash, maybe.

He remembered the rumors about Beuford and Detroit.
That until 1933, the farm had been a front for a lucrative
rum-running business operated by his sons, and Finest once
told him of some Chicago types that used to come around.
Al Capone had even stayed here once, it was said. In his
glory days before he went to prison and got dementia. It

was his kind of hideout, thinks Gus. Back then it was, anyway. A long winding lane swallowed by a Great Wall of trees the only way in. The river running through the glen in back with a boat tie-up for a quick escape. A catwalk across the roof chimney to chimney for lookout posts and gun turrets. But rumors were like taxes in Tradition. Everyone was subject to them. The damaged and the rich more so than most. Finest and the Simlers suffered more scrutiny than the entire town combined.

"Somebody went looking for something," he says through his handkerchief. He steps around the pyres of plaster and enters the back stairwell. "Was it you, Finest? Searching for buried treasure?"

The first flight of stairs is missing. What's left of the banister looks as though it were hacked at with an axe. In the ballroom, as he enters the house proper, chunks of plaster, ash and charred pieces of banister and the missing staircase fill the grate in the fireplace. The walls in the library and dining room have been gutted like the kitchen.

Thunder claps and drums across the sky. He can hear the rain pelting against the plywood. Lightning slices flash and crisscross the room and all around him slivered reminders of his own time served in places like this flare up and go dark in the shadows. Discarded milk cartons. Beer cans, bottles. Though it has been years since anyone has strayed here. McDonalds bags. The petrified excrement in the corners, the needles and broken meth pipes tell him it was once a gallery of sorts and he wonders if Finest were still here then. If they had that in common as well.

He climbs the main staircase to the second floor, thinking of all the things he'd burned in desperation for warmth.
Mattresses. Picture frames and photographs. Fear. Hunger.
Every once in awhile someone would drag in a couple of
pallets from one of the supermarket bins and for a time they
would have a real fire.

On the second floor the plaster pyres are smaller, and in
the bedrooms the walls remain intact. He has given up hoping
to find him. Now he searches only for a sign that he was here.

"Of course," he whispers when he reaches the attic. "Got
the whole house all to yourself and where do you hole up?
Where else?"

There is more light here than on the lower floors. Save the
thick carpet of dust growing over every surface like moss in
a bog, the attic is just as he remembers it. Beatrice's bed, the
four poster, headboard flush against the center of the west
facing wall. The divan under the window and the chairs and
tea table across from it. Finest's cot and hutch in the alcove.

In the alcove, stuck behind a shelf in Finest's hutch, he
finds the sign he is looking for: a faded old Polaroid of
Sojourner, all grown up, waving goodbye in front of a Ford
station wagon loaded down with boxes and furniture. Her
hair picked out into a 'fro. A head scarf tied around it.

He backs into the center of the room and looks for a
sliver of daylight and holds the photograph under it and
stares at it awhile. Wipes away the layers of dust with his
thumb. Rain washing steady over the roof above his head,
calming the thunder.

She looks just like her, like she was cloned from her. A little heavier maybe. Unfinished in spots. Not as refined. But the mystery in the eyes, the skin color, the smile and the ability to make you fall in love with her even from a dusty photograph, a spot-on match.

He must be dead, he thinks. Has to be. No way he'd ever go away from here willingly and leave this behind. He slides the photo into his wallet then fits the wallet back into his pocket and looks around the room again. Nods his head up and down a time or two and walks to the door.

WHEN HE CRAWLS back through the window the thunder is quiet and the wind has died, but the rain is coming down in sheets, showing no sign of letting up. He takes off his jacket and holds it over his head and jogs to the grass line, then stops and turns back one more time before jogging on.

*You said before sunup. Where you been?*

*Never mind where I been. She wake up?*

*No. She sat up.*

*What you mean sat up?*

*Just sat up. One minute she was lyin' there. Next she was sittin' up. What happened to you?*

*Nothin'. She open her eyes?*

*No. She opened her mouth. Why you so late gettin' back?*

*Got held up. She say anything?*

*No. She tried to. Nothin' came out. Held up how?*

*Don't pay no mind to it. What you mean tried to?*

*Just kept openin' it and closin' it. Like this. Nothin' comin' out of it... and she sniffed me.*

*She sniff you?*

*I thought she was wakin' up so I went over to get the pills.*

*And her eyes was closed?*

*The whole time.*

*And she never said one word? You sure? Just sniff you?*

*Sniffed me.*

*You give her the pill?*

*Didn't have to. After she sniffed me, she lay back down and fell back asleep. What's that cut on your face?*

*Nothin'. After how long?*

*How long what?*

*How long 'fore she lay back down?*

*I don't know. Few minutes, maybe.*

*And that's all she did was sniff you?*

*Yeah.*

*And she been sleep ever since?*

*Never even rolled over.*

*Okay. Okay. Ain't moved. You sure? Okay. Good. You done good, Schoolboy. Might be we can do business again sometime.*

*What's that?*

*Your pay.*

*Where'd you get all that money?*

*Never mind 'bout that. Make sure nobody see you on the way out.*

HE SLOSHES FREE of the grass and crosses to the gate and opens and closes it behind him. A man he's never seen before leans against the grill of a red F-150 parked behind the Edsel. A white man. Old. Wrinkled. He has a rain parka on. The hood pulled up over the bill of a John Deere cap. And chews on a wet blade of grass. Gus stops in front of the Edsel and the man crosses to him. He stands there and watches him from under his jacket, water dripping onto his face and head.

"Gus?" he says. "Gus Weesfree?"

Gus looks at him.

"I know you?"

"Guess I am kinda hard to recognize these days. 'Specially in this getup. Sometimes when I look in the mirror I don't even recognize myself." He holds out his hand, shaking and spotted. Blue-veined. Water drips from the bill in his cap. "It's Luke," he says to him. "Luke Simler."

# 1931

On both days. The morning they find him and the day that his strength recovers to the point where he can grab hold of an axe and raise the blade above his head high enough to swing it down on a log and split it in two. The Pastor is preaching.

"How clean is thy house?"

Gus can hear him over the crunching of the leaves beneath the leather peeling and flapping on the soles of his boots as he runs through the cemetery.

"I say how cleeeean? Is thy house, Church?"

Over the sound of the bark chipping away and cascading to the ground on top of the leaves as he scales the trunk of the big climbing elm to the place where it was struck by lightning.

"Are your dishes washed? Your pots and pans scoured? Dried and put away in the cupboard?"

Over the voice in his head urging him to get down from that elm and hurry over to the sugar maple tree at the edge of the cemetery because he sees something sticking out from behind one of the headstones down there.

"Your clothes off the line? Pressed and folded? Tucked away inside the drawers of your bureau. Creased and hung on the hooks in your closet?"

He climbs down from the elm and jumps to the ground and raises his arm in the air in imitation of The Pastor. His right arm. So that it bends at the elbow. His forearm and fingers pointing to the heavens. His palm facing the congregation of unmarked headstones as if he is swearing on a Bible and he pallbearer slides. Once to the right and back to the left with a dip in the knees between each slide and a jump in the air after every fifth and he walks in that manner all the way down to the scarecrow bare branches of the sugar maple tree, spooking the birds from the back of the cemetery, reciting in perfect synchronization the sermon The Pastor preaches the mornings after he beats his wife.

"How clean is thy house, Sisters? What will the good Lord find when He comes to call on you in thy house? Will He find the curtains finished? Cleaned and mended and starched? The beds turned down? Catalog pages or newspaper a plenty in the outhouse? Or... Will He find abominations of grease and grime? Dust on the sideboards? Breadcrumbs on the countertop? Mold and mildew and jealousy hiding inside the walls? Festering in the basement?

Cobwebs and secrets huddled up and whispering in the corners? How clean is thy house, Brothers? Will there be a gleam in the eye of the glass in your windows? Or will the good Lord have to clear a circle in the dirt with the palm of His hand before He can look out on all His holiness has created? Will He glide across your floors on His anointed bare feet? Or will He risk rashes and lockjaw? Head lice? Impetigo?"

Gus sees his legs first.

"How clean is thy house, Church?" he whispers.

Sticking out from behind the headstone and splayed apart like the limbs on a rag doll. His hands crooked. Boot-blacked with soot.

"We have been remiss, Church."

The smell of smoke and fire simmers over the grave. The embers of a soul caught in limbo, unsure whether to move on to the life ahead or back to the one just left to give it another chance.

"Neglectful in our chores and responsibilities, Church."

He slides around the headstone and dips at the knees and stops behind it and stares at him. At his clothes shredded and torn from his body. The welts. Raised and angry. Beaten into his back.

It's the Coon boy.

"But it is not our house to neglect, Brothers and Sisters."

Pus and blood ooze from the side of his face and neck and the gash where his eyebrow used to be. The eye below stares bloody and lifeless at the buzzards circling the sky overhead.

Gus kicks him with the toe of his boot to see if he's dead.

"Your house does not belong to you, Church," he sings along with The Pastor. "Let the congregation say amen. Amen. Your house does not belong to you. Church."

After kicking him a second time he runs to the house to get Mabel.

He bursts through her door and drops his head over his knees and gasps for his breath and looks at her. The air rank and bloated. Hanging over the room like the ankles of people with sugar over a porch at the end of a long day. Thick and swollen.

"Get up," he gasps at her.

The glass of water and bowl of potatoes and gravy are still on the floor where he left them. The mop bucket still at the foot of the bed.

"You got to!" he yells at her.

She stares through the window watching the leaves turn from yellow to brown on the tulip poplar on the other side of the glass. The fingers on her hands clasped together in the rumbling hollow of her belly.

"I found something," he says to her. "A body."

She rolls her eyes from the window and looks at him, then rolls them back to the tree.

"The Coon boy's," he adds, then watches her.

She stares at the window and pushes her tongue through her mouth and licks and sucks her lips and blinks her eyes and flexes her foot back toward her face. Then licks and sucks her lips again and blinks her eyes and sighs. "Where?" she says to the window.

"In the cemetery. I think he's dead."

"IS HE?"

"Is he what?"

"Dead?"

She eases down on her hands and knees and rolls him over on his back and presses her ear against his chest.

"Not yet," she whispers. "But if he stay out here much longer he will be. Grab a hold of his legs."

"What you gonna do?"

"See if I can save him."

"Why?"

"What you mean why? Why not?"

Gus grabs him by the ankles and raises his feet into the air and hoists them onto his shoulders and slides and dips along behind her. He never expected she would bring him back to the house. He never expected she would get up from the bed. Let alone leave the room, step onto the porch and cross the yard. He doesn't know what he expected. But it wasn't that she would say, "Grab a hold of his legs," and drag him back to the house. Cut away the rest of his clothing and clean and salve his wounds and bandage and nurse him back to life. He just wanted to tell her he'd found a dead body. See if the news of it might move her somehow. Shock her into turning her head from the window and looking at him for a change. If he could get her to say something to him other than "Naw."

SHE SMILED WELL enough when the Missionary Ladies paraded onto the porch followed by the procession of well-wishers, arms overflowing with mourning food: Roasting pans of ham and fried chicken. Collard and turnip and mustard greens. Macaroni and cheese. Mashed potatoes and gravy. Biscuits, fresh from the oven in dishtowels, dripping with butter. Even managed a "Thank you." Followed by the requisite "You shouldn't have," when presented with the thirty-two dollars and thirteen cents and two spools of thread taken up in collection. Nodded and laughed at all the right moments through the exaggerated stories of remembrance. "I remember when your daddy…" "Sure was something your daddy…" "Your daddy ever tell you 'bout the time he dove head first into a pile a pig shit tryin' to prove he could fly?" Promised she would call. Even though everybody knew she wouldn't. If the two of them should ever need anything. Anything at all. But as soon as the Missionary Ladies left on their way and the well-wishers re-passed back into their lives, she Nawed.

"You not gonna eat?" he asked her. He stood in the middle of the doorway chewing on a leg of fried chicken, a thick slice of ham and talking all at the same time.

"Naw," she said.

"You not gettin up?" he asked her the next morning.

"Naw," she said.

"Tomorrow?"

"Naw."

When he asked her what was wrong with her she didn't even bother to respond and the house breathed and settled through her as if like his parents she were no longer in it.

"Go put some dirt in a bucket," she said to him one day. He watched her, staring at the tree outside the window.

"What bucket?"

"Mop bucket."

"What for?"

"Never mind what for."

"What you want me to do with the mop?"

She shrugged her shoulders. "Sell it."

"Sell it? A mop? You lyin'. Who gonna buy it?"

"See if Sister Tremble want it."

He watched her. She lay in the bed with her hands clasped and resting on her stomach. Her head back on the pillow facing the window. Her eyes. Unblinking. Cicadas and grasshoppers rattling in the trees and weeds outside.

"You not gonna mop no more?" he asked her.

"Naw," she said to the window.

He did as she told him, then leaned the shovel against the side of the work shed and carried the bucket back into the house into her room.

"Leave it on the floor by the window," she said to him. "And shut the door behind you."

Out in the hall he stood outside the room with his ear pressed to her door and listened. The rustling of sheets. The bed frame creaking. Floorboards moaning under feet. He heard the window slide open and fall back down then slide back open again. A shuffling and tearing of something. Newspaper, maybe, and the floorboards again followed by a straining sound. Grunting. The floorboards. More straining, followed by a sigh. The crumpling of paper. The window closing. The bed frame creaking. Sheets rustling.

He stepped away from the door and tiptoed through the hall into the kitchen and grabbed another leg of chicken, then went outside and swung his legs over the back porch. For the second night in a row he sat there swinging his legs back and forth watching the twilight lower like a curtain over the sunset and darken the house. The lamps unlit. The rugs unbeaten. Repast plates still on the table. Bats diving and swooping through the shadows.

In time she started to eat again and he would leave on the floor by the head of the bed glasses of well water and plates of whatever Sister Tremble brought over that day, which she would pick at whenever he came into the room to empty and refill the mop bucket, and everyday until this morning when the leaves started to turn and he burst into her room reeking of fire and brimstone to tell her about the Coon boy, he would slide the fresh bucket of dirt back on the floor under the window and ask her the same question. "You not gettin' up?" And every time he asked she would look out the window and stare at the tulip poplar tree and say, "Naw."

FOR THE PAST three days. Over the nine colored boys in Alabama convicted of raping two white prostitutes. The dedication of the Empire State Building in New York City as the tallest building in the world. The sentencing of Al Capone to eleven years in prison for tax evasion. The death of George Coon, The Womanizer, was all anybody talked about. Mabel lay there staring at the clover pattern on the leaves, listening to the fear laced inside the outrage in the voices carrying through her window.

"To go like that?"

"Can you imagine?"

"Set on fire by your own child in the middle of the night while you sleepin'?"

"After you birthed them and nursed them. Housed them and clothed them?"

"Worse than *white people*."

The uneasiness swallowed with the knowledge that the Coon boy had always been trouble. Capable of almost anything. But this? This kicked trouble and capable's butt. This right here was evil, pure and simple. The very definition of it. The work of the Devil himself. The Womanizer was a terrible man. The worst kind. But that was still no cause to be done like that. By your child? Nothing was cause to be done like that. And then to have the nerve to run away and hide? And all that smoke! Oh that smoke! And the smell! They would never get over that smell. Sweet. Like burning sugar.

She lay there. Listening to the voices. Thinking that the first time she saw Finest Coon and every time after he was fighting. Sometimes three or four boys all at once. Beating the living breath out of every one of them. One time he broke Junebug Marston's jaw. Junk Man's boy. In two places. Straddled and stood above him begging him to get back up. To please! Get back up! So he could break his face a third time. But Junebug just lay there crying out for Junk

Man and Finest got up and called him a sissy and left him alone. When Junk Man and the rest of the parents marched over to Justice Street to have a talk with Finest's father, The Womanizer met them at the door with a shotgun. Junebug brought it all on himself, he said. His boy never messed with anybody who didn't have it comin' and as far as he was concerned the whole goddamn town had it comin'. The way they all mocked and laughed at him all the time. Junebug Marston got exactly what he deserved. No more. No less.

Before the news of the fire, other than the fighting, Mabel had never given the Coon boy much thought. But now as she sat there listening to the voices shuddering in horror through her window, she believed she understood why he was so mean. Meanness was the logical destination for a boy forced to travel his whole life long clothed in such a ridiculous name. Finest Coon. Because even before he lost half his face in a fire, he was never what anybody would call "fine." Just the opposite. Finest Coon was ugly. He was born ugly. In the middle of the birthing something tore in his mother's womb and she started bleeding and died with the baby stuck halfway inside her, and Doc Agee had to use a pair of forceps to pull him the rest of the way out. But the pressure from the forceps caused his head to become disfigured. Top heavy. As if a small watermelon dented on either side where the forceps found their grip had been mounted to the front of it. Its weight forcing everything below his eyes. Nose. Cheekbones. Mouth. Jaw. To bunch into an angry indistinguishable mass. The Womanizer looked at the twisted-up face on his new baby boy. The blood spurting out of the mutilated womb of his wife dead on the table and he cried out in an anguish the whole town could hear. She was sorry, Doc Agee told him. So sorry. But there was just no way they could have known that she was bleeding inside. They were lucky she was able to save the boy. Regarding his face, she said, there will always be some disfigurement. But in time the muscles and bones should relax a little and ease into a less contorted shape.

They never did and at first the south side took pity on them. Empathized with the father. But for the grace of God, they whispered. But for the grace of God. The birthing of babies was a risky business. It was a miracle any woman survived the process. Let alone gave birth to a child possessing the appropriate number of all the right parts. It could have happened to any one of them, and though they glanced at each other sideways upon learning the boy's ill-given name, for the dead mother's funeral they turned out in full force. As if it had been their own mothers who'd perished in the act of giving life, spouting a litany of kind and soothing words to the grieving father and husband as well as to his monstrous son. In the receiving line single south side women offered up their services. Their soft supple bodies as cups of comfort. Chalices into which the doleful widower could woefully pour his grief. To the boy, nursing mothers yielded the milk from their breasts believing that the life-giving nutrients within them, of which he'd been so wrongfully deprived, might lessen the severity of his deformity. But once the father proved a little too anxious to accept the single women's offers and was branded a womanizer, and the boy who sucked so desperately on the nipples of yielded breasts grew into the neighborhood's worst nightmare. As swiftly as it had been given, the south side's pity was withdrawn and both father and son were regarded as lepers. Outcasts to be avoided. Ridiculed and shunned.

SHE SITS THERE on the edge of the cushion on her father's chair. Her feet tucked inside the moth-eaten slippers. Soles flat on the footrest. Knees pulled up to her chin. Watching the chest rising up and down on the boy clinging to life on her sofa, thinking about tulip poplar leaves and luck. Wondering if it is true. If he did all the things they said. Deciding as soon as she wonders that it doesn't matter. Because even if the answer is yes it could have been a mercy killing. Or the other way around. The father who tried to set the son on fire and killed himself instead. Besides. Grieving for a dead wife or not, a father who could subject such an ugly son to a lifetime of ridicule by naming him Finest was capable of even worse forms of cruelty. Deserving of any revenge the tortured and mutilated son decided to exact.

"Why you doin' it?" Gus asks her.

"Doin' what?"

"Savin' him?"

"Ain't saved him yet."

"Why you tryin' to?"

"Why you always askin' the same stupid questions over and over?"

She looks at him. The Coon boy. Lying there on the sofa. The same sheet and blanket that covered her father pulled up to his chin. The muslin strips wrapped around his head. The sound of his breath. Struggling through his lips. Dry and cracked and parted on his open mouth. The sun low in the sky. The room sketched in shadow.

The truth is she doesn't know why. She knows why it is not and it is not because she feels sorry for him. Nor does she care one way or the other whether he lives or dies. Maybe it's because he killed his father and she is tied to him somehow. Leg to leg in kinship. Not because of the killing part. Mercy killing is mercy killing. Even when the soul being put out of its misery resides in the body doing the killing instead of the one doing the dying. Sooner or later, if we live long enough on one side or the other, everybody comes to the crossroads of a mercy killing. What binds her to him is the choice each of them made before the killing. The courage to quit a road going nowhere and pick up a new one with no mind to where it is headed. If it will prove better or worse. So long as when it gets there it is someplace other than where they've been.

A strange thing happened at her father's funeral. When it was time to get up from the church pews and walk the length of the aisle and line up behind the pallbearers to escort the casket to the cemetery, her legs stopped working. Twice she stumbled and fell before The Colonel scooped her up off the ground and carried her in his arms the rest of the way. At the interment ceremony after The Pastor pronounced ashes to ashes and dust to dust and The

Colonel ferried her to the gravesite to throw the first fistful of dirt on the coffin, her hands were locked in the position in which they had been frozen the entire time The Pastor was delivering the Eulogy. Fingers rigid. Extended and spread apart. Palms flattened against her thighs as if she were in trouble. Awaiting punishment. And she was incapable of making the fist necessary to throw the dirt, and at the repast, though she knew from experience that the people talking to her and patting the backs of her locked and frozen hands were offering their condolences, she recognized no meaning nor order to the jumble of pops and ticks and hisses and suckles clucking out of their mouths. One by one it seemed the parts of her body echoed the "No!" she had hollered when she crushed up a jarful of pills and fed them to her already-dying father. No. To keeping folks alive just to preserve them for the grave. No. To following caskets and pallbearers into cemeteries. No. To dirt-throwing rituals and collection plates of sympathy. No. To keeping to the same old dead-end road. So she lay down. She smiled and nodded and laughed until the well-wishers condoled themselves through the door and back into their own lives, and then she asked Junior to help her to her feet and down to the end of the hall where she kicked off her shoes into the room where her parents once handled their business and got out of her funeral clothes and back into her housedress and crawled into the bed in which the old road had been conceived and she lay there and she waited for the new one.

FOR FINEST THE new road began as a blessing. The heat more than the flames so damaged his face that everyone seemed to forget about the original deformity. They never allowed themselves to go so far as pity. But after the fire it was agreed. The disparagement of Finest Coon was no longer necessary. He had received punishment enough, they whispered to each other in private. Who would have thought that a boy that ugly could be made any uglier? Besides, they reasoned, if he could do such a thing to his own flesh and blood, what might he be willing to do to them? So they left him alone. And he was grateful for it. People still stared when they passed him in the street. But people will always stare. It is our nature.

HE OPENS HIS eyes and blinks into focus the ceiling and the molding on the walls framing the smile on the blurred half face of Mabel Weesfree's little brother. Fix-it Man's boy. Looking down on him.

"You awake!"

He closes his eyes and opens them again and looks at the ceiling and the moldings, then back at the little brother and back to the ceiling and breathes. His breath whistling through his throat, anxious in coming. He can see out of only one eye. The left. Something is blocking or covering the right. He pulls his hand from under the blanket and winces at the pellets of pain searing like buckshot up through his side, into his shoulder, the muscles in his neck.

He touches and traces with the tips of his fingers the wide strips of muslin wrapped around his head and face.

"Don't," yells the little brother. "My sister say not to."

"What's wrong with me?" he asks. But nothing comes out. Nothing but the same broken and strangled whistling he hears when he breathes only louder and he opens his mouth again and asks the question a second time. Slower. Pushing and pulling the words up through his throat and out past his lips like a baby refusing to be born. "What's wrong with me?" he screams and still, no sound. Save the broken and strangled whistling.

"You can't talk," says the little brother. "Your throat got burned and closed up on ya."

"What you mean burned?"

"I told you. You can't talk. My sister say you might not be able to no more."

He pushes the sheet and blanket down to his waist and opens his mouth and whistles through the searing jolts of pain and tries to sit up and swing his legs over the edge of the sofa, intending to get to his feet and find his clothes and get the hell out of there, and he whistles and whistles and whistles again and again until he falls back down on the pillows on the sofa. Sweat dripping from the bandage-free side of his face. Pellets burning through his ribs and his head like fire.

He opens his eyes and stares into the dark and breathes and whistles and listens to the voices. Loud. Fighting with each other in another part of the house. The air cool and dry.

"Can't leave you alone for two seconds without somethin' gettin' broke or burnt?"

"I'm tellin' you. He opened his eyes and everything."

"Well he ain't now, is he?"

He braces the back and the side of the sofa with his hands and stiffens his arms and waits and whistles through the pellets and tries to sit up again. This time managing to slide his left calf over the edge of the cushions all the way up to the bend in his knee and dangle his foot just above the floor before his arms buckle and the pellets sink deeper into his flesh and he falls back down onto the pillows again.

"No. You cannot go ask him if he did it. How many times I gotta tell you. It don't matter. If he want to tell you on his own someday, that's his business. But the last thing he need right now is you up in his face askin' all kinda stupid questions."

THIS TIME THERE are two faces. A whole one leaning over him on the left and half of one hovering on the right. Foreheads touching.

He blinks at them.

"Hey there, Finest!" says the one on the left.

It's the sister. She smiles at him as if they are standing in line at the market. As if she has just looked up from calculating in her head the cost of her purchases and is surprised but pleased to see him there.

"It's me, Mabel," she says. "For a minute there we didn't think you was gonna make it." She steps back away from him and places a soup pan with steam rising over the top and washrags draped around the rim on the table she's drug around from the end of the sofa. Next to the pan she lays a rusted old pair of scissors and a canning jar filled with something that looks like the creek water he steals sips of when his father is sleeping.

The half face of the little brother disappears from view then reappears whole next to the sister on the left, gripping the wooden handle of a mop bucket containing a brown and curdling paste. The little brother stands there staring down at it. The paste. Holding his breath. In the daylight spilling through the window their images are clearer now. Behind them he can see a chair and a footrest. A rocking chair rocking and a side table turned at an angle to it. The entrance to the kitchen. The china cabinet.

"What happened to me?" he whistles at her.

"See. Told you he was tryin' to talk."

"Shut up!"

She unscrews the lid from the canning jar and lowers it down to his mouth. "Drink some of this," she says then pulls the jar away before he has a chance to sip from it and shakes it in front of his eye. His good eye so that he can see the little white flecks of powder sloshing and dissolving and settling in the bottom of it, then lowers it back to his mouth. "Slow," she orders. "Small sips. Gonna burn goin' down.

"Inhalin' all that smoke," she says as he sips and whistles between swallows. "Caused your throat to swell. Took some of your air away. Your voice and your smell, too, I expect. Might not get 'em back."

He sips on the creek water and whistles and looks at her and blinks and fluid fills and spills from his eye and burns and rolls down his cheek as she speaks.

"You was in a fire," she tells him and he lies there and watches her. Cutting jagged strips of muslin with the rusted pair of the scissors. "Your house burned down with your daddy inside it. Folks think you the one set it on fire. But Sheriff Newsome say he can't prove nothin'. Can't or won't."

He looks at her and blinks.

"You was in the cemetery three days when we found you. Today makes seven since you been here. Sleep the whole time. Got to cut off these bandages now," she says. "Keep sippin' on that medicine. It'll help with the pain. If it get to be too much, hold tight to Junior's hand. And if that don't work." She stops and stares at the empty rocking chair rocking in the corner, then turns back to the sofa and shrugs her shoulders and with her eyes fixed on the wall just beyond his head she says, "Think of somethin' else."

The little brother sets the bucket of paste on the floor and steps up to the sofa beside the sister and holds out his hand.

The first time his father took him hunting he was five years old. He had never taken him anywhere before. He stood in the doorway with his jacket on. The one with all the pockets. His shotgun slung over his shoulder. His night lamp swinging in his hand. "Get your clothes on," he said then stood there and lit a cigarette and smoked and watched him while he dressed.

It was dark out and cold. The leaves gone from the trees. The ground hard as limestone. They were checking the traps his father put out the day before and they walked. One behind the other. Father first, then son. Twigs snapping under his feet, over the sticks and branches felled onto the rock hard soil. Breath clouding in puffs in front of his face as he trailed along behind. Tying ropes gripped in his hands. Shoved inside the pockets of his jacket.

"Probly won't need it," his father said of the gun. "But a Negro alone in the woods can never be too careful." He was hoping for rabbit, he said. Possum. Raccoon. Though he would settle for whatever he got. Long as he could do something with the hide and stew some part of the flesh. Weasel. Skunk. Anything.

But the traps were empty. All except the last, and the first two were sprung yet held nothing captive. His father cursed and kicked at the ground with the toe of his boot, leaving a dimple in the earth there. He kicked at the traps and slid the gun off his shoulder and crouched on the ground like a cat, holding the night lamp out in front of him. Scanning the dark tangle of woods surrounding them for signs of movement. His face. Glowing in the backdraft of light from the lamp. The barrel of the shotgun aimed as if he were planning to stab somebody. A crow cawed and swooped after another crow through the tangle of tree branches, wrangling with each other above their heads. A barred owl hooted. The air laced with the smoke from a cook stove. The wind. Stirring as if it might snow. His father stood and swung the shotgun back over his shoulder and thrust the lamp in front of him in place of the gun barrel and turned and said, "Let's go." And Finest followed behind him, running at times to keep up. Until they were deep into the woods and his father stopped and squatted and cursed again and dropped to his knees on the ground in front of the last trap, staring at nothing he had hoped for. Not possum. Not rabbit. Not weasel. Not raccoon. Not even skunk. But dog. Somebody's hound. Twisted on his side. Blood saturating the fur around the wounds from where the worn iron teeth on the jaws of the trap punctured his skull. His belly rising up and down as though he were panting with thirst. Legs twitching as if he were dreaming. It was never clear how or why the dog got his head down so low to the ground to trigger the trap. Nor why his owner left him there to bleed to death instead of ending his misery. But for the second time that morning, after smoking a cigarette and watching him dress, his father swung from his shoulder the shotgun he wasn't supposed to need and scanned once more the shadows in the naked woods for movement. When he was satisfied no one was watching, his father said, "Hold this," and held the night lamp behind him and Finest took it and watched him as he placed the mouth of the gun barrel against the saturated and punctured skull of the dog and pulled the trigger.

All that morning and the rest of the day into the darkness of the night and the morning of the day following, he heard that shot. He heard it as they marched back through the woods in silence. Daybreak waking. Peeking hesitant over the frayed blanket of treetops to the east. Dragging behind him by its legs, the hound on the end of one of the tying ropes. He heard it when they waded across the river and returned to the house and his father put his shotgun away and took out his knife and wiped clean the blade and cut through the hide down the center of the belly from the breastbone to the tail, scraping the guts and the organs into a wash pail. The heart. The lungs. The spleen. Tasted it in the bile in the vomit gushing into his throat from the smell. Erupting from his mouth like a geyser. He heard it through breakfast, through the frying of the eggs and the buttering of the bread. The washing of the dishes after. The sweeping of the floors and the porch. In the setting of the table, in the chewing and swallowing of the stewed and leathery hound meat his father slopped on his plate for supper and he heard it in his sleep, folded into his dreams. The memory of it. The shot rebounding off the shadows of the trees. Hammering back into his ears. The rise and fall of the belly. The legs twitching. The dark and the light. Suddenly gone from the eyes. Playing over and over like newsreel footage at the beginning of a picture show.

Head propped up on the Fix-it Man's sofa, he lies there, pellets burning, and squeezes hold of the little brother's hand while the sister cuts and peels away the muslin stuck to the burns on the side of his face and head. Blinking and whistling between burning sips of creek water. Thinking of the legs twitching on that hound. Wishing that instead of a pair of rusted scissors against his head, the Fix-it Man's daughter held the barrel of a gun.

"IT'S SUPPOSED TO be cow dung," she says of the paste curdling in the bucket. "Cow dung. Cod liver oil and spit." She dips a strip of muslin into the paste and drains it through her fingers like a shirt wet from washing through the rollers on a scrub board. Smoothes it over his eye and the bridge of his flattened nose, then grabs another strip of muslin and dips and squeezes and pastes it to the side of his head. "Closest cows is over at the Simlers," she says and she dips and squeezes and pastes until his head and the right side of his face and his neck are lathered in muslin. "North side. Wasn't no time. Had to make do with what I had around the house."

It wasn't hard to figure out what "around the house" meant, with the little brother looking at him and shaking his head and wrinkling up his nose the way he was.

"Mama used to use it to cool the skin and draw out infection," she says and she leans over him, over his face. Arms and hands working dry layers of cloth over the wet strips pasted around his head.

Her voice is far away now. Wobbly. As if she crawled into the jar in his hands and is talking to him from under the creek water and he has to strain to make out the words bubbling up to the surface from the depths of her mouth. He whistles still when he breathes and whenever he tries to speak, and his eye still blinks and cries when he drinks. But the pain seems to have followed the trail of her voice into the creek water, and though a fire still burns when he lifts his arm and raises his head, it is a slow burn. Taking its time like the voice to bubble to the surface.

"Too soon to tell if it's doin' any good," she says. "I only ever saw Mama use it on stove burns."

The following days pass in a haze of sleep and half-sleep and pills crushed into powder. Doctored into creek water. The sister floating in and out of the room and back in again. Rolling him. Turning him and changing the muslin. His undershorts and bedding. The face of the little brother staring at him every time he opens his eyes. But if asked at some point when she decided the muslin wraps were no longer necessary and switched to rubbing aloe on his burns instead of her own shit, he could not say. Nor could he say with any certainty when he started eating again. Smelling. Making trips with a walking stick to the outhouse to relieve himself. Or when his voice came back and his sight returned and the itching started and she was forced to tie his hands behind his back with a piece of clothesline when he slept at night to keep him from scratching out his eye and blinding himself all over again.

HE WAITS FOR the little brother to place the log on the stump then raises the axe in the air and brings it back down. The wood splitting in time with the beat of the sermon drumming away in the background.

"People say you the Devil," says the little brother.

He waits. Then raises the axe and brings it back down. Waits. Raises the axe and brings it down.

"Are you?"

"Am I what?"

"The Devil."

"That's what they say," he says and he clears his throat several times before raising the axe above his head and slicing it through the log.

He is not yet used to his new voice. The scraping and scratching of it. As if he is sawing through two-by-fours or filing the edge down on the rim of a pipe, and the way that it catches in his throat. Always as if it is snagged on something. A nail or a broken piece of glass. Something jagged.

The little brother stacks the splits on the woodpile and places another log on the stump.

"They say you killed your daddy."

"Who they?"

"Everybody."

He looks off into the distance through the cold and naked branches on the trees in the cemetery and stands there. Listening to the far-off voice of The Pastor, and he imagines himself with horns and smoke coming out of his ears. Hogtied and squirming on the floor between the pews and the pulpit in the church beyond. The Devil burning alive on the pyre. The congregation on its feet. Eyes closed. Hands raised. Heads shaking and nodding. And mouths howling Amen into the chill of sanctified winter air burning up the room.

"You think I'm the Devil?" he says and he clears his throat.

The little brother sets another log on the stump and shrugs his shoulders.

Finest raises the axe head and brings it down. "Your sister think I'm the Devil?"

"No. She say you just a boy. Like me."

Raises it and brings it down. "She think I killed my daddy?"

"She say it don't matter. Say everybody gotta die sometime."

"Why she let me live?"

"Cuz you the new road."

He lets the axe head fall and rest on the ground and leans on the handle and looks at him.

"The new what?"

"That's what she call you. Her new road."

"Road?"

The little brother nods.

"What kinda road?"

The little brother shrugs his shoulders.

He turns from the stump and stares at the house and sees her through the kitchen window, moving back and forth between the sink and the icebox. The icebox into the pantry closet.

The little brother places another log on the stump.

"You miss him?" he says.

"Who?"

"Your daddy."

He waits until she reappears at the sink in front of the window and looks at her, then turns and plants his feet in front of the stump again and raises the axe high above his head and grunts. Throat snagging. Back arching. Voice scratching out the word "Sometimes" as he brings it down.

# may 6, 2007

When he reaches the turnoff he slows and stops and glances again at the apparition sitting beside him in the passenger seat, then rotates the steering wheel twice to the left and once to the right. The long nose of the Edsel dipping. Listing. Descending onto The Bone. Half-light settling like fog in the gaps between the birch trees lining the road.

*What's wrong with him?* he asked Luke.

*Doc Rawlins said it was some kind of dementia. Somethin' to do with the veins.*

*He sat there. Glancing back and forth between the eyes of the white man who was speaking. Murky. Capsized in waves. Violent folds and wrinkles breaking the length of his face into tide pools gathered beneath his chin. And the black man seated next to him. A ghost of a man. Pasty. Bones showing through his skin.*

*Reduced and evaporated like gravy meat after the water boils off.*
*Recognizing neither.*

*Can he talk? he asked him.*

*Ain't since I got to him. But the doc don't think it's the*
*dementia. Says he don't know what's causin' it. Can I get you*
*somethin' to drink? Ice water or punch or somethin'?*

The Edsel rocks to the right then down to the left and
up and back and to the right again, rising and falling and
leaning. Deer leaping into the headlights. The tarmac rolling and disappearing beneath the tires like a conveyor belt.

He steps on the brake to let the deer pass and the ghost
man he doesn't recognize, safety belt harnessed around his
waist, pitches forward slightly then back against the seatback and sits there. Rigid. Hands clasped around the cane in
his lap. Staring through the windshield as if it is a portal. As
if any minute now he expects the glass to vibrate and a giant
hand, clawed like the talon of a bird, to reach through the
opening and snatch him back to the underworld.

*I don't understand.*

*Don't much either, said Luke. Daddy wasn't in the ground*
*one day 'fore she run us off the place. Fired the whole damn*
*house 'cept Sara and sold all the livestock. Pigs. Cattle. Gave*
*away everything else. Everything. Furniture. Tractors. The*
*picker. Combine went to old Schumacher out there on Jacoby*
*Road and she let the cornfields go to grass. Daniel tried to fight*
*her for it. Took her to court, but the judge upheld the will and*
*sided with Mama. I just went on and left. Never was much*
*for stayin' where I wasn't wanted. Never that much for farmin'*
*either. Wasn't for Daddy I'da been gone long before. Always*

*wanted to try actin'. You know. Go to Hollywood like everyone used to say. Shame the way he had them trees cut down though. He crossed his arms and nodded his head and stroked the stubble on the tide pools jiggling under his chin. Always wondered what he did with the money.*

*What money?*

*From the sale of the lumber. Never spent a penny of it, far as I could tell. The old man looked at him and smiled, showing yellowed and missing teeth. Thought I was talkin' about that Capone business, didn't ya? That's somethin' that'll never change. Enough people say a thing often enough and loud enough, pretty soon everybody starts believin' in it. Even Daniel started believin' it there for a minute.*

*Once Sara passed, he said, Mama started showin' up in town more. Must be when she run into him. One of them trips into town. No way to know how long he was out there 'fore she got the cough. All Doc Rawlins knew was Finest was the one made the call. Guess you know all the rest, or you wouldn't a gone out there.*

He eases back on the gas and accelerates into the bend and considers the man sitting next to him. If he only had the lump. Or the holes in the beard where the hair couldn't grow through the scar tissue. The smell or the nose alone all by itself, he never would have agreed to take him. But as he sat in that house. Ripe with the odors of loss and age and permanent body filth. The identity of the white man may have been suspect. But even though he didn't recognize him, there was no mistaking the black man sitting next to him. Rigid on the sofa. Even without hearing the voice that defined him so, and as much as he had hoped to find him alive so they could right what they had wronged, now he's no longer sure he wants to. What's the point of it anyway? Dredging up the past after all these years just to give it a proper burial. Will it change anything? The life his sister had? Finest? He got on, didn't he? Maybe not great, but he got on. They all did, and now that they were standing at the precipice of Gethsemane, what was the point?

He rolls to the end of The Bone and makes a right on Justice Street and a left on Hope and another left midway through the block into the driveway and coasts to a stop on the side of the house and cuts off the engine and sits there, staring at the ghost man staring through the window into nothing. Night falling down around them like a blanket. Wind whistling through the raised blades of the bulldozers towering above the piles of debris. Prostrate on the ground next door.

IT IS DARK when the gravel crunches and the brakes squeak and the wheels on the Edsel creep to a stop outside the kitchen window. Rain pelting the drainpipe and the siding. The glow of the television the only light in the house. She sits in her rocker in her jogging suit with her feet up and listens to the man on the TV screen telling her about gas prices hitting record highs and twelve more soldiers dead on the other side of the world in a place with a name she is unable to pronounce, and she traces with her forefinger the rim on her coffee mug and waits for the door to open, wondering what about right here? How many died on the streets of Columbus today? Or Dayton? Springfield?

"'Bout time," she hollers when she hears the chimes ring on the kitchen door. "Beginnin' to think they sent you off to one a them places in I-raq."

Footsteps approach across the floor behind her from the kitchen and like magic he materializes out of the darkness and stands in front of her. Television light splashing and dancing across the jagged angles of his face like lightning in a thunder storm. A grocery bag. Paper. Cradled in his arm. The word Caleb's flashing at an angle across the front like neon. He reaches inside the bag and pulls out the bottle and unscrews the cap and fills the coffee mug halfway to the top with whiskey and sets the bottle on the side table and stands there while she drinks, wondering how to tell her.

"My Pick Three?" she says.

From the bottom of the grocery bag he fishes out the lottery ticket. Wet with sweat from the milk carton, and hands it to her.

"It's wet," she says to him.

"He's alive," he answers.

"What?"

"He's alive."

"Who's alive?"

"Finest. Been livin' over at Luke Simler's all this time. He's alive."

"Bullshit."

"Look behind you," he tells her.

She reaches for her coffee mug and brings it to her lips and sips and swallows and sips again and swallows and sets the mug back down and lays the ticket on the table to dry beside the bottle then belches. Twice. And instead of looking behind her, continues to stare straight ahead at an invisible spot just above the television.

He puts down the grocery bag and slides the table away from her and switches on the lamp and lifts her feet from the footrest and swivels her chair around so that she is now facing the entrance to the kitchen and she sits there. Staring. At the evaporated black man with his hat in his hand inside the doorframe. Leaning on a walking cane staring back at her, and she looks at him. The lump on his head and the holes in his beard, and she takes him in. The nose and the skin. Shrink-wrapped over the bones, and after all these years, that smell wafting across the room again like it never left, and she gropes in the air for her coffee mug in the empty space beside her chair where the table would be if he hadn't moved it out of the way and turned her around the way he did, and she looks at him standing above and just to the left of her shoulder and says, "Who the hell is that?"

"I just told you. It's Finest."

"Finest who?"

"How many Finests you know?"

"Take him back," she says.

"Do *what*?"

"Return him. To wherever you bought him from and turn me back to my television and give me back my table and my mug."

He stands there and looks at her, then rotates the chair so that she is facing the television again and slides the side table back in its place and hands her the coffee mug. Hands trembling as she raises the mug to her mouth. Eyes filling with water as he retrieves Finest from the doorframe and guides him over to the sofa.

"Don't know who you think you got there," she says to the spot above the television. Dabbing the water from her eyes with the handkerchief she keeps in her pocket. "But that ain't Finest Coon."

"Mae," he says to her.

"Finest Coon's dead."

"Mae?"

"No."

"Look at him, Mae."

"Already have. Finest Coon been dead too many years to count. Last thing I need right now is some been-dead little brother fetchin' some raggedy sack of bones into my house tryin' to conjure him back to life."

"But it's Finest, Mae."

"Oh no, it ain't."

"He's family."

"None of mine, he ain't. Only family I got is Sojourner."

"Sojourner? What about me?"

"Who you?"

"Come on, Mae."

She shrugs her shoulders and looks at them both, then returns to her spot above the television. "You say you my little brother," she says. "But I don't know. Ain't seen my little brother in sixty years. Don't even know what he look like now. Then here you come out of nowhere, talkin' that long-lost shit. Maybe you my little brother. Maybe you not."

"Mae."

"Every other day the man on the TV tell about somebody showin' up on some other somebody's doorstep pretendin' to be somebody they not. Got a driver's license. Credit cards. Next thing you know somebody's dead. Raped. Or locked up in a cellar somewhere livin' as somebody's sex slave."

"Mae."

"Could be workin' for the bulldozer man, for all I know."

"The bulldozer man?"

"Coulda sent the two of you up in here to try to confuse me. Trick me into sellin'."

He sits there and stares at her and shakes and lowers his head.

Finest is silent and rigid beside him on the sofa. Hands gripping his cane. Feet spread apart on the floor. As if any minute now he is going to spring up and dance away. Hypnotized by the images flashing on the television.

"Nobody's tryin' to confuse you, Mae," Gus says to her. "And I damn sure ain't tryin' to turn you into a slave. Of any kind."

"Why you here?"

"What?"

"Why you here? All these years. Coulda come back any time. When a body still cared about a thing. Bein' alive. Missin' folk. Wonderin' where they got off to. Why now? When a body don't care no more?" She reaches for her coffee mug. "Couldn't care less."

He looks across the room at the photographs of Sojourner flickering in the television light on the picture shelf. Cap and gown. Crawling in the grass. A third one similar to the one he has in his wallet. He looks at the television screen, at the black man pumping his fist in the air on a golf course. The footage of another black man. The first with a chance to become president of the country. Leader of the world, if he doesn't get shot first. He's been asking himself that same question since he picked up Finest, who is staring at the same footage.

"Been everywhere else," he says to her. "Wasn't any place left to go but home."

"Home, huh? That what you callin' it?"

He looks at her.

"Wasn't sure you'd be here. Thought maybe…"

"I'd be dead?"

He shrugs his shoulders and lowers his eyes.

"Wish I was," she says and sips from her mug and swallows. "Always figured death woulda come for me early after what I did to Daddy. What I done since. Sit up here sometimes and wonder if he got lost someplace. Or hijacked by Bin Laden."

"Soon as you answered the door," he tells her, "I started thinking about Finest. Thought maybe if he was still around, you know the three of us could…"

She looks at him.

"The three of us could what?"

"You know. Sit down…"

"And what?"

"Talk about stuff."

"What stuff?"

"Stuff. Before I…"

She shakes her head at him.

"There's something I gotta tell ya, Mae."

Again she shakes her head and raises her coffee mug and empties it, then picks up the bottle and refills the mug and drains it a second time.

"You look in a mirror lately?" she says to him. "Before is gone, Junior. Time done marched on into now and I ain't sittin' down with nobody," she slurs. "'Cept ol' man Death, Bin Laden ever turn him loose."

She takes another swig of whiskey and looks at Finest and watches him watching the young black golfer on the television. Expressionless and still as a statue. Eyes riveted on the screen as if he is seeing through it. Beyond the glass into the tubes and chips semiconducting and transmitting the images.

"What you got in that bag?" she asks him.

He looks down at the Caleb's bag and smiles.

"Grits," he says.

"Grits? What you know 'bout grits?"

"A thing or two."

"They any good?"

He nods and shrugs his shoulders.

"You use milk?"

He reaches into the bag and produces the carton of milk. "Probably bad by now," he says.

"Butter?"

He shows her the butter.

"What you do with the leftovers?"

He places the milk and the butter back in the bag. "Mix 'em with a little flour and egg," he says. "Fry 'em up in a pan."

She laughs and nods her head in approval and picks up the bottle and pours herself another half mug of whiskey, and he laughs too and he welcomes the distraction of things that don't matter, even if it is only briefly.

"What else you got in there?"

"Orange juice. Razors. Toothbrush. Greens." He'd spent the last of his check and most of her change.

She lifts the mug to her mouth and drinks and swallows and wipes the residue from her lip with the back of her hand and sets the mug back on the table and turns back to Finest.

"What's wrong with him?" she slurs.

"Some kind of dementia."

"Dementia? What? He forget things? Who don't?"

"More than that. Something to do with the veins."

"His veins forget things?"

"Luke says pretty soon he won't even know his name. Remember how to walk or hold his head up."

"Can he talk?"

He shrugs his shoulders. "Hasn't since he's been with Luke."

"You ain't heard his voice?"

He shakes his head.

"How you know it's him then?"

"It's him."

"How you know? Anybody can grow a lump they get hit in the head hard enough."

"It's him, Mae. You know it's him."

"I don't know nothin'," she says and reaches for the mug. "'Til I hear him talk and see what he look like under all that hair on his face. What you plannin' on doin' with him?"

He looks at Finest then back at Mabel. Finest: unmoving still, staring at the television. Mabel: hands wrapped around the coffee mug, staring at the two of them on the sofa. The house dark but for the TV and lamplight. The night outside. Rainless and quiet.

"Was thinking maybe we could hole up here for awhile."

She drinks from her mug.

He watches her.

"How long awhile?" she says finally.

He shrugs his shoulders. "Little while. 'Til I can figure things out."

She drinks from her mug again.

"Don't want no permanent house guests," she says. "Program on television talk all the time 'bout folks droppin' in for a visit and never leavin'. Pretty soon, you the one packin' up and movin' 'stead a the house guests."

"Just for a little while," he says. "Promise."

"You got any money?"

He looks at her.

"Nothin' from the government?"

He shakes his head.

She drains the rest of her mug, picks up the bottle and lottery ticket and spills all three into the basket on her walker, then slides her feet off the foot rest into her slippers and rises from the chair and push-shuffles her way into the kitchen. Feet stepping on the bottoms of the pant legs on her jogging suit as she goes. Scuffling along with the tennis balls scooting across the hardwood.

**book two**

# 1935 – the simlers

They tie the sow's front legs across her chest and listen to her squeal as they drag her from the pen into the slaughter yard, and watching their breath cloud silent in front of their faces they manage to loop a second rope around her hind legs without getting kicked and they pull back on her legs and expose the breadth of her neck and steel their minds against their hearts. Their stomachs against their eyes and their ears, and they do not flinch nor blink nor any of them stop breathing when Hog unsheathes the sticker from its case and buries it at an angle deep into her throat until the blade disappears and he pulls it back out again releasing her blood, and she squeals and she squeals and she squeals until she stops. Like wheels braking on a freight train. Screaming into the depot.

Finest holds her head down by the snout against the cold and hardening ground and whispers to the sow into her ear until the twitching ceases, while Luke cuts the wire from around the bale of hay and in the frigid and biting silence they blanket her body in a shroud of straw which Hog sets afire with the match he took from his pocket to light his cigarette and they cup their noses with their hands to ward off the smell and they back away from the flames, from the smoke watering their eyes, and they repeat this sacrament over and over until between burnings they have scraped with a knife all the hair from her body. On a soiled slab of plywood they drag the expired sow from the slaughter yard and heft her onto the table outside the barn and peel off her hooves and pluck out her eyes and drain the last of her blood, and they scrub away the charred and stubborn remnants of hair with a bootblack brush and saw off her head and drop it into the soup pail, and using a crank winch they fix a gambrel between her legs and hoist her into the air and wash down her hide with well water from the buckets they fill and refill at the pump atop the cistern behind the barn, and when they are finished they drink in turn from the tap and Hog takes out his tobacco pouch and they stand there and stare for awhile at the cornfields. Soil turned down like bedding for the winter. Breath clouding the air in front of them in the cold gray morning.

"What's with all the whisperin', Coon?" asks Hog.

Hands red with blood, he reaches into the tobacco pouch and pinches off a plug of shag then offers the pouch to Luke, who breaks off a knob and passes it to Finest, who reaches in and hands it back.

Finest clears his throat several times before answering.

"What you mean?" he asks.

"Whisperin'," says Hog. "To the swine. What the hell's the point of it?"

"Calm 'em down," says Finest.

Hog laughs, breath fogging in front of his face. And he pats at his coat pockets and the pockets on his pants trying to remember where he placed the matches.

"Calm 'em down?" he says.

"Relax 'em," says Finest.

"They's dead, Coon. Can't get much more relaxed than dead."

"Let him alone, Daniel," says Luke. "He ain't hurtin' nothin' by it."

"Let him alone? Am I botherin' you, Coon?"

"Naw," says Finest.

"I'm just askin' a simple question, little brother." And he spits and looks over at Finest and steps around past Luke and stands in front of him. The tips of their boots near touching. Watered-down blood dripping on the ground from the sow, hanging upside down by her ankles behind them. And he rolls up his cigarette and licks and stares over the gum on the edge of the paper and seals it over and runs it through his mouth and glances at the sow, at the blood, then rolls his eyes back to Finest. To the lump shaped like someone stuck a melon on his head, and smiles at it. "Coon don't mind answerin' a simple question. Do you, Coon?"

Finest clears his throat and lowers his eyes and stares at the piece of earth hardening like water seeping between their boots and he shakes his head and he looks at the deadened piece of earth and says, "Naw" again.

"What's the point of it then? If they's already dead?"

"Keeps they soul calm," says Finest.

"They soul?"

"For the crossin'," says Finest.

Hog looks at the sow and spits. "You know what, Coon?" he says. "Headless and all, even that ol' gal back there's better lookin' than you are."

"Let him alone, Daniel."

Hog sniffs at him. "Smells better, too," he says.

"Daniel."

"The thing of it, Coon," says Hog. "Swine ain't got no soul. So seems to me you just wastin' your breath."

"He ain't hurtin' nothin' by it, Daniel."

"Maybe I don't want him doin' it. Maybe I don't like hearin' it."

"Everybody got a soul," says Finest, voice churning in the cold like a frozen feed grinder.

"Everybody?"

Finest clears his throat and turns up his collar and coughs at the earth between them.

"Even you, Coon?" says Hog. "Under all that ugly? You got a soul somewhere?"

"Let him be, Daniel."

"What about bastards, Coon?"

"Daniel!"

"Do bastards got souls, too, Coon? When we close our eyes for the last time and die, do all us ugly and bastard souls get to go to some ugly and bastard heaven together? Like a Prom? At a school fulla queers and retards?"

Luke steps in between them and urges Hog away and separates them. Finest just stands there. Knees bending. Weight shifting back and forth on his legs to warm his feet. His collar turned up. The scars on his face twitching in the cold. His eyes. Staring into the morning. The sow headless behind them under the silent and smoky sky. Filthy and bloody with clouds.

Hog finds his matches and shakes his head and lights his cigarette and glares up to the heavens at the dirty patch of sky where Pegasus would fly if it were cloudless and dark out, and he thinks about stargazing in haylofts with Mary Jo Christopher. Souls and the word bastard. The shape of it. Balanced. Like a seesaw. Shared and equal burden end to end and the way she stood there and talked to him from behind the door and refused to come out to the porch, laying it out thick and long across her tongue. Stretching it through her lips with the "a" drawn out in a lamb's bleat without the stutter as the reason her daddy refused to let her see him anymore. "'Cause you a baaastard," she said to him and he is in the middle of thinking about all that. Stars and souls and bastards and Mary Jo, and he is looking at the sky, at the streaks of blood dried on the backs of his hands, and he is passing the box of matches on to Luke who is passing him back his tobacco pouch when all three hear something that sounds like rifle fire and just in time from his thoughts and his blood-dried hands he looks up to see the door bang shut on the side of the house. The white hot flash of his mother's bare feet disappearing around the corner of the porch. Vanishing into the thinning guard of tulip poplar and sycamore trees. Sugar maple and cedar. Defending the house against the onlookers. And he drags on his cigarette and blows the smoke through his nose into a cloud that evaporates in front of his face and he nods his head a time or two and he stands there. Nodding at the corner of the porch and the place where her feet flashed white just before she vanished, and he inhales another drag from his cigarette and nods his head again and picks up his skinning knife and turns back to the sow.

"What do you think it is this time?" asks Luke.

"Hell if I know," says Hog, and with his back to them, to the house, he slips the knife inside the slit in the sow's tendon where he fixed the gambrel and from each of her ankles he cuts over her tendons around her feet and slices down her legs to her centerline, cutting the tail of the "Y". Formed by joining the three lines together down the length of her body to her neck. Coon's wild notions of souls on his mind. Stars and bastards and Mary Jo...

"You goin' after her?" asks Luke.

...and the way she stood there on the other side of the door chewing on that word. Stretching it out and snapping it back like taffy. Baaastard. And him just standing there saying nothing. Staring at that door saying nothing. Not a goddamn thing. Not Mary Jo. Not but. Not nothing. Just standing there. Wishing she would stop all that yelling and come out to the porch and talk to him. Quiet. Like they did in the hayloft that night when she taught him the stars. Or at least open the goddamn door and look at him. And stop yelling. Please! Stop! Yelling! that word and he takes another drag from his cigarette and exhales the smoke through his nose, and with the nail of his little finger he picks off the ribbons of shag from his tongue and between his teeth, then wedges the cigarette back into his mouth, into the corner between his lips, and motions for Finest to come around and brace the sow from behind, and he tips back his hat and jabs his hand into the centerline cut and he grabs and he holds and he pulls at her skin as he begins to sever her hide.

"You goin'?" says Luke.

"Goin' where?"

"After Mama."

"No."

"Someone ought to."

"So go," says Hog, cigarette bobbing up and down in his mouth as he works and he holds and pulls and saws between the gristles of skin and fat and holds and pulls and saws and grabs and holds until he succeeds, finally, in sectioning off her belly.

"You ain't comin'?"

"I *look* like I'm comin'?"

"Someone ought to go get her."

"Not me. I got work to do, little brother. So do you. Case you forgot."

"I ain't forgot," says Luke and he stubs out his cigarette and tosses the butt into the chew tin and steps into the driveway and looks down the lane toward the gate, at the cars pulling up and the crowd beginning to gather on the other side of it, and he turns and squats and cups his hands over his eyes and squints into the leaves. Changing and thinning on the tulip poplar guard and sycamore. Maple and cedar. Then stands and wipes his hands on his pants and looks back down the lane. To the gate and the gathering crowd.

"You think she actually hit somethin'?" he asks.

"Hard to pull a trigger without hittin' somethin'. Even with the barrel pointed straight up in the air."

"What do you think she shot?"

"Nothin' worth nothin'. Otherwise Sara'd be out here. Screamin'."

"Maybe she shot Sara."

"Blew a hole in one of Beuford's old socks, more likely. Couldn't stand the smell."

Luke laughs and spits on the ground and laughs again and looks at the gate. "Which one?" he says, and breath collects in his front of his face.

"Which one what?"

"Which sock?"

"Hell, Lucas. I don't know. But I'll tell you what."

"What?"

He opens his mouth and lets the cigarette fall to the ground between his boots and steps on it. "You can stand there pickin' your nose and wonderin'," he says. "Or you can get back to workin'. Either way. I guarantee ya won't be long 'fore you find out."

"Still think they can't see nothin' from out there?" says Luke.

"Do it matter?"

"She won't come for me," says Luke.

"Guess she'll have to wait on Beuford then."

"Maybe we ought to."

"Or maybe Coon ought to," says Hog. "Maybe we ought to send the nigger to go fetch her. Makes about as much sense as everything else goes on around here. What do you say, Coon? Wanna go fetch my looney-toon mama?"

"She ain't gonna come for him either, Daniel. We all ought to go."

"All is one too many people, little brother. Wait on Beuford. Fetch her yourself. Or go on with Coon and take that pail with ol' gal's head in it up to Sara when you go. For the sausage."

Luke walks around behind Finest and picks up the pail with the sow's head in it. "I think we should all go, Daniel," he says. "Won't take but a minute. Take no time to dress the rest of them hogs, neither. Not with the three of us, if you let us each take one."

Hog ignores him. From her belly and the junction of the "Y" he works up over the sow's crotch, around her anus, over to her tailbone and jerks up on her tail to release her spine, then shakes his head and spits again, working the blade fast and easy now around the rest of her body to her forelegs, skinning from outside to front. "Ready, Coon," he says and, after muscling the knife around her neck and slicing down the insides of her forelegs, he digs in and plants the heels of his boots into the frozen dirt and he braces himself and pulls and peels off her hide.

SHE WENT AWAY. She went away and she came back and she never said where she'd gone nor why she left, and then she went away a second time. Though he could see her there. Moving about the house, and smell her there. Wet summer mornings wrapped around the lavender water she spritzed into her hair, drifting through his room onto the sleeping porch where he lay with his chest bare, and feel her there. Her presence, hovering above his head, then vanishing. Just as he opened his eyes, and hear her there. Screaming throughout the small hours like a pig stuck for slaughter. The muffled voices of Beuford and Sara hushing. Quieting. From that journey she never returned.

"To her sister's," said Beuford the first time and he never said when she left nor how long she'd be gone. When she was coming back.

He ran across the lane from the barn where every-day after Mrs. Perry rang the bell on the schoolhouse he went to look at the hogs and fetch them some water and he wiped his feet on the mat before going inside and he dropped his satchel by the door and kicked off his boots and hung up his coat and took off his hat and stuffed it into his coat pocket and he ran up the stairs and washed his hands in the basin and combed his hair and changed his shirt for supper and even though he was hurrying. When he came back down she had already gone, and he was halfway through his second piece of pie with ice cream before Beuford looked up from his plate and said, "To her sister's," and something about his grandmother coming to stay and he finished his pie and carried his dirty dishes in to Sara, who took them from his hands and patted the top of his head and gave him a piece of butterscotch, and he put his boots back on and went back to the barn. Leaving his coat and his hat behind, and he sat against the wall across from the feed pens where he unwrapped the paper from the butterscotch Sarah gave him and he stuck it in his mouth and he looked at the hogs.

By the time she returned to him his grandmother had come and gone. Snow fell and melted and replenished the soil and the fields had been harrowed and plowed. Sown and harvested. Grains threshed and milled into feed for the stock. Stubble ground turned over, and leaves rained down from the treetops like firework embers shimmering brilliance against the crisp blue sky. He was all grown up now, she said. "A real little gentleman," and she bent at the waist until they were face to face with each other and she straightened his collar and smoothed down his hair and told him that she loved him, which she had never done before and had not done since, then Beuford stepped up beside her, holding her suitcase, and held out his hand and she let her fingers trail over his head through his smoothed down hair, down the nape of his neck and onto his shoulder, and she took Beuford's hand and she walked onto the porch and into the house and she closed the door behind her and she left him there. Standing. In a rain of shimmering leaves.

SHE SAT THERE curled up on the divan in her summer dress with her legs folded up behind her thighs and her feet. Bare. Crossed at her ankles and rubbing against each other. Soft. Like a worn kerchief gripped in the palm of a hand absent-mindedly stroked between the thumb and forefinger, and she sat there rubbing her feet together, stroking the outside of her forefinger in place of the imagined kerchief and she listened to the wind. Braying through the chimneys. Like donkeys. Careening around the pillars on the porch. Shutters banging. Loose. In another part of the house, and the hammer, controlled and measured. Pounding outside the window in the braying gusts of wind. Mending the shingles on the roof on the barn across the lane and she sat there gazing through the window, listening to the rhythm of the hammer pound and she held out her hand with her palm turned up and her fingers scissored apart the way she'd seen the ladies hold their hands in the catalogue pages and the *Woman's Home Companion* and she held her hand like that and she accepted the cigarette her sister offered as though she had curled up on divans and welcomed such offerings all her life. And she sat there rubbing her feet. Stroking her finger. Smoking like the ladies in the catalogue pages. Staring through the window as she listened to the hammer pound and the shutters bang. The wind braying and her sister pacing back and forth across the room. Demanding between rabid draws on the end of her cigarette holder to know What the hell! was she thinking? and How far along was she? and What! was she planning to tell Beuford? The heels of her shoes clopping like donkeys' hooves against the hardwood and she sat there. Smoking like ladies, inhaling and exhaling. Listening to her sister. The pounding of the hammer. Staring through the window at the colored man silhouetted against the evening sun. The Fix-it Man her husband hired. Straddled over the apex. Defying wind and gravity to replace the shingles broken on the barn before the first snowfall, and she watched him. His blackened shadow. Riding the dark horse of the roof. Raise up the hammer and bring it down. Smoke flavoring the room from the cigarettes. Pine crackling in the fireplace.

"Beatrice!"

"What?"

"Are you listening to me?"

Beatrice turned from the colored man and looked at her sister, then stared down at her hands at the cigarette burning between her fingers.

"I'm listening," she said.

"God, Bea!" said her sister. "A nigger? You couldn't come up with anyone better to fuck than the help? Could you be any less original?"

Her sister looked at her.

"Was it rape? Did he rape you?"

"It wasn't rape."

"'Cause if he raped you…"

She could see her sister's mind working. Spinning. Pacing it out. Marching back and forth across the floor in step with her feet.

"It wasn't rape," said Beatrice.

Whetting the stone they would throw to accuse him.

"I said it wasn't rape."

Her sister stopped pacing and stood there. Silent save the suckling arrangement her mouth composed on the end of her cigarette holder, and when her shoulders dropped the way they did and she let her arms fall to her sides and turned to face her, she looked no older than a child standing there. The holder a salve. A teething ring. Against the ache of the world coming in.

"He'll put you out," said her sister. "You know that, don't you? You know he will. He'll put you out. And then what will you do?"

Beatrice looked at her.

"And that nigger's good as dead. Jesus, Beatrice. First Hog…"

"Daniel."

"Now this."

"His name is Daniel."

"What?"

"My son, Mona Ruth."

"I don't know how much you expect him to take, Beatrice."

"His name is Daniel."

"To put up with."

"Say it, Mona Ruth."

"You'll have to get rid of it."

"He has a name, Mona."

"What else can you do?"

"Mona!"

"Damn it, Beatrice! There isn't time for this."

"What's my son's name, Mona?" she said and she crushed the rest of her cigarette into the ashtray on the table in front of the divan and she leaned her head back against the window ledge and she closed her eyes and crossed her arms and she sat there. Listening. Waiting for her sister to answer.

"Daniel," said Mona Ruth.

Beatrice opened her eyes and looked at her.

"Daniel," her sister repeated and she was so small standing there in the middle of a room in the middle of the world coming in. So insignificant. They both were. "Okay?" said Mona Ruth and she stood there. Staring at her. Daubing the water staining her cheeks with the back of her hand. "Satisfied?"

Beatrice smiled at her.

"Is it still so hard, Mona Ruth?"

"What now, Beatrice?"

"Is it still so hard?"

"I said I don't know what you're…"

"I named him after Daddy, you know. I thought it would make him happy. Think I could have another one those cigarettes?" And she sat there. Inhaling and exhaling as if she were smoking, and she stared at her sister. Holding her hand like that as if she were a sketch rendered on a catalogue page, listening to the shutters bang and the hammer pound. The wood hissing and popping in the fireplace. Wind. Braying through the flue. Worrying the flames below.

Her sister put out her cigarette and crossed the room and sat beside her on the divan and reached for her hands and drew them together and held them. "Beuford Simler's a good man, Bea," she said. She patted her hands and waited for Beatrice to look at her. "But even good men ain't that good. You've got to get rid of it. You know you do. You have no choice."

Beatrice sat there, staring into the room at nothing, and for a time, at least, the world coming in began to quiet some. The wind calmed. Sara or Beuford had seen to the shutters and the pounding ceased. Through the window she glanced out at the dark horse of the barn. Riderless under the evening sky, and she saw that the Fix-it Man's shadow had gone for the day. The sun ducked low beneath the tree line, halving the light. And the only way she knew that her sister was patting the backs of her hands and talking to her was because when she looked at her, she could see her mouth moving, her fingers patting.

THEY SAID SHE went around naked under her clothes. Beatrice Simler went around naked and she heard voices. Talking to her inside her head, and that at night, if you stood outside the gate and waited long enough and listened, you would hear screaming. Nails clawing at the walls. Kids told each other ghost stories and witch tales and swore oaths upon the Bible that she was both. A ghost and a witch, and that they could prove it. And over bonfires and roast-outs they dared one another to climb up over the gate and spend the night out there and make it through 'til morning. Alive. Double dared if the night was Halloween, and the rite of it soon became passage. A Hallows Eve spent alone at the Simlers, or the claiming of it at least requisite. To the granting of the first kiss. Women wondered if she might be stingy in the bedroom, several noting that when he came into town of late, Beuford had begun holding onto their hands much longer than usual when he met them by chance in the street. She drank and smoked, some said. Opium with the Chinaman doctor in Cleveland she paid to prescribe it to her, and that her son. The eldest. The one they called Hog, nursed an unsavory passion for his animals and was a bastard. Fathered by his own grandfather, and a few went so far as to claim that she slept with niggers and that she'd had three children and not just the two boys. The third out of wedlock and that she smothered it. With a pillow as soon as it was born. That it was buried somewhere in the yard out there and if you stood real quiet, you could sometimes hear the cries of it, while the devout believed she was possessed and they warned that if the evil was not rooted out—exorcised!—every soul in the house would be lost. And sometimes, they said, she remained in bed for weeks at a time. Months. With the shutters drawn. Then she woke and never slept at all, wandering the nights like the damned, suckling dreams like blood from the slumbered. She was prone to fits, they said, and had to be tended to often in public and that one day out of the blue she might walk up to you and block your path and stop you in the street with her hand raised up toward your face as if she were going to brush your cheek with the backs of her bent fingers and she would look into your eyes and utter not a single word, while on another she might waltz up and thrust her hand through your arm and inquire if you had been waiting long, then call you by some other name and talk with you awhile and walk with you a ways before turning and drifting away. This is what was said of her.

What was not said because it was never suspected, or considered of little importance, was that she counted. Footsteps and stairs. The number of them. Between where she came from and where she was going. Forty-six from the base of the stairs to the attic. Thirteen from the front door into the drawing room. Sixteen. Plus another fourteen. Back to Sara's staircase and into the basement or ten plus eight plus seven plus four. Into the kitchen, onto the back porch, through the screen, down the stairs, into the yard. So if ever she needed to turn and run someplace, she knew the exact number of steps to safety, and whether inside or outside, in the dark she knew when someone had come around or entered a room she was in by the way the ether shifted. The scent of it, its weight, and that she could walk forty paces into the kitchen and tell Sara to cut back on the rosemary or the garlic. Add a little sugar, just by sniffing the air. And although she knew the difference between the sounds of a stair and a floorboard creaking, a door and a box spring hinging, and could tell apart the crows in a roost by the pitch of their caws. Close her eyes and know if another body has joined her in the rain by the interruption in the drops of the water falling on the ground around her. There were times when she heard nothing at all or only every other word spoken to her, and she turned her head to the side and tilted it so that her ear raised up a little closer to the source of the sound and asked that you repeat yourself or that you walk on the left side of her rather than the right whenever you accompany her. That her eyes were wont to cut the edges off things. The corners of book pages, the beginnings and endings of words. Faces and moldings on the fringes of ceilings and walls.

HE UNCRANKED THE winch on the gambrel and lowered the sow, and with his short knife now he cut around her anus, taking care not to puncture her intestine, and when he cleared it and was free of it, the intestine, he pulled part of it out and Finest came around to tie it off, and from her anus he cut down the length of her belly. Inside to out as before, and with the hand not working the knife, he reached in and held the rest of the viscera to the side away from the point of the blade and he cut through her belly fat all the way down to her breastbone and waited for Finest to place the pail underneath her before releasing her entrails. Which were swelling and spilling out of her body, and the cold dry air filled with a foulness that made them thankful it was the end of November instead of July and each fought the urge to cup his hand over his mouth and retch. Hog filled his lungs and held his breath down inside his chest as he cut away the offal and took out her kidneys and her liver and handed them to Finest, who dropped them into the keeper pail along with the entrails, and he sliced through the last of the flesh connecting her stomach to her body, which was all that remained in the cavity, and he stepped back and let what was left of her fall and slosh into the bucket and he did not free his breath until Beuford came home, when under the cold sober glare of the dirty gray sky he told him about the thing that sounded like rifle fire and the white hot flash of his mother's bare feet vanishing around the porch and they stopped what they were doing and one by one filed into the house behind Beuford. And none of them, not even Luke, glanced down the lane toward the crowd that had gathered to watch them on the other side of the gate.

ONE TWO THREE four five six seven eight nine ten eleven. Beatrice ducks behind the cedar tree and leans against the trunk and waits and listens and feels for the shifts in the ground, changes in the ether. Then runs and counts off one two three four five plus another six plus nine plus eight equals twenty-eight to the scant leaves and near bare branches on the sugar maple and now she can see them. Two of them through the trees. Coming for her. And she scans the trunks of the rest of the guard. The tulip poplar and elm. Sugar maple and cedar. Birch. Spruce and walnut. And she spies three more. Two together and one by himself, closing in from either side, and she looks back behind her and calculates the distance, and she runs and she counts and she is fourteen thirteen twelve more steps from freedom. Breath clamoring in front of her face like the crowd of onlookers outside the gate, when her wind goes out of her and she is knocked from her feet and taken down from behind.

THEY PULL HER arms across her chest and hold her hands together and listen to her scream and, watching their breath cloud silent in front of their faces, they manage to get a hold of each of her ankles without getting kicked and Hog quiets her hands while Luke stills her legs and Finest holds her head down against the cold and hardening ground and whispers to her into her ear and they steel their heads against their hearts and their viscera against their eyes and their ears and they do not flinch nor blink nor any of them stop breathing when Doc Rawlins unsheathes the needle from his case and buries it into her buttocks until it disappears into her flesh, and he pulls it back out again and she screams and she screams and she screams. Until she stops.

# may 7, 2007

*He hears what sounds like gun shots and comes up from the millrace from cleaning the grate between the race and the flume and follows the sound into the woods. He is running but suspended in place. He can hear his breath strain, his heart pound. His feet crunching over twigs and branches. But the scenery around him never changes. The red leaves on the maple trees never give way to the river birches as he nears the water. The clearing behind him remains only feet away. He hears the shots again, then a scream he can place as neither human nor animal, and though he tries to run faster, lengthening his stride, he is never able to reach it.*

When he wakes he is sweating and Mabel is standing over him in her walker. Staring at him as if he is a corpse in the bottom of an open casket, and he looks at her. Staring at him like that, like he is dead, and he lies there a moment and thinks about it and he wonders if he is.

"You late," she says to him.

Corpses don't sweat, he decides, and though he's not a hundred percent on this, he's fairly certain they no longer have to go to work either. He blinks and rubs his hand over his eyes and over the scratch of stubble on his face and chin. His neck, and he stares at her and shifts himself so that he is sitting and he leans back on the pillows squished against the headboard and rubs his eyes again.

"For what?" he says.

"Work," she answers.

"Work?"

"Your charge," she says. "He's waitin' on you. In your office." She backs away from the bed and struggles through the doorframe and he watches her. Hunched and frail and small. Lost in the desolate folds of the jogging suit, dragging beneath her feet behind the walker. Thinking about how strong she used to be. Solid and sturdy. As if a bomb could go off beneath her and she would not budge.

He slides his legs over the edge of the bed and puts his feet on the floor and sits there awhile and waits for the blood to trickle down into his toes and his fingers, then pushes himself up and stands and listens to his joints crack and pop as he rotates his shoulders around and back a couple of times, flexes his knees and fingers to ensure that everything is still working alright. He crosses to the chair on the other side of the room and looks out the window as he reaches for his suit pants.

The bulldozers have moved on to the house across the street on the corner. The Colonel's house with the SOLD sign in front and the flagpole saluting the day without its flag. The Sentinel's Shack, Finest used to call it, and the cracking and splintering and collapsing of it sounds further away than it is.

He dresses and follows after her and stops when he enters the kitchen and sees the table stood on end and shoved against the door to the driveway. Mabel is already in the sitting room, jawing back and forth with someone on the television.

"Voluntary!" she hollers. "That lady ain't gonna see no prison cell!"

He stands there and listens to her as he surveys the room.

"White people got to kill a whole bunch a folk," she hollers, "Fore they get put away! Or children. Don't nobody get a pass on children."

The chairs, stacked in two-highs, are pushed against the table. Books and magazines and video tapes from the bookcase in the sitting room and dishes emptied from the cupboards stack to the ceiling on the countertops in front of the windows. Tinfoil, secured by duct tape, blocks out the light and covers the glass.

In the sitting room the back of the rocking chair is wedged beneath the front doorknob. The side tables are piled on top of the chair and in the dining area the china cabinet and bookcase block the windows while the table barricades the door to the back porch. The entire house looks as if it is hunkered down in preparation for a siege or a catastrophic storm blowing in. And in the middle of it, still and calm inside the eye of the chaos, sit Mabel and Finest, side by side on the sofa, watching television. The sofa, the television, the coffee table and the remote control the only objects still in place.

He stares at them. Mabel on one end. Lost in the folds and creases in her jogging suit. Sipping from her coffee mug. Finest on the other end. The ghost man. Rigid and silent on the edge of the couch cushions. Frayed and dusty as if he spent the last sixty years stored in a box in the attic. And he looks at him and thinks maybe he made a mistake. Maybe he did die this morning and this is what hell looks like.

"What happened?" he asks her.

She looks up from the television and sweeps her eyes over the room. Her hands shake as she raises the coffee mug to her mouth and she looks at him and turns back to the television.

"That preacher's wife," she says. "Got manslaughter. Voluntary."

"Preacher's wife?"

"Mmm hmm. Pulpit preacher in Tennessee. Murdered him in his sleep. Claims she snapped."

"What?"

"Snapped! Shot him in the back with a shotgun. Twelve gauge. Now you know if it was a colored woman…"

"What happened to the furniture?"

She drinks from her mug and picks up the remote from the coffee table and switches the channels back and forth and drinks again. "You got to ask ol' Superman here about that one," she says. "And while you at it," she tells him, "ask him for me when he's plannin' to put it back."

He looks around the room again then back to Finest. Sitting there as thin and straight as a board. Fixed. Like the woodcarvings he passed along the Avenue of the Giants on his way up to Seattle. As if he were petrified, whittled in wood or stone, and could not lift a finger if you ordered him to at gunpoint. Let alone raise a table on end and push it against a door. Two tables. A bookcase and a china cabinet.

"But how?" he says.

"Sundowners," says Mabel.

"Sun what?"

"Sundowners. Lucille Sutton had it 'fore she went back to bein' a baby again."

"Lucille Sutton?"

"The Colonel and Puddin's little girl. Same grade as you was, wasn't she?"

"What's Sundowners?"

"The Superman Syndrome."

"Superman?"

She unscrews the cap on the bottle and refills the coffee mug.

"Comes on after sundown. Old folks and crazy people get it. Clovis had to put double-sided locks on the doors and a gate at the bottom of the stairs just to keep Lucille in the house."

"Who's Clovis?"

"Lucille's daughter. Had her out a wedlock. The Colonel and Puddin hushed it up. Locked Lucille in her room like it was some kind of prison. Made her raise little Clovis in secret. You'd a been here all this time, you'd know it already."

He takes one of the chairs off the dining table and sits in it.

"What's that got to do with Finest?" He is almost afraid to ask.

She picks up the coffee mug and drinks. "When Lucille wasn't around no more," she says, "everybody figured she run off somewhere. Eloped maybe. Then one day. Sometime after The Colonel passed. Puddin went first. Right after Precious. Out walks Clovis. A full grown woman. Talkin' 'bout her mama Lucille caught the Alzheimer's and wandered off. Next morning Clovis got a call from Sheriff Newsome."

"Newsome?"

"Grandson," she says. "Original died in sixty-four. Told her he had Lucille locked up in his holdin' cell and to come down and get her. Said one of the Bent brothers came on her in the woods when he was huntin'. Walkin' around in circles like one of her feet was pegged to the ground. She was so messed up. Dehydrated and all. They didn't know if she would make it. When she did, and Sheriff Newsome started wonderin' 'bout elder abuse, Clovis went out and bought the locks. Ain't that life?" she says to the television. "Jailed by the parents. Jailed by the law. Jailed by the child."

"You sayin' Finest has Alzheimer's?"

"No. I'm sayin he got the Sundowners."

"What's wandering got to do with moving the furniture?"

"Some people wander," she says. "Like Lucille. Others get strong. Real strong. Look like your Superman friend here got a bit o' both."

He looks at Finest and shakes his head back and forth. "He can barely walk," he says to her. "I had to help him out of the car! Into the house!"

"You got some other explanation for how my furniture got this way?"

He looks around at the hunkered down furniture bracing the room. The rocking chair and the side tables. The bookcase and china cabinet. Then back at Finest. At Mabel, sipping from her coffee mug, and at himself. An old man in a musty Goodwill suit afraid to close his eyes at night for all the nightmares haunting his sleep and he doesn't have an explanation for any of it.

*He is the last to come off. Duffle bag slung over his shoulder like a hunting rifle. Staring out at the empty street as if he were listening for game. Shaking loose a cigarette from the pack he'd just fished from his left breast pocket. Dipping his head down to pull it free with his teeth and light it. Gus stands across the street from him, rainwater trickling into his eyes and blurring his vision, as he watches him standing there in his uniform in the wet exhaust of the bus. Lighting his cigarette as if he were basking in sunshine on an island someplace in the middle of the tropics. Looking out at the sea instead of the deserted main drag of an old blockhouse town seized by wind and rain.*

*Head down, hands in his pockets, books under his arm, wrapped in Pliofilm, he jogs across the street and stops in front of him. Smiling. They stand there awhile, staring at each other, neither one speaking. Then Finest takes another drag from his cigarette and exhales the smoke and his scars twitch and glisten with rainwater and he smiles back as if he's only just seen him and nods his head toward the books under his arm and in that mangled grating voice he says, "You ever read them things, or they just for show?"*

*"For show," says Gus, and like that they pick up where they left off, as if Finest never went away and the war never happened, and without another word in the gusting seizing rain they make their way through town to The Bone.*

*Halfway across Finest shifts his duffle bag from his right shoulder to his left and looks straight ahead in front of him when he says, "You ever kill anything?"*

*Gus stares up the road and shakes his head no.*

*"Nothin'? Not even a animal?"*

*Gus plods through the rain-soaked gravel and shakes his head. Finest slows his stride. "Deer? Rabbit? Field mouse?"*

*No.*

*"Your daddy never take you huntin'?"*

*Gus shakes his head and Finest turns silent again and alongside the silence Gus hears something else fall in between them. A click of sorts, like tumblers in a lock sliding into place, a lock that will never again open, and he understands now that it wasn't the war that separated them but events that took place long before, and they hoof the rest of the way in silence, keeping to the rim of the shoulder, heads down, ducked under the wind like birds preening. Rainwater slapping the napes of their necks, running down into their shirt collars. The smell of sulfur rising up from the spring in the gorge below.*

*When they finally reach the house, they are soaked through to the bone. Belle is home and when she sees them she runs out into the rain and throws her arms around them, then steps back and takes a look at them, at Finest. An old Model T sedan, red with the top down, sits in the driveway collecting rainwater. Mabel stands in the doorway laughing and watching them.*

*"Well, don't just stand there looking like a couple of soggy statues," Belle says to them. "Get in here." And she slips her arms through theirs and ushers them inside.*

*"Now," she says to Finest, "let me take a proper look at you."*

*Finest drops his duffle bag on the floor and stands in the middle of the kitchen at ease, feet whispered apart and hands cinched behind his back, dripping water on the linoleum.*

*Belle steps back and onces him over.*

*Mabel stands next to Belle and drapes her arm around her.*

*"You look good," Belle says to him. "Filled out some. Handsome. Doesn't he look handsome?" she says to Mabel.*

*"A regular Native Son," Mabel tells him. Then asks how many Nazis he killed.*

*Finest winces and his scars twitch as he laughs and smiles and rain pelts hard against the window.*

HE WAS IN love with her even then, thinks Gus. They all were.

The doorbell is ringing.

He rolls up his shirtsleeves and takes down the side tables from atop the rocking chair. The back of the chair from under the doorknob.

"Let it be," says Mabel.

"What?" says Gus.

"Don't answer it."

"Don't answer it? Why not?"

"'Cause I said so."

"You don't want to know who it is?"

"Know who it is."

"Who is it?"

She drinks from her mug.

"Who is it?" he says.

"Bulldozer man."

"Bulldozer man? Well, don't you want to see what he wants?"

"Know what he want," she says and she sits there on the end of the sofa nearest the door and she looks at him. "What you think he want?" and she turns back to the television and tells him to put her chair back under the doorknob where he found it and he stands there and stares at her. Listening to the doorbell ring. The voices blaring on the television, and he looks down at the binding on the back of the rocking chair still gripped in his hands, and over to Finest. Hibernal. Watching on the opposite end of the sofa next to her.

"He make you an offer?" says Gus.

She picks up her mug and glances at him over the rim and sets it back on the table and rotates her eyes to the television.

"Chris Rock in another movie," she says.

"What did he offer you?"

"You know Chris Rock?"

"How much?"

"That boy is funny. Remind me a Richard Pryor."

Knocking. Loud. Insistent. Replaces the ringing.

"Did you even talk to him?" he says.

"'Specially that bit 'bout bein' afraid a white boys."

He sets aside the chair and wraps his hand around the doorknob. "Maybe we should see what he has to say," he says.

"The one where he talk about all them school shootin's and how the last place he ever wanna be trapped someplace is in a elevator with a couple a seventeen-year-old white boys? Now that shit is funny," she says and she laughs and from the coffee table she picks up her mug and she drinks.

"No harm in listening to what he's got to say," says Gus.

She sets down the mug and she looks at him.

"We can at least hear the man out, Mae."

"We?" she says to him. "Wasn't no *we* a couple a days ago."

He stands there and stares at her as the knocking picks up speed. Rises in volume like the slow rumble of kettle drums at the beginning of a movement, and he stares at her and he looks at the door, then turns back to Mabel and he glances down at the space of floor between them and thinks what harm could it be? It's his house as much as it is hers. Maybe he could work out a good price for them. For all of them. Finest included. Maybe that's how he can bury her. Work out a price so they can all be comfortable and let the bulldozers have it. Turn it over like a field of stubble and plant something new.

"We're the only ones left, Mae," he says. "Not much choice but to hear him out," and she looks at him and he nods his head a few times. To convince himself more so than Mabel. And he nods his head and he looks away from her and he turns the doorknob and he opens the door.

"Ain't so urgent as it sounds," says Luke. "It's the arthritis." And he lifts up his hand and tears up his face as he expands and contracts his fingers to demonstrate. "Once I get it goin'," he says. "I can't seem to get it to stop. Plus," he adds, baring his teeth somewhere between grin and grimace, "saw the car outside and heard the television on so I knew somebody was home."

He wears the same baseball cap and coveralls as yesterday and Gus stares at him, trying to find the brooding long-legged boy he remembers in the vague beacons of blue pulsing in the fogs of milk in his eyes. Gary Cooper, they used to call him, and in his other arthritic hand, angry and misshapen fingers clutch the worn creased folds of a brown paper lunch bag. The kind kids used to carry to elementary school, and Gus sees the bag and he steps back from the door and he asks him in.

"I see you figured it out," says Luke when he sees Mabel and Finest.

Mabel picks up her coffee mug and drinks from it and looks at him over the rim.

Gus closes the door behind him and follows him into the room.

"You remember my sister," he says.

Luke takes his cap from his head. His hair. Thinned and greasy, gray. And he holds the cap in both hands with the bag against his chest and bows as much as much as much as his arthritis will let him toward the sofa. "Course I do," he says. "How are you, Mabel? You know you ain't aged a day."

Mabel sips from her mug and nods her head at him. "Sorry to hear about your mother," she slurs.

Luke stares at her a moment, looking confused, then bares his teeth again and turns to Gus and laughs out loud. "Guess it has been that long since we seen each other," he says.

"Figured what out?" says Gus.

"The television," answers Luke. "Only thing keeps him put." He pivots around in a circle and whistles to himself as he scans the disorder in the room. "Guess I come too late with these," he says and he hands the lunch bag to Gus and Gus opens it and reaches inside and pulls out two plastic bottles full of pills. Childproof caps and a pair of fur-lined metal handcuffs. Pink with a set of skeleton keys turned inside the lock, and he holds them up so Mabel can see them, and Finest sits there. Hands on his cane. Staring at the television.

"Hard to believe, isn't it?" says Luke. He looks at Finest and shakes his head. "First time he did it with me I wouldn't even consider it. Shoot. He was skinnier then than he is now. Figured it was kids got in," he says to Mabel. "Messed up the place on a dare."

The bulldozers beep and grind across the street. Mabel watches him from the sofa.

"Then he did it again," he says. "And I thought 'You are a goddamn lie, Lucas.' I still wouldn't believe it. Had to catch him in the act. Made myself a pot a coffee the next night. Turned the lights out and sat in the dark at the dining table and waited.

"It was the pacin' got to me more than anything else. That's how it starts. He gets all fidgety and he starts pacin'. Like he's mad at something and he don't know what or he has to get someplace but he can't remember where or how it is he's s'posed to get there. Then after while he just starts movin' things. Like he don't feel safe no more. Chairs under the doors. Tables on top the chairs. Hell!" he says and he looks around the room again. "I ain't got to tell you," and he takes off his hat and wipes his forehead with his sleeve and fits his cap back on. "Wanderin's the other thing," he says.

"Wandering?" says Gus and Mabel picks up her coffee mug and looks at him and sips from it and says "Hmph" after she swallows. And Gus stands there, staring at Finest. Fingering the pink fur on the handcuffs.

"'Fore I came to my senses and wrapped my head around what was happenin', I woke up one night and heard him fussin' with the deadbolt. It was cold out. There was snow on the ground. Figured by the time he got it sorted. The lock. I could get to him and stop him." He shakes his head back and forth and whistles. "Wasn't even close," he says. "Barely had my feet stuck in my slippers and he was out the door and loose over the fence. When I finally caught up to him, up the street and around the corner, he was pacin'. It's the most amazin' thing," he says. "To see him go like that," and he looks down at the floor in front of his feet and he shakes his head again when he adds, "I think when he wanders. For a time anyway. He's remembered where it was he was s'posed to be."

Gus looks at him and Luke looks up from the floor and points to the pill bottles Gus is holding in his hands and he reaches into one of his coverall pockets and pulls out his eye glasses.

"These'll keep him calm during the day," he says. "And two a these 'fore bed at night knocks him out cold, and you know what them are for. Backup. Mostly. Case the pills wear off. Had a time findin' ones with fur. Figured it would be more comfortable for him. Wouldn't chafe him. Ended up havin' to go down to the library and buy 'em off the Internet from a place in California calls itself a Fetish store. Thought I was orderin' black, but when they got to me they was pink. Coulda sent 'em back, I know. But I never saw the point. Cuffs was cuffs, far as I was concerned, and fur was fur, fake or not so long as it was soft and I knew Finest wouldn't mind."

Gus looks at the handcuffs.

"He will eat for ya," says Luke. "Pretty much whatever you put in front of him. You'll have to feed it to him. But he'll open up his mouth and chew and swallow just like everybody else, and so long as you show him what it is beforehand, he'll drink for ya without spillin' and he'll bang on the floor with his cane when he's ready to go to the toilet. Other than that, just stick him in front of the television and lock him down at night. Bathe him and trim his beard once in awhile. If you want," he says, easing his glasses back in his pocket, "'fore I go I can help you put the furniture back."

# 1939

When they hear about the white lady coming, walking across The Bone with a suitcase in her hand, accompanied by a swarm of migrating blackbirds, nobody believes it. Especially after that business with the Martians last year. Obliterating New Jersey, and though none would confess to being fooled by it, all would agree that even beings from outer space, crashing to the earth in giant cylindrical pea pods and blasting everybody to death with heat rays from the tips of tentacled fingers, was easier to sell than a white lady walking The Bone to the south side. Carrying a suitcase as if she were planning to stay awhile. Borne by a pall of blackbirds or not. And when Mabel peers through the curtains on the sitting room window to determine the source of all the fuss outside and sees her. Standing there on the

rim of Hope Street. The ground and the road beyond paved
with the squawking birds. The sky doused in shadow as
though a bulb burned out in the sun. Rippled. Screeching.
She still won't believe it. But there she is, standing there for
all the world. Flanked by the birds. Staring at the FOR LET
sign Gus hammered to the trunk of the tulip poplar tree at
the edge of the yard. The suitcase on the rim of the road
beside her feet, and as Mabel watches through the gap in
the curtains, she picks up the suitcase and stares for awhile
at the house then steps from the road into the yard and the
birds flutter into the air and land again on the ground as
she passes. Leaves. Fallen from the trees. Crumbling under
the spikes of her heels into the earth, and she walks past the
tulip poplar, across the yard, up the stairs to the porch, and
Mabel steps back from the window and lets the curtain fall
back to the sill and she stands at the door and looks at the
doorknob and she waits for the lady to knock.

"Hello," she says when Mabel answers. "I saw your sign. Is
the room already taken?"

Through the half-open door Mabel stares at the lady, at
the birds flitting and scavenging and molting in the trees
beyond. Cold chilling her face. Dishtowel slung over her
shoulder. The knife she was using to cut up the potatoes for
the pot roast still gripped in her hand.

"Beg your pardon?" she says.

The lady looks at the towel and the knife and smiles.
"The sign," she answers. "Posted on the tree out there," and
she half turns and points toward the birds. Milling and flying about like windup toy sentries around the base of the

tulip poplar tree where the sign is posted, then she turns back to Mabel and she smiles again. "Says you have a room for let. Is it still available?"

Mabel looks down at her hands and moves the knife and the towel behind her back and holds them there out of sight and she stares at the lady then past her. Over her shoulder, across the yard, past the sign and the leaves fallen and the birds squawking, and she looks at the houses on the other side of the street. Facing her. At the curtains parting and whiffling in the windows. The sky beyond. Rolling in swells of black.

"Yes, ma'am," she says. "But it ain't really a room."

"No?" says the lady.

"No, ma'am. It's a shed. Old work shed."

"Oh. I didn't realize."

"Yes, ma'am."

"But you're looking for somebody to live in it?"

"Yes, ma'am. But it's really just a shed. My daddy's before he passed."

"How big is it?"

"It's just a old shed, ma'am."

"Is it clean?"

"Yes, ma'am."

"And it has a bed?"

"Yes, ma'am and a chest a drawers and some shelvin'."

"May I see it?"

Mabel looks at her. Standing there in a tweed skirt and matching jacket the color of pine needles. Dressed like Christmas with gloves and a scarf around her neck the red of plum wine. On her head she wears a shoe hat. Black. Of wool in the shape of an upside down high-heeled pump. The toe bending forward and down. Hanging over her eyebrows like the bill on a ball cap. Sole and heel plumed toward the sky. The shoes on her feet are as the one on her head. Black. The leather cinched around the toes. Her lips are painted and she smells like a combination of ginger and cigarettes.

"Yes, ma'am," says Mabel. "But they got a roomin' house over on north side I expect be more comfortable. Sign say they got indoor toilets. The Colonel go over that way some-time. If you want I can see if he can run you back with him so you ain't gotta walk it twice."

"Belle," she says.

"Ma'am?"

"I want you to call me Belle," she says to her. "Ma'am makes me feel old, like my mother."

Mabel looks at her.

"And what do I call you?"

"My name is Mabel, ma'am. I mean…" She lowers her eyes and says, "Weesfree. Mabel Weesfree."

"How do you do, Mabel Weesfree?" she says to her and she holds out her hand and leaves it there, and Mabel looks at her, at the plum wine glove staining the pale white skin. Hovering in the air in front of her. Not sure what to do with it, and she stands there a moment and stares at it and when it stays there, hovering like that, like a bad idea. Lending no indication that it is planning on going anywhere until she tends to it, she sets the knife and the dishrag on the side table beside the door and as she reaches for it. The hand. To shake it. She glances across the street at the curtains dancing and fidgeting in the windows and she imagines Sister Tremble behind one of them. Paying a visit to the Mill Worker's Widow. The two of them shaking their heads together. Whispering the words *white people*. The Colonel. Stationed on his porch in his uniform, making out his report, and as she stands there in view of the parted windows of Hope Street, shaking a white plum hand reeking of ginger and cigarettes, Belle tells her that she is not partial, never has been, to rooming houses and that if it wouldn't be too much trouble she would like to see the room anyway. And she releases Mabel's hand and Mabel stares at her and looks around at all the curtains parting on the houses. The staging of blackbirds crowding on rooftops. Lining the tree branches in place of the leaves fallen. And finding no other way but to follow this migration and see where it takes her, she picks up the knife and the dishtowel and she leads the lady through the sitting room to a small squat building in back by the outhouse, at the edge of the cemetery. A stovepipe pushing up through the meager apex of the roof. Gabled after a barn.

Belle steps inside and sets her bag down and looks around. There are four walls with a single push-up window in the center of each. A bed. Twin with a cast iron frame pushed against one. The highboy against another and on the third, a column of four shelves each. Plywood. Nailed to the plaster a foot apart on either side of the window. The fourth, empty save another window, and the potbellied stove back in the corner. The floor is pine. Slat. A rag rug tossed in the middle of it. And, of course, it is spotless. Belle looks around the room and over at the stove and around the room again.

"I'll take it," she says.

By the time they return to the kitchen and come to an arrangement, Belle insisting that three dollars a month is far too little and Mabel repeating it's just a shed. A work shed, and it's not too late to see if The Colonel will run her over to the rooming house if she wants. The birds are gone and the trees look sickly. Gaunt and spare, rent of their dark quilted leaves like hunger-stricken captives stripped of clothing. Before a death march, and the sky has lulled from black into a kind of gray. The ashen of bones piled. Bleached by the sun in the shallows of open graves. A couple of crows flying. Chasing the silence of a hawk through the stark and arid branches.

They settle on five plus another three for her board and as Mabel shows her the outhouse and the rear entrance to the kitchen where she will take her meals with them, the temperature drops and an icy mist begins to fall, and when they hurry into the kitchen out of the wet and the cold into the heavy warmth of the house, while Mabel puts another log in the stove and pours the milk and chocolate into the sauce pan, Belle takes off her gloves and removes the shoe hat from her head and long thick wires of string. Black. Spring out and bound in all directions as she roots out an overwhelmed bobby pin and untwists the bun that was hiding inside the heel of the shoe and she pulls at it and combs the course black strands with her fingers and tames it back and smoothes it down and grabs it in her hands and twists it up again and she sticks the bobby pin down and up into the rewrapped bun and she pats it with her hand and sits at the table.

"Is it just you and your brother?" she says, undoing her scarf and the buttons on her jacket.

Mabel stands at the stove and stirs the hot chocolate and stares at her, and as she watches her, removing her scarf first and then her jacket, she sees what she might have missed had she never witnessed the taming of the hair. The high curved rise in her forehead, for instance, and the shape of her nostrils. The width of the bridge of her nose and the fullness of her lips. Painted. And Belle repeats the question: "Is it just you and your brother who live here?"

Mabel stares at her, at the pale white skin encasing her hands and her neck and doesn't it look a bit more yellow in this light? And the lips and the nose. The forehead and the feet. Stockinged. Coming out of the shoes now. Toes flexing above the floor for warmth. The ease with which she sits there in her body. As though she has lived in it for lifetimes. And as she stirs the milk and chocolate and pours in the sugar, she stares at this root-and-cigarette-scented woman before her and she wonders how it might feel to walk on the other side of something.

"Did you want any of that sugar in the pan?" Belle says to her. "Or is sweetening the stove first part of the recipe?" and she looks at her and laughs and Mabel smells the sugar burning and looks down at the pan to see a deep copper residue spreading over the stovetop, and she curses herself and reaches for the dishrag and snatches the pan from the flame.

Belle falls quiet and stares at her then smiles a little when she says, "It's a bit of a shock at first. Was for me anyway. Takes some getting used to."

Mabel looks at the stovetop and scrubs at the stain. "I thought you was…"

"I know," says Belle. "Most people do. Shall I help you with these potatoes?" she says to her, and before Mabel can say no she stands and picks up the cutting knife Mabel dropped on the table with the dishtowel when they ran inside to escape the drizzling cold, and for awhile there is silence between them save the clip of the knife blade against the wood of the cutting board. The scrubbing of the dishrag against the stove.

"Everybody but the people who look for that sort of thing," says Belle. "The ones who look for it tend to call it out right away," and she scrapes the cut-up wedges of potato from the cutting board into the soup pot and she reaches for another one and she holds it there in her hand for a moment and stands there. Staring at the window at the rain freezing on the pane. "Funny thing is," she says after a time, "most days I'm lucky if I feel like much of anything at all, let alone one particular thing or another. But people seem to need you to be. Want you to choose like it's a game of sides or something and if you refuse, they'll choose for you. It comforts them somehow. Lessens their burden. So that's what I do," she says. "I lighten people's loads and let them choose for themselves. Makes the way a little easier sometimes."

Mabel sets the dishrag aside and places the chocolate pan back on the burner and she stands there and she watches her, and there is something about the way she is slicing the potatoes. Holding the knife, that reminds her of her father. Something to do with the wrist maybe, though she is unable to place it, and she stands at the stove and she watches her and the rain drizzles and freezes on the window.

DRIZZLE. THAT'S WHAT her mother called the weather the day her father came home and told her that he quit his job with the Simlers. It wasn't a downpour, she said. Or a thunderstorm. That might have made sense somehow, but what fell from the sky that day was hard pressed to pass as moisture much less some kind of a rain. It was drizzle, she said. A freezing of sorts. Growing colder and damper by the hour. He came in out of the drizzle and hung up his jacket and he sat down in his chair and put his feet up on the footrest and unscrewed the cap on his bottle, and when she came in from the kitchen to ask what he was doing home so early in the day, he turned to her and he looked at her and he said, "I quit."

"Quit what?"

"Beuford."

"What for?"

He looked away from her and drank from the bottle.

"Quit or got fired?" she said to him.

"Quit," he said and he drank again.

"He do somethin' to you?"

"Didn't do nothin'."

She looked at him. "Then he must've said somethin'," she said.

"Didn't say nothin'. Didn't do nothin'. Nothin'," and he sat there staring at the empty picture shelf on the other side of the room and he tilted his bottle back, and Mabel memorized the look on her mother's face as she stood there staring at him. Belly swollen full with her baby brother Gus and she stood there and she stared at him and she opened her mouth a couple of times to say something but nothing came out, and Mabel stood in the doorjamb between the kitchen and the sitting room and watched her. Opening and closing her mouth and looking at him. Her father just sitting there. Drinking from his bottle. Saying nothing along with her. Drizzle. Freezing on the windows.

"This ain't about that mess they been talkin'?" she said to him.

Her father was silent.

"Tell me this is not that mess."

He sat there with his feet up and his bottle in his hand and he stared at the picture shelf and her mother bit down on her lip and pressed on the small of her back with her fingers, then held herself by her arms. Rubbing her shoulders, and when she saw Mabel standing there, watching them from the doorway, she hollered at her and ordered her to her room, and Mabel ran down the hall and closed the door behind her and sat on her bed and kicked her feet back and forth above the floor and watched them. Her feet. The shadow of them. Crossed at the ankles. Swinging through the uneven grain in the hardwood like peculiar burdens weighted on threadbare souls. And as she sat there, watching the burden of her feet swing, she listened to the muffled barking of her mother. Chasing her father's silence through the wall gristle like crows. Dogging hawks through the skeletons of barren landscapes. Useless, and she sat there and she listened to her mother bark through the walls and the house chasing after silence. Her feet rocking back and forth above the floor like a pendulum. Drizzle seeping through the cracks in the glass pane in her window.

The following morning the drizzle was gone, but her father remained in his chair. Staring at the picture shelf with his feet up. The bottle was empty, and sometime during the night a chill settled into her mother's chest that never thawed, and as soon as Gus Junior was walking good, on his own without the boards, she started to cough and her chest began to hurt and in the middle of hanging wash or shoveling the outhouse, she had to stop from time to time and sit for a minute on a stump or a stool, and she'd wake in the night awash in the puddles of her own sweat and she would have to get up and change the bedding before she could go back to sleep, and when she looked at her handkerchief in the mornings after a bad coughing spell, most of the time it was stained with blood. And soon she started to lose weight and it wasn't long before Doc Agee called in the men from the asylum and quarantined the house for a month after they took her away.

In the days before she died, they were forbidden to see her. Sister Tremble and The Pastor put them in the back of The Pastor's Model A and drove them to Cincinnati to say goodbye. Mabel and Gus Junior. Her father stayed behind, and when they arrived in Cincinnati, The Pastor kept the motor running and waited in the car while The Sister took hold of their hands and hurried them along the sidewalk past the courtyard, around to the back of a tall brick building where she stood them together in front of her and squatted and bent down behind them and she put her arms around them and Mabel could smell the Sweet Georgia Brown frying in her hair as she looked up and pointed to a window high above their heads and she told them to look at it and wave to it. "Come on," she said. "Wave to your mother now. She's been waiting on you. Waiting for you to come so she could say goodbye to you and tell you that she loves you before she passes on to heaven to be with Jesus. Come on, Junior. Wave now. Wave your hand and say goodbye to your mother."

And they stood there on a sidewalk in the back of a tall brick building in Cincinnati. Eyes burning as they squinted into the sun to stare at a window Sister Tremble kept insisting was their mother, and they stood there and they squinted at it and they raised their hands above their heads and waved to it and when they finished, The Sister hurried them back along the sidewalk, back to The Pastor's Model A and he drove them back to the south side and dropped them in front of their house, and when they got out of the car, before he drove off The Pastor stuck his head out of the window and said, "Tell your father I'll be around." And they stood at the edge of the yard in front of the house and they watched the Model A drive away, and when it turned the corner from Hope Street onto Justice, they looked up toward the sky and they went inside. The sun. A fireball. Blazing above their heads.

THE FIRST SNOW never sticks. The flakes are large like popcorn or torn up bits of paper drifting down from a giant cardboard box tipped on its side somewhere over a stage in the rigging high above the clouds in the theater of the heavens, and they melt as soon as they catch the ground. The sky is white and the air smells of sweat and Finest's stench and the waste matter of horses and the barn door claps and rattles open on its track as the rollers squeak and sing in the wind. Finest stabs the pitchfork into the bedding and scoops the muck of soiled hay and horse dung into the wheelbarrow while Gus sits against the wall opposite the stall with his knees up and stares down the aisle way past the mare tied to the hitching post, through the door rattling, and watches the snow. His lessons notebook on the ground beneath his knees.

"She white?" says Finest and he grunts and clears his throat as he pitches a scoop of horse dung into the wheelbarrow.

"Naw," says Gus. "She just looks white."

"How you know?"

"Know what?"

"She ain't white."

"You just do," says Gus. "You'll see. Not at first. You gotta look at her some. You'll see it," he says. "But you gotta look for it." He turns away from the snow and looks across the aisle way. Fingers rubbing the length of the spine on his notebook, and he watches him. Stooped over in the stall. Cap turned on his head like an old man save the ease with which he skewers and tosses horse shit into a wheelbarrow.

"Thought you didn't have to do that no more," says Gus.

"This all I do gotta do," says Finest. "Sides keep a eye on Beatrice."

"Everyday?"

"Naw," says Finest. "Once a week. Gotta shovel the shit every day, but that don't take no time."

Gus sits there and stares at him. "You notn shovelin' shit right now?" he says.

"Naw," says Finest and he stabs at the straw and pierces it with the prongs and pitches another forkful into the wheelbarrow, and Gus looks at him and watches him and laughs.

"You not muckin' out horse shit right now?"

"Naw," says Finest as fist-sized rocks of horse manure thunk into the bottom of the wheelbarrow.

"Then what you doin' then?"

"Right now?"

"Naw, Ace. What you doin' tomorrow? Day before yesterday? Yeah! right now," says Gus and he laughs into his chest and shakes his head at the ground, and Finest leans the pitchfork against the wall inside the door to the stall and he grins at him and his scars twitch in the scattered gray light of afternoon.

"Right now," he says and he clears his throat and pulls up on the handles of the wheelbarrow. "I'm swappin' out beddin'" and he guides the cart of excrement down the aisle way toward the entrance to the barn.

Gus leaves his notebook on the ground and jumps to his feet and catches up to him and walks with him past the snow white mare tied to the hitching post who cakewalks and swishes her tail at them as they pass into the snow falling outside, and they slog around to the dung pile in the yard in back of the barn through the mud and the slush. Faces turned in against the wind and Finest dips the nose on the wheelbarrow and dumps the horse muck onto the dung heap, and snowflakes land and turn to ice water on their caps and shoulders and the backs of their coats.

Gus pulls his collar tight around his neck.

"And that ain't the same as shovelin' shit?" he says.

"Naw," says Finest and he turns the nose around on the wheelbarrow and points it in the other direction and trudges back through the slush the way they came. "If I was shovelin' shit," he says, "'stead of a pitchfork I'd be usin' a shovel. And only scoopin' out the wet muck. By itself. Mixin' in a new bale with the leftover dry."

Gus tugs on his collar and follows.

"When I'm swappin' beddin'," says Finest, and he stops and he puts his hand to his mouth and coughs and clears his throat then lifts up on the wheelbarrow handles again and continues. "Got to empty out everything. The whole stall. Then I got to sweep and mop it clean and lay it all back fresh. Beddin'. Feed tub. Water bucket full from the pump. And after this one I got to do the same for the other three. Day's damn near gone 'fore I'm through." When they reach the stall door he turns the wheelbarrow so that the nose is facing the entrance again, toward the mare and the door rattling, and he steps back into the stall and reaches for the pitchfork. "Then I gotta go inside and spend the night lookin' after ol' gal," he says over his shoulder. "Shovelin' shit? That ain't nothin'. A hour tops. All four stalls. Whole day still in front of me," and he stabs the pitchfork into the soiled hay and he tosses it into the wheelbarrow.

Gus stands there. Leaning against the stall watching horse shit fly into the cart beside him. "You ain't gotta do the pigs?" he says.

Finest sticks his head out of the stall and looks around and up and down the aisle way before answering. "Shoot," he says, spearing the pitchfork back into the bedding. "'Cept when he come to pick 'em out for slaughter, Hog don't even let Beuford near them things."

Gus looks down the aisle way at the pens roped off at the other end of the barn then back at Finest. "Still looks like you shovelin' shit to me," he says.

"That's cuz you don't know nothin' bout it, schoolboy."

"'Bout what?"

"Workin'. Division of tasks and labor and such. You too busy sittin' up in that schoolhouse. Lookin' in all them books don't learn you nothin'."

"Beats shovelin' shit."

"Maybe so," says Finest and his throat catches and it sounds like someone is ripping a sheet of paper in half. "But come the end of the week," he says. "You still got a empty pocket."

Gus looks at the mare, and Finest leans the pitchfork against the wall and grabs hold of the wheelbarrow and pushes the cart up the aisle way and Gus walks alongside him, and when they step outside into the disappearing snow, he glances up toward the attic to the window imbedded in the dormer in the roof on the side of the house.

"Who's up there with her now?" he says.

"Sara," says Finest, and they trudge around the barn through the mud and the slush and Finest dumps the wheelbarrow onto the dung heap and turns it back around the way they came.

"Hog and Luke never watch her?" says Gus.

Finest stands there a moment and stares into the snow dissolving into the soil turned over in the field on the other side of the dung heap, and he stands there and he watches the flakes rain down like powdered sugar and he sticks his tongue out of his mouth and tries to catch one and when he does he says, "Hog don't want nothin' to do with her," and he sticks his tongue out again and darts his head about until he catches another and another. "And she don't want nothin' to do with Luke. And Beuford," he says, catching a fourth, he don't want nothin' to do with none of em." And he turns away from the field and lifts up on the handles on the wheelbarrow, and as they tramp back around the barn, Gus glances up to the attic again and when they walk back inside, past the mare, down the aisle way, and he bends to retrieve his lessons book, he thinks about his father. The last time he saw him. Propped up in the bed like he was sleeping, and the migration into their lives of the white-looking woman to whom his sister let his old work shed.

THEY HEARD THE squawking from inside the schoolhouse. The Pettiford boys were first to get up from their desks and go to the window and look, and when Junebug Marston jumped up and next Lucille Sutton copied them, the whole class followed behind. All twenty-seven of them, and the deafening noise of it forced Sister Tremble to open the door and change the lesson plan and teach the class outside for the day. And they put on their coats and their scarves and their caps and their jackets and she led them out into the schoolyard where they bunched around her in a half-drawn circle and she told them that the birds they were seeing, congregating and swooping before them, were migrating. Leaving their homes for the winter to live in the warmer temperatures of the south, and that not just birds, she said, which were the most common. From geese to brambling finches and owls. But every kind of creature. Elephants and whales. Earthworms and turtles, too. When it got too cold or wet or dry or the food supply ran low. Went off in search of a better place to live. All God's children. Even people, she said. Migrated when conditions warranted. Some just to get a look at the other side of the road. What they were seeing this morning, she told them, was special. It was a laying up. A holdover after a long day's journey in a place deemed free of predators, where the birds, exhausted, could fatten themselves and bathe their feathers and rest up their wings for the next leg of the passage. They ought to consider it an honor, she said. To be chosen as a stopping place. For it meant that above all else. The noise and the disruption. The extravagance and excrement. Ravaged and plundered gardens and crops left in their wake. The birds felt safe here.

"Sorry to hear about your mother and father," she said to him.

He had just come in from witnessing the birds in the schoolyard and the two of them were sitting there together at the kitchen table. Mabel and a white lady who called herself Belle. Drinking hot chocolate, and he stood there and he looked at them and they looked at him and Mabel turned to the white lady and said, "This is my little brother. Gus," and the white lady looked at him and smiled and he looked at her, at her mouth moving, and in a warm and scratchy voice that seemed born out of thin air, he heard the words "Nice to meet you," and something about "sorry" and "mother" and "father" and he stood there. Looking at her. Watching her mouth move, and there was something about her, about the way his sister sat there with her at the table instead of serving her. Holding her coffee mug. The two of them drinking hot chocolate together.

"Will you join us for a cup of cocoa?" she said to him, and then he saw it, and before he could answer, she had risen already from her chair and crossed to the other side of the kitchen to the cupboard and he watched her, and along the way she brushed her hand across his sister's shoulder and she reached in the cupboard and took down another coffee mug. And from the sauce pan warming atop the stove, she poured him a cup of hot chocolate and set it on the table, and she pulled out a chair for him and patted the seat on it and she looked at him. Standing there in the doorway with his lessons book in his hand. Watching her, and she smiled again and told him to put down his workbook and come on over there and sit with them awhile.

# may 8, 2007

The bulldozers are quiet today. Mabel pushes her walker so that the side of the basket flushes clean against the edge of the countertop, and as the bottle and the coffee mug rattle inside the cage, she turns and leans and braces herself on the counter with her hand and with the other she reaches up and rummages through the cupboard next to the refrigerator. Finding nothing save the chipped mugs and saucers that have lived in the house longer than she has, she slides the basket and the walker to the left along the countertop, past the windowsill and the placid blue of a day coming in unfettered by bulldozer dust, and she braces herself and she reaches in and ferrets around the next cupboard.

She is hunting for ginger. The root of it. Because all day long she has been smelling it. Fresh ginger. Above the leftover tinges of things lingering in the air. Cinnamon toast. Coffee. Butter. Forgotten too long in the pan. Bacon grease and cigarette smoke. The stain of it. Yellowed and brown. Steeped over the years into the baseboards and walls and all of it save the ginger. Cut with the edge of body filth. The ginger hovers by itself and was so insistent this morning that it woke her from a dead sleep a full hour earlier than she had planned to get up, and when she opened her eyes she half expected to see it there. The cloven hoof of it dangling above her head from a string attached to the yellowed and paint-chipped ceiling.

So far she has searched the pantry. The refrigerator. The drawers beneath the countertop. The cupboards below the drawers. In the dining room she scoured the china cabinet, the bookcase and side tables. Emptied the medicine chest in the bathroom and twice now she has patted down and strip-searched the linen and hall closets like an overzealous police officer or customs agent looking for drugs or terrorists. She has interrogated the dresser and the drawers in her night stand. Sought out for questioning the shelves in her wardrobe. She has even eyed the cobwebs harboring who knows what in darkened corners. Hollows and the cracks in the walls. Boards loose in the floorboards, and after she has finished with the kitchen she will push down the hallway and shakedown the usual suspects in Junior's room, and after Junior's room she will re-interview the bathroom and her bedroom, and by the time she is satisfied that she has turned out every crevice and followed up every lead, she will have coerced to near confession the rails on the balustrades of both porches. The garbage cans. Sojourner's shed and the interior of the Edsel. The sun quit for the day, replaced by the stars and a flaxen crescent moon slivered against a blackened sky, and she will be no closer to finding the source of the ginger than she was when she started.

When she pushed her walker into the kitchen this morning Junior was standing in front of the stove stirring a pot on the burner and Finest was handcuffed to the leg of the kitchen table watching him.

"What you makin' calls for ginger?" she asked him.

"Ginger?" He looked at her like she was crazy.

"You ain't cookin' with ginger?"

"In the grits? Maybe it's time for you to put down that bottle."

She looked around the room.

"Then where's it comin' from?"

"Where's what comin' from?"

"The ginger."

"What ginger?"

"You don't smell ginger?"

"Fresh ginger? Naw."

"You smell some other kinda ginger?" she said and she looked at him, at the sunlight glaring over his shoulder through the window. Shadowing his face.

"Mae, I don't smell no ginger, period."

He stirred the grits and she put her hand in front of her eyes to block the glare of the harsh morning sun and she held her hand up and she looked at him awhile to make sure he was telling the truth, then over at Finest who sat at the table looking at the two of them as if they were a television screen and he sat there. Staring at them as fixed and straight as he sat on the sofa in front of the real television. Eyes blinking now and again to adjust to the pace of the images changing. Fractured and clipped. Like pages flashing in a giant electronic flipbook and she looked at the handcuffs pink and furry around the black ash of his ankle shackled to the blond of the table leg and she thought about Clovis Sutton. A full-grown woman, and her mama Lucille. Gates at the bottoms of staircases, holding cells and prisons, and she wondered if either of them was still living somewhere.

"Simler boy said you only had to lock him down at night," she said.

Gus stirred the grits. "Not takin' any chances," he said. "Not after yesterday. Wasn't for Luke comin' by, all that stuff still be where it was."

A whisk of ginger brushed at her nose as if someone had bottled it and stroked the breeze with a test sample, the way twin engines and puddle jumpers trail banners across the sky advertising sunscreen at air shows.

"You don't smell that?" she said to him and she turned her walker a bit so she could take in more of the room.

"I smell grits and bacon," he answered. "And I'm about to start smellin' eggs."

"Thought you didn't have no money," she said to him.

He stared into the pan and talked as he stirred. "Don't," said Gus. "Used the money in the silverware drawer. Wanted to surprise you. After we went to the bathroom this morning," he added as if he and Finest had been relieving themselves together the whole of their lives, "I sat ol Superman here in front of the television and cuffed him to the sofa, then drove into Caleb's while you were still sleep. Open the refrigerator," he told her.

It was full. She lowered her head down and sniffed it. The freezer was filled with meat but no ginger.

"Picked you up another couple of bottles," he said to her back. "Receipt's on the table. Put the change back in the drawer. Hope you hungry."

She looked at him, wondering what he was up to, and just as she was about to ask, another promotion for ginger streaked by and instead she turned away from him and stood there jutting her nose back and forth toward the sitting room. Furrowing the air the way a possum ruts the ground in search of beetles and snails, and after Junior insisted that she sit down to breakfast and put something in her stomach besides creek water, when she picked up a piece and held it to her nose even the bacon smelled like ginger and she sat there. Picking around the food going cold on her plate. Sipping from her coffee mug, while Junior sat across from her, scooting his chair closer to Finest in order to feed him, and she sat there, sipping creek water and huffing ginger. Watching them. Junior: dipping forkfuls of eggs into Finest's grits and holding them in front of his face. Finest: opening and closing his mouth around them, then chewing and swallowing and opening it again, waiting for the next bite to come like a hatchling, mute and shriveled, clamoring for the next worm.

"He talk yet?" she asked him.

The sun was high in the sky now and the glare coming through the window was gone.

"Nope," said Gus and he picked up another bit of egg and dipped it into the grits, and she held on to her coffee mug and she watched him and each time he raised the fork in the air he studied Finest's open mouth the way a surgeon considers the place he's supposed to cut before inserting the scalpel, as though he were resolving the best way to go about it. Spill the least blood.

"You still sure it's him?" she said. She rutted her nose toward them and sniffed at the air.

"Yep," he said and he sectioned a strip of bacon and forked a ration into Finest's mouth and her eyes followed the lance of the sunbeam as she turned away from them, cutting across the threshold through the doorway into the sitting room, and she looked into the sitting room and she stared at the picture shelf. Empty on the opposite wall.

"You didn't put my pictures back?" she said to him.

"What?"

"My pictures of Sojourner. On the shelf. You didn't put 'em back."

Her hands shook as she took up her mug and pushed back from the table, and she stood up and pushed her way past them into the sitting room to the picture shelf and she looked at it and she ran her fingers across the vacancy of it. Upsetting the dust settled on the surface between the missing pictures, and now she is worrying cupboards. Bedeviling drawers and the insides of pillowcases. The sun high and the bulldozers quiet. Planes flying overhead. The coffee mug and bottle rattling inside the basket of her walker.

*THE CHIMES RANG on the back of the kitchen door as she entered and again when she left. The suitcase was in her hand. Alligator. She stood inside the doorsill holding the worn and faded bag down by her ankles. By the handle. The way Mr. Metzger carried his briefcase when Mabel passed him on the walkway in the mornings and Mrs. Metzger stood on the porch behind him. Waving goodbye as he backed out of the driveway, holding the door for Mabel as he drove off to work.*

*Belle pushed the door closed and stood there. Her overcoat draped over her forearm. She wore a skirt suit of soft brown wool and a hat on her head with a feather in it and a mesh net veil that hung down over her face.*

*"I have to go away," she said.*

*Mabel sat on the edge of her chair. Bending over the washtubs. Running a pair of undershorts back and forth against the ridges in the scrub board, and she sat there beneath the socks and the handkerchiefs. Pant legs and shirtsleeves. Dripping from the clotheslines strung above her head from corner to corner across the kitchen. Slicing the room into an X shape. She rubbed the undershorts against the washboard and she sat on the edge of the chair and she looked at her through the dripping and drying wash.*

*"Back to Cleveland," said Belle. "Something I have to see to."*

*Mabel stared at her.*

"It shouldn't take long," she said. She set the bag on the floor and ducked beneath the X of the clotheslines and stood there. Smiling. Shaking her head at the washtubs and the clothes hanging all over the place. The rags. Spread over the linoleum to catch the water. "But just in case," she said, "I wanted to pay up the rent in advance." And from her purse she withdrew a thick cache of five- and one-dollar bills and left them on the table. Mabel scrubbed the undershorts against the washboard's ridges and looked at her, at the bills on the table, and watched her. "Didn't want you to think I was skipping out on you," said Belle and she looked at the clothes and the water dripping onto the rag-covered linoleum and she stepped back under the X and smiled and shook her head again and took up her bag and left. Cold rushing in. Chimes ringing behind her as she pulled the door closed. The memory of ginger milling inside the sill where she'd stood.

One week she was with them. One week. Scenting the house with the redolence of ginger. Their hearts with all the stories she told them of all the places she'd seen. New York. Chicago. The men she knew in Detroit who gathered together in each other's houses so they could dress up like women. "Even down to their drawers," she told them. "Lacy. Frilly. Pretty little things. Ordered them from the pages of a magazine. Pinks. Lavenders. Reds." Of women who changed their names from Lucinda to Lou and Alison to Al. Georgia to George, and spent the whole of their lives moving through the world as men. She told them of circus freaks. Bearded ladies and acrobats, she called them. Who jumped up from the ground and turned summersaults. Backwards in the air before landing on each other's shoulders.

*Flipping and stacking like chairs sometimes one on top of the other, three and four high. Contortionists who lay flat on their bellies with their chins mounted on the ground like trophies on walls and their legs raised up over their shoulders beyond their heads. The soles of their feet level with the earth in front of them. Hiding their faces and mounted chins like praying mantises. Beheaded and skewered for mating, and she told them of colored people like themselves only she used the word "black" instead of "colored" in a place called Harlem who were writing books and plays and essays about their lives. Making music and movies and getting paid for it, and to prove it she gave to Gus Junior a two-inch thick sheaf of papers she carried around in her suitcase she called a manuscript and said that the author was a friend of hers. It was a story, she told them, about a young black man named Bigger who was not much older than Gus and she asked him to read it and tell her what he thought of it. And then she was gone and she was away so long they thought she had burrowed under the ground someplace and lapsed into sleep for the winter, and just as they began to wonder if she was ever coming back or had ever been there at all, after the leaves began to bud and the snow trillium posies bloomed, she returned to them and this time she held two suitcases in her hands. The alligator and a square black box with metal hinges on the back and a compartment inside the lid from which she took out a record and fit the hole in the center of it over a spindle in the middle of a flat round pad she called a turntable and she fit the record over the spindle and cranked around in circles an arm on the side of the box crooked in the shape of a spider's leg and she cranked the crooked arm and when the record began to spin she swiveled a long tube over it that narrowed into a cylinder and something resembling a bicycle bell on the end of it and she placed the bell and the cylinder on a groove in the record and, from somewhere in the box she could not comprehend, Mabel began to hear music, and before she had time to figure out which part of the contraption was making the sound, Belle waltzed over to where she was standing in the doorway and led her into the sitting room and when they reached the middle of the floor, Belle turned to face her and threw her head back and laughed. Showing all thirty-two of her glowing white teeth, and she placed one of Mabel's hands in hers. The other on her shoulder and as they started to dance, Mabel stared at the floor and stepped and crossed and followed Belle's feet as best she could and Belle pressed her hand into Mabel's hip and steered her around the room and a cloud of ginger rose about them like dust kicking up in a desiccated field during a wind storm, and Belle pressed and stepped and crossed and skipped and Mabel followed and as she wondered whether this lightness coming over her was the same that rushed over the birds when they took to the air in flight, in a warm and scratchy discordant voice wrapped in ginger, Belle started to sing.*

*"No one to walk with, all by myself. No one to talk with, I'm happy on the shelf. Ain't misbehavin'. Savin' my love for you..."*

*The second time she left she said it was business. She wore a coat with rounded shoulders. Beige with a pocket sewn on the left over the bosom and no collar, and Mabel began to feel the ache that remains after being chosen for a time only to be discarded. The hole in the heart claimed when abandoned, and the third time Belle just stood there. Alligator bag hanging from her hand down by her ankles.*

*Mabel looked at her, at the bills as they landed on the table.*

*"Rent's already paid," she said.*

*"Extra," said Belle. "In case something comes up," and this time her teeth were veiled when she smiled and she turned and picked up her bag and Mabel sat there and stared at the cache of bills lying in front of her and the door swung open and the chimes rang behind it. And after the fourth time she left, although the opening of the hole began to skim over and harden, the hole itself festered and tunneled deeper.*

*The last time she took the car. Sister Tremble was there and rain threatened and the wind kicked up. Harrying the drainpipe on the side of the house and, save a couple of crows cawing, silenced the sky. The door was open and Mabel looked outside through the screen and for a time the late-morning day was cast into the half-light of night falling, and whenever the crows cawed and she caught sight of the shadows of time creeping past the trunks of the tulip poplar trees swaying back and forth in the mocking and swirling wind, she turned and glanced at the hands on the clock ticking on the wall above the sink to verify the hour.*

*Sister Tremble sat at the end of the table and stared at the windowsill awhile at the radio. Playing the stories in the background, then turned back to Mabel and let her eyes fall on the formula bottle perched on the table in front of the high chair stationed midway between them. A scarf was tied around her arm below her elbow. Knotted into a sling on her shoulder, and as she sat there across from her, holding onto Sojourner, asleep in her arms, Mabel looked away from the makeshift bandage and all the broken wing it held implied and trained her eyes instead on the baby.*

*"She always this quiet?" said Sister Tremble.*

*"She sleep," said Mabel.*

*Sister Tremble shifted in her chair.*

*"I know she's asleep," she said. "But even sleeping babies make a sound now and then."*

*Mabel glanced at the clock.*

*"Hiccups. Gurgles. Maybe you ought to check and see if she's breathing."*

*"She breathin'."*

*Sister Tremble set her mouth in a smirk and stared at her, at the baby and the black wisps of hair sticking up over the pale white skin like fine curls of smoke drifting up from an exhausted fire. She looked at the backs of the baby's hands. The fingers. Small and doll-like. Gripping Mabel's shirt collar. The flesh on the knuckles wrinkled as if they had been scrubbed too hard in the effort to get them so pale and white rather than age-shriveled.*

*"Looks just like her, doesn't she?" said Sister Tremble.*

*"Mmm hmm," said Mabel.*

*"Like she thought her up in her head then made her appear. Just like that. Like magic."*

*"Mmm hmm," said Mabel.*

*"Except for the mouth," said Sister Tremble. "The lips," she added. "And the forehead is all wrong.*

*"She said anything yet?"*

*"Who?" said Mabel. "The baby?"*

*Sister Tremble shook her head and smiled. "About the father,"
she said.*

*"Nope," said Mabel and stared at the clock.*

*"The Pastor and I used to talk about children," said The Sis-
ter and she held her arm in her lap and turned and stared at
the radio again, at the window. Stella Dallas was trapped in
a submarine at the bottom of the sea somewhere on the other
side of the world. "But the good Lord never blessed us that way,"
said Sister Tremble.*

*Sojourner shifted and started to cry. Mabel held her above
her head and sniffed at her diaper, then placed her in the high
chair and tied her bib around her neck.*

*"We were given other blessings," said the Sister. "More than
we ever deserved," and she turned back to Sojourner, flashing the forsaken grin of a woman who accepts she will never
bear children. "Like the schoolhouse," she said. "Maybe I'll get a
chance to teach this little bit one day."*

*The forehead was wrong, thought Mabel. But also familiar
in a way she couldn't quite place...*

*Sister Tremble looked through the window. "What do you
think it's doing out there?" she said.*

*...and the mouth and the lips were off as well and she
searched her mind to recall where she had seen them before, but
came up blank.*

*"Hard to say," said Mabel. She rolled her eyes away from
the baby toward the screen. The day eclipsed by half-light still.
Wind swirling. "Seem like it's still decidin'."*

*Sister Tremble nodded.*

*"Well, I wish it would hurry up and make up its mind," she said. "Can't tell if I ought to go on home now and risk getting caught in it or wait and see what it does."*

*She looked at the clock. Ticking loudly above the sink.*

*"That time true?" she said.*

*Mabel nodded and Sister Tremble nodded in turn, then stood from her chair and with the arm that was not broken she smoothed out her dress. "Suppose I could wait a little while longer," she said and she looked at the clock again and sat back down. "See if it blows over," and drummed her fingertips against the table top.*

*But now as she fed her, the baby, Mabel saw it. Not in the lips or the mouth or the all-wrong forehead, but in the jaw.*

*"Seems like she should've been back by now," said The Sister. "Where'd she say she was going again?"*

*"Town," said Mabel.*

*The defiance of it as the baby sucked at the nipple of the bottle and swallowed. The way it jutted out in front of her. Not so much in greeting but in warning. She had seen that jaw in only one other face and the hole in her heart that had festered and tunneled deeper now began to put down roots and spread itself into a gorge.*

*"She's not walking, is she?"*

*Mabel stared at the child.*

*"Took the car," she said.*

*"Probably waiting it out somewhere," said The Sister.*

*Mabel tilted the bottle and stared.*

*"They're so precious when they're that age, aren't they?"*

*Mabel didn't answer.*

*The hands ticked on the clock.*

*Sister Tremble glanced at her broken arm. "Good thing the Lord didn't bless me with one," she said. "So clumsy I'd be afraid I'd break it."*

*When the Milk of Magnesia announcer came on she asked Sister Tremble to turn off the radio, and when she did Mabel turned away from the baby and stared into the almost-night falling in the middle of the day and ran her fingers through the wisps of smoke rising up from the baby's head. Bent. Like teeth on a rake. Rasping leaves into a pile to burn, and she stood there as she hefted Sojourner back onto her shoulder and stared into the almost-night. The trees. And thought about how easy things go from one to the other. Day into night. Night into day.*

*First she stopped sleeping and no matter what hour she woke, when Mabel walked into the kitchen in the mornings, she would find her. Sitting at the table. Smoking. In the dark. Listening to torch songs on the radio. Ellington on the Victrola. Next she asked them to repeat what they said to her. She would sit across the porch from them atop the balustrade. The sun red behind her. Kicking her feet back and forth. Or next to them on the swing. Inside on the sofa, and she would look at them and they her and talk to them. Inquire about their day. How they slept, and when they answered her she would stare at them awhile as if they had not spoken and her eyes would dull against the hallowed glow of the sun and she would sit there a moment. Still and quiet. And they would watch her as she shook her head and swept her hand in front of her face as though she'd walked into a cobweb and after sweeping the unseen tangle aside her face would relight and she would smile again and ask, "I'm sorry. Did you say*

something?" Then the water ran from her eyes. With no warning, for no apparent reason. Trails of it slid down her cheeks
and tracked through her makeup like the heels of boots skidding
through mud down embankments, and no matter what they
tried or offered she would not be comforted, and after the water
ran, her appetite left off in search of it and what she did eat
she retched into her napkin. The cupped palm of her hand. And
when the ground went hard, the air above it sweat with cold,
her belly grew big and she moved into the house into Junior's
room and Gus Junior moved into the shed.

In the months before the birth she left them again. Her body
remained but the rest of her had gone to a place just beyond
their reach, returning now and then through a flash of remembrance. Warm and fleeting across her eyes. The low rasp of a
chuckle from her mouth as if she were poking her head in the
door on her way to somewhere else just to make sure they were
home still. The rest of the time she had someone cover for her. A
substitute. Like a teacher in the classroom. For though she looked
at them and words came out of her mouth when she opened it
and they could see her there. Standing in front of them, and
smell her. Moving throughout the house trailing ginger and cigarette smoke behind her like twin trains on a bridal gown, and
feel her. Her absence. Hovering in every room. When she spoke
to them they had no idea who she was nor she they and they
slogged through the motions together like stand-in blackboard
lessons on which they would be tested later.

When the baby came she left them for good. She held it
alright when Doc Agee placed it with the cord on her belly and
told her it was a little girl. The afterbirth still attached in the

*bucket on the floor beside the bed, and she stared at her and fed her long enough to look up and smile one day and announce that her name was Sojourner. But after the naming, when the cord dried up and broke off into the afterbirth bucket, she was gone and Mabel went about the business of mothering the newborn the same way she went about feeding and diapering the others she had cared for. Cooing and pacifying, and she wondered how much time would pass before they looked up and saw that her body had left them as well.*

*The morning she took the car she stood in the doorway between the hall and the kitchen and watched as Mabel secured Sojourner in her high chair and fastened her bib around her neck. The one with all the pretty horses on it. Her arms were folded in front of her and she wore a yellow cotton dress. Sleeveless with a matching patent leather belt buckled around her waist, and her shoes were brown with red polished nails peeping through the holes cut into the toes. Her hair was pulled back from her face and she stood there. Watching as Mabel dipped her finger into the bowl of mashed rice and milk and rubbed it on Sojourner's lips.*

*"I have to go into town," she said.*

*Mabel looked at her, at the dress. The shoes. Then wiped away the dribble from Sojourner's chin. The dried kernels of rice stuck to her fingers and the curls in her hair.*

*"It's fixin' to storm," she said.*

*Belle turned and looked toward the window.*

*"I'll drive," she said.*

*Mabel pushed the bowl away and reached for the formula bottle.*

*"What about lunch?"*

*"I'll get something in town."*

*"Supper?"*

*"I'm just going to town,"* said Belle, and Mabel looked at her and Sojourner fit her mouth over the nipple on the formula bottle. Jutted her jaw forward, sucked on it and swallowed.

# 1941

"Wake up, Coon!"

When Finest opens his eyes Hog is standing over him. Whisper-yelling and kicking at his feet with the toe of his boot. In one hand he holds a coffee mug. Steam curling over the rim like smoke. In the other the looped end of the rope he slipped off Finest's wrist. He smells of horses and cigarettes. The coffee in the mug. A day's growth of stubble the red and blonde of unripe strawberries grazes his face.

Finest looks at him and closes his eyes. A waning quarter-moon light slices through the window.

"It ain't no nightmare, Coon!" whispers Hog and he kicks at his feet again. Harder this time. "Wake your ugly ass up!"

Finest shifts and coughs and sits up in his chair and stares at the rope loop shoved in front of his face.

"What the hell is this?" says Hog.

Finest looks at Beatrice. Asleep in the bed across the room. The other end of the rope slip-knotted around her ankle, sticking out from beneath the covers at the foot of the bed.

Hog hands him the coffee mug.

Finest takes it.

"You lucky it's me standin' here and not Beuford. Now get up and put your goddamn boots on!"

"Where we goin'?"

"Snowflake's down."

"From what?"

Hog glances across the room at the rope tied around his mother's ankle then turns back to Finest. "Colic," he says.

Finest looks at him.

"I'da woke if she'da moved."

"Get your goddamn boots on!"

Finest sets the mug on the floor and reaches for his boots. He looks into the dark outside the window.

"What time is it?" he says.

"What? You don't know?"

He pulls on his boots and laces them.

Hog sticks a toothpick in his mouth and chews on it and watches him.

"You was awake every night," he says, "like you was paid to be, you would."

The scars pulse and twitch on Finest's face as he rolls his trouser legs down over the uppers on his boots and rises from the chair and tucks his shirt in.

"It's four o'clock in the mornin'," says Hog.

He chews on his toothpick and turns and studies his mother.

Finest slips on his sweater and looks at Beatrice again as he buttons it. Then bends down to the floor and picks up the coffee mug and drinks from it and they stand there awhile shoulder to shoulder and they stare at her. Lying there on the bed on her back under the covers with her hands folded flat atop the turned down spread, one inside the other. Her eyes creased closed with her head raised and fluffed on the pillow. The suggestion of a smile on her lips as if, save the rope noosed around her ankle and the rise and fall of her chest as she breathes, she were placed in repose for public viewing, and Hog takes off his hat and holds it in front of him and Finest's scars twitch and jump and they stand there together in the quiet of the room, in the dark of early morning. Hog chewing on his toothpick. Finest sipping his coffee. Staring and saying nothing until after awhile Finest cups his fist to his mouth and clears his throat.

"Who gonna stay with her?" he says.

Hog stands there. Watching her. Fingers fondling the looped end of the rope he holds in his hands with his hat.

"Doc Rawlins come by last night?" he says.

Finest sips from his coffee mug and nods.

Hog nods in turn and stares at her a moment longer, then hands Finest the rope.

"Tie her to the bedpost," he says. "Somethin' simple Sara can undo, but that she can't get out of," and he puts on his hat and turns away from them and marches toward the door.

Finest swallows the last of his coffee and ties an anchor bend through the middle of the bedpost then grabs his cap and jacket from the hook by the door and follows.

"We'll wake Sara on the way," says Hog.

Halfway down the staircase he stops and takes his toothpick from his mouth and turns his head toward the banister as if he hears something creeping through the shadows on the quarter-moon lit floor below.

Finest stops behind him.

"Coon?"

"Yeah?"

"I catch you sleepin' again and it ain't daylight, you gonna wish it was Beuford standin' over you up there." His voice is calm and low. "And you so much as think about puttin' a rope on any part of my mother again, I'll kill ya," and he sticks the toothpick back in his mouth and turns and continues down the staircase, and Finest pulls down on the bill of his cap and shoves his hands inside his pockets and clears his throat and follows.

When they emerge from the house, cold splashes their faces and shocks them to life like the dead wrenched from slumber, and Hog spits the toothpick on the ground and lights a cigarette and smokes it while they walk. The air reeking of earth and fireplaces, and when they reach the door to the barn he inhales one last drag, then spits on his fingers and douses the cherry on top with his calluses and drops it into the butt can as they enter.

Beuford's white mare is cast on her side against the rear wall of her stall with her lip curled back, and Beuford and

Luke have the rope lines around her legs, around her fet-
locks, and they stand back and dig their heels into the dirt
and brace themselves in the doorway to the stall and pull
and roll her by her ankles and flip her, and as soon as she
clears her withers, with no warning, she kicks and leaps to
her feet and lunges at them and paws the ground and blows
horse snot through her nose, and when they let go the rope
lines and back away from the stall to keep from being tram-
pled, her legs buckle beneath her and she collapses and
crumbles to the dirt as if she were made of match sticks
rather than flesh and blood. Felled by a breath of wind.

Beuford sees Hog and Finest standing there and orders
them to get the halters and lead ropes on the bay and the
filly and the roan and walk them.

"What about the pens?" says Hog, and he looks down the
aisle way toward the roped-off section at the other end of
the barn.

"What about 'em?"

Beuford and Luke scramble for the rope lines again.

"You don't want me to check on 'em?"

"Check on 'em for what?"

"Make sure the swine ain't got it."

"It's colic, Daniel!"

"I know but…"

"But what? Walk the goddamn horses like I told you 'fore
we got four animals cast instead a one. And don't you dare
stop 'til Doc Hoover gets here and one or the other of us
tells you to. Not even to piss. And for God sake don't let 'em
drop on ya."

Finest takes the bay while Hog handles the filly and the roan until Beuford and Luke get the mare to her feet and Beuford gets the lead on her and guides her from the stall, managing to keep her from dropping again when Luke lets go of her and takes over the roan from Hog and they walk together. Staggered one back from the other behind Beuford and the mare, up and down the length of the aisle way from one end of the barn to the other in the bitter chill of early morning, in silence for a time and darkness save the hushed clip of horse hooves and work boots against the hard black soil. Nose blusters and the wan glow of oil lamps hung from the nails rusted between the stalls.

"You give any more thought to it?" says Luke.

Hog stares in front of him and walks and pulls on the lead.

"Any more thought to what?"

Finest follows.

"You know. What we talked about before."

"No more thought to give it, little brother."

"So you still goin' to then?"

Hog sticks a toothpick in his mouth and chews on it.

"Got no choice, Lucas. You won't either when your number gets called."

They reach the rope separating the farrowing pens from the rest of the barn and lead the horses in a semicircle and turn them back the other way. Hog chews on his toothpick and they stare ahead at Beuford, at the mare. The white of her coat and her mane sullied with dirt and the red from the cedar walls of the stall, and they watch as she ducks her head several times and paws the ground with her hooves, and Beuford wrestles with the lead and halter to keep her upright.

"Sign up early, I mean," says Luke.

Hog stares ahead. "Rather be where I'm wanted than where I ain't," he says. "Even if it's killin' Nazis halfway across the world."

At the barn door Beuford and the mare turn around ahead of them and eclipse them with their shadows on their way back toward the pens, and as they pass, Hog stares through the opening in the door into the unlit morning and chews his toothpick.

"When?" says Luke.

"First of the year. I don't get called sooner."

They make the turn.

"I'm goin'," says Finest.

"Goin' where?" says Hog.

"Killin' Nazis."

"The hell you are!"

"I'm goin'," says Finest.

Hog takes his toothpick out of his mouth and slows and almost stops.

"How you figure?"

"Went to the place and filled out the form."

Hog looks at him and laughs, then sticks his toothpick back in his mouth and shakes his head as he jerks on the filly's lead and catches them up again.

"For a minute there you almost got me, Coon."

Finest clears his throat.

"Notice say every man twenty-one to thirty gotta go down and fill out the form," he says. "Made twenty-one December last. 'Bout to make twenty-two. So…" He looks back at the bay and shrugs his shoulders. "Went down and filled out the form."

"You twenty-two years old, Coon?"

"Will be come next month."

"What day?"

"Christmas."

"Christmas?"

"Twenty-fifth a December."

"Now I know you a goddamn lie! Let me see your card."

They make the turn and Finest reaches in his pants pocket and shows Hog his draft card and Hog takes it in hand and looks at it, then glances up the aisle way at Beuford and gives it back and they walk and lead the horses in silence for awhile save the hooves hushing against the soil. The work boots and the nose blusters coming from Beuford's mare up ahead.

"I'm objectin'," says Luke.

"Objectin' to what?"

"The war."

"What do you know about it, little brother?"

"Daddy says it ain't our fight."

Hog stares ahead of him.

"Says neither was the last one," adds Luke. "Says it's okay to help 'em some. Send 'em weapons. Food and stuff. But when it comes to doin' the fightin', let 'em send their own sons off to die."

Hog watches as Beuford and the mare make the turn.

"I don't wanna die, Daniel. Don't wanna kill no one neither. Not when it ain't my fight. Plus I ain't…"

He lowers his eyes and falls silent as Beuford and the mare cross between them.

"You ain't what?" says Hog.

They make the turn.

"You ain't what, Lucas?"

Luke stares ahead at Beuford.

Hog looks at him.

"Never?" he says.

Luke is silent.

"Shit, little brother," and they continue on without talking for awhile. All three staring up ahead at Beuford and the mare.

"Have you?" says Luke.

"What?" says Hog. "Broke a filly?"

Finest glances at the farrowing pens then down at his feet as they make the turn.

Hog takes his toothpick from his mouth and spits.

"What do you think, little brother?" And they follow Beuford's lead and walk the rest of the way in silence. The horse hooves and the work boots. The blusters. Thinking about fighting and killing and dying and not dying. Virgins. Until sometime after sunup Doc Hoover rattles down the lane in his pickup truck and forces a tube down the mare's throat and fills it with some kind of liquid while Beuford and Hog hold her still and push her head up so that her nose and her mouth point toward the pitch in the barn roof and she is unable to spit it out, and she paws at the ground and peels her lip back and the liquid drains from the tube into her belly and he fills it again and at some point when the sun is high and washed out wisps of blue tease through the breaks in the clouds above, she calms some and Doc Hoover pulls the tube from her throat and massages her belly with his hands, and after awhile her gut sounds return and her stools soften and she releases them and when he examines the other horses and pronounces them clear, he packs up his case and his truck and turns back to Beuford and nods his head at him and says, "We were lucky this time, Beuf. Real lucky."

BELLE STANDS BACK in the shadows between the sycamore and elm trees. Watching them. Finest and the older one. The one they call Hog, as they cross the lane and disappear into the barn with the others, and with her thumb she traces the creases in the photograph she carries tucked inside the lining of her coat pocket. The words Mona and Bea, Tradition scrawled in a foreign hand across the border. White around the edges. It will be light soon and she stands there concealed by the shadows and the skeletons of the trees. The past. And her eyes rove from the barn to the house where she can almost see them. The two of them. Sitting there together in front of her as they sit in the photograph: on the porch on the steps. Squinting into the camera with their hats pulled low on their foreheads. Collars wide and flat on the lapels on their day dresses. The trees have grown and the barn, now that she can see it whole, stands taller than she expected. But everything else save the two of them. Sitting there. Squinting. Remains as it is pictured. The lane. The catwalk and the railings between the chimneys. The shutters. Even the ivy scaling the face of the brick, resembling ropes thrown down as a means of escape in case of fire from the rooms behind the windows in the dormers. She looks at the barn then steps from the shadows from the past out into the yard, into the present. The pale light of the wee-hour sky, and she crosses to the side of the house to the place where she saw them exit. Beuford first followed by the younger boy, then Hog and Finest.

She opens the door and the hinges creak when she enters and closes it behind her. Otherwise it is the dormant quiet of winter inside and she can hear herself. Breathing in the stillness of the slumber, and she stands there. Holding onto the door handle. Listening to it. The breathing, until her eyes adapt to the dark.

She is in a stairwell. The steps down and to the right lead to the basement. Up onto the landing and to the left to a door opposite the staircase. A closet and another door ahead at the foot of the stairs. She opens the door on the left and peers into the entry hall. There is more light here and warmth. The cackle and hiss of a dying fire. She looks to her left and finds the dining room, the library and the sitting room. To her right, another set of stairs. Decorated and carpeted. The family's staircase, and a ballroom the length of the house beside it. Ahead of her in the center, an extinguished chandelier, the bronze of deer skin hangs over the foyer and the main entrance to the manor and beyond it the porch at which just a short while before, hidden by shadows and the veil of the past, she stood staring, and in front of her, stowed away like a fugitive in a closet under the stairs: an indoor toilet and wash basin with a tap and running water.

She closes the door and returns to the stairwell. Crosses the landing past the closet and other door to the foot of the cook's staircase. The floorboards groan beneath her feet under the weight of unexpected burden, and when she reaches the second floor she pauses again and listens for a moment for signs of movement, then passes into the living quarters when she hears none. The bedrooms. Three for the boys and Beuford and a fourth made up for guests. Empty. And she continues climbing the back stairway to the top, to a third landing which leads to another, and three quick steps to the right past the crest of the family's staircase to the door to the attic, in front of which she stops and stands for awhile and looks at it.

She has made this journey before. Every night for the past eight years in her mind. Rubbing time creases into the photograph she stole the night she ran. The routes may vary from time to time. The room and the state in which she finds her. The number of other children she has. But the door is always the same and when she reaches it, instead of turning the knob and entering, she stands there as she does now and stares at it.

"WE CAN'T JUST get rid of her, Henry."

"We got no choice, Mona Ruth."

"What if I take a job?"

"A job? Doing what?"

"I don't know. Something."

"You've never worked a day in your life. Thirteen million people out there begging for bread and change. More if you count their children, and you'll just go somewhere and take a job. Just like that. Doing something. There are no jobs, Mona Ruth! I'm lucky I still have mine!"

"I can't do it, Henry."

"Then I will. Sniveling over some colored gal like she was your own flesh and blood. People are going hungry, Mona."

"She is my flesh and blood."

"Don't know how on earth I ever let you talk me into it. Must have been out of my mind."

"Just because I didn't birth her."

"Or sick with fever."

"She's my sister's child, Henry."

"Felt sorry for you, that's what."

"Henry!"

"Then give her back to her!"

"I can't!"

"Look. I don't give a good goddamn whose child it is. It's not ours. Is it, Mona Ruth? We don't have any children now,

have we, Mona Ruth? And I am through pretending that we
have. What was the word the doctor used? Damaged?"

"What do you want me to do with her?"

"Take her to the Catholics like you should've done in the
first place. Hell, Mona Ruth, what do I care? Hang a sign
around her neck and leave her on a goddamn curb somewhere."

"And what am I supposed to say to her?"

"To her? To her?"

SHE WALKS INTO the middle of the room and stops and stares
at the rope cinched around the bedpost and follows it with
her eyes to the ankle sticking out from beneath the covers and
the woman attached to it asleep in the bed. Hands folded in
repose atop the spread. In the distance somewhere she hears
a door close and footsteps. The moaning of floorboards, and
she crosses to the bed and she fingers the creases in the photograph and she looks at her, at her hands. The one nestled inside
the other. The shape of the nails. The footsteps and the floorboards moaning in the stairwell. From her hands she moves on
to her shoulders and the arc of her collarbone. The pale white
skin of her neck. She looks at her mouth, at her lips. Parted
slightly, and the hint of a dimple in her chin. The bump midway down the ridge of her nose. She looks at her hair. Black
like her own. Thick and fine and tangled on the pillow beneath
her head. Her eyes, she imagines, hidden behind the creases in
the eyelids closed under the eyebrows, arched and harrowed,

are blue, and she stands there awhile and she looks at her and she reaches her hand out and holds it over her face as if to touch her. Her cheek. Rearrange the lie of her hair, and the footsteps and the floorboards are loud now and she stands there. Staring at her. Holding her hand out suspended there over her face like that, and she fingers the photograph in the lining of her coat pocket. And when the footsteps approach the landing and the three quick steps to the right, the door to the attic, and enter and cross the room to the bed, she is gone and she hurries down the last flight of the family's staircase as if she has been keeping someone waiting, a gentleman come to call, past the ballroom and library, through the main entrance, across the deck of the porch and back into the shadows. Fingering in her coat pocket the creases of her past she carries tucked inside the lining of the present.

FINEST SMELLS THE ginger and leaps the stairs two at a time to the attic where he bursts through the door and charges into the room and stops when he sees Sara. Sitting in the same chair in which Hog caught him sleeping twelve hours before.

The rope is gone and Beatrice is awake now. Lounging on the divan with her knees bent and her back turned to him. Staring out of the window.

He glances at Sara, then sniffs at the air and looks around the room.

Sara watches him.

"She's gone already," she says.

He hangs up his cap and coat and walks to the chair nearest him and sits, facing her. Beatrice and the window.

"Who is?" he says.

"Whoever you had up in here when they come to get you this morning."

He looks over at Beatrice, then scans the room again with his eyes.

"Don't know what you talkin' 'bout there, Sara."

She crosses her arms in front of her. "Know exactly what I'm talkin' 'bout," she says. "Less you started wearin' ginger water all of a sudden. And I know it ain't ol' girl over there." She glances at Beatrice at the window. "Her scent is lavender."

She looks at him.

"Whoever it was, she smokes."

Finest clears his throat and looks at her, at her arms folded in front of her below her bosom. He looks at her bosom. Small and firm and round in her dress, and her legs crossed over one another in her chair. The skin on her knees showing between the folds in her stockings and the hemline of her dress. The smile forming on her lips.

He shifts in his chair and the scars twitch on his face as he nods toward Beatrice.

"Only one up here 'sides me and ol' gal right there was Hog," he says and he shrugs his shoulders and clears his throat again. "Hog smokes. Must be Hog wearin' that perfume water you say you smellin'," and he licks his lips and smiles back at her and smoothes down the moss of hair sprouting over the lump on his head with his hand.

"Must be," she says and she looks over at Beatrice. "Must be why you was breakin' your neck trying to get up them stairs a flight at a time, too."

Finest laughs and hikes up his pant leg and crosses his ankle over his knee and says, "Go ahead, you don't believe me. Next time you see him, ask him what I was doin' up here when he come to get me this mornin'. He'll tell you."

"I ain't got to ask him nothin'. My nose know what it smells. Never been wrong and never forget. And his name is Daniel," she says to him, "and I'm sure he will appreciate knowin' you goin' around telling folks he up here wearin' ladies' perfume." And she smiles at him, then rises from her chair and smoothes out her dress and crosses the room to the window to gather and collect Beatrice, and he watches her. The shimmy of her dress as she glides across the floor. The way she places her hands on the backs of Beatrice's shoulders. Soft as not to startle her, and tells her that it's time to go down stairs now and get supper ready for the boys and Beuford. The way she glances through the window as she helps her to her feet to see what she's been staring at all this time.

"How long she been awake?" he says.

"Three four hours maybe."

"She say anything?"

Sara shakes her head.

"Not today," she says and she takes her by the arm and leads her across the floor in front of him and they leave, and when the door closes behind them he sits there awhile and stares at it and listens to their footsteps fall away down the staircase, then stands and searches the room. He looks in the wardrobe. He looks in the water closet. Under the bed. His cot. Nothing. From the cot he walks to the divan in the dormer and looks out the window into the cold steel daylight and he stands there. Staring at the wintry skeletons of tulip poplar and maple. Sycamore and elm. Breathing in the smell of ginger water and cigarette smoke. Wondering what she was doing here. If anybody saw her.

**book three**

# may 9, 2007

Mabel fell while rooting through the house for ginger.

"Ginger?" says Doc Rawlins. "What the hell you need ginger so bad for, Mabel? Next time send Gus here down to Caleb's to buy you some."

"Was trying to find it so I could get rid of it," she slurs to him.

"Get rid of it?" He looks at her and shakes his head. "Never will understand you people," he says.

Gus and Luke stand on either side of her on opposite sides of the bed, watching as Doc Rawlins examines her injuries: the swelling around her hip and ankle, the bruising on her elbow and the cut lashed across her lip. Overhead they can hear the engines screaming on the

Flying Dutchmen, the F-16s of the Royal Netherlands Air Force, shrieking through the cloud cover, training for the upcoming Air Rendezvous in Springfield. Moisture, baked by the hidden sun, hangs damp and warm in the room and sweat drips from their chins and from their foreheads to the floor and they pat themselves about their necks and faces with their handkerchiefs and stick them back in their pockets, and for the second day in a row the bulldozers are quiet and Mabel lies there in the bed. Pain dulled by the tincture in her coffee mug and the distraction of ginger, and she stares at the hunched and withered sweat-glistened men standing over her as if they are specters. Tending vigil over the barely living. Waiting for the final breath to expire to lead the soul into the afterlife, and she lies there. Propped up on the pillows, and she stares at them, at the doctor, at his hands. Soft and age-spotted. Dull on her hip.

"Well, you didn't break anything," he says to her and he straightens himself and reaches for his handkerchief. "But you damn sure ought of," and wipes off his glasses. "It's a miracle you didn't," and holds them up to the light. "That's the good news."

She sniffs the air and looks at him as he fits them back on his face.

"Bad news is," he says to her, "sometimes not breaking something is a whole lot worse. The pain tends to never fully go away. Just sits there and hangs on ya. Nagging and chewing at ya 'til it wears you so thin you don't know whether you've come or gone."

From his bag he pulls out his prescription pad and stares over the rims of his glasses at the half-empty whiskey bottle next to the coffee mug on the nightstand as he scribbles on it.

"'Fraid you're about to be laid up awhile, Mabel," he tells her and he tears off the top page of the pad and hands it to Luke, who passes it to Gus. "I'm giving you something here to help with the pain," he says. "I want you to take it as needed."

He looks at Gus and stares at him.

"Nobody else here to help you with her?"

Gus shakes his head.

Doc Rawlins frowns and looks at Luke.

"Well," he says. "Hope you all are comfortable with each other then. Gonna learn to be if you're not. Less she changes her mind about the rehab center, you'll have to help her do everything. Everything," he says to Gus. "Eat. Bathe. Dress. Sit on the toilet." He looks at the bottle again. The coffee mug on the nightstand. Through the window he glances out at the bulldozers. Idle in the empty lot that used to be The Colonel's house. "Saw they started building already," he says. "Over on Prosper. Got stuck behind one of the cement trucks on my way in."

Gus looks at Mabel and wipes off his face again. His neck with his handkerchief.

"Hard to believe it's only May, isn't it?" The doctor reaches into his bag and pulls out a bottle from it, palm-sized, and dabs a little iodine on the cut slashed across Mabel's mouth with a Q-tip. "Hate to think what it's got in store for us come July."

Gus and Luke watch as he sits on the mattress beside her. He wraps an Ace bandage loose around her elbow and tells her when she sleeps at night to keep a pillow under her knees, and they step back to let him pass as he rises. Like an overworked deity he makes his way around to the other side of the bed where he leaves the iodine bottle next to the half-empty bottle of whiskey and the coffee mug on the nightstand.

"Spread a little of that on it three times a day," he says to Gus.

He reaches in his wallet and takes out a business card and passes it to him.

Gus looks at it.

"Young gal just happened to give me that the other day," he says. "Number for a new service in town provides home care. You know, cooking and cleaning and such," and he closes his bag and latches it, then takes it in hand and Gus and Luke follow him to the doorway, where he stops and turns back to Mabel and grins at her and says, "I'll check in with Luke next week to see how you're doing. So don't get any ideas on me now and try to go out dancing tonight." He laughs and Luke laughs with him and Gus just stands there and she stares at them. The three of them. Standing there in the doorway.

"Running to the pharmacy," says Gus, and when they turn to leave she lies there a moment. Staring at the place where they stood before they disappeared down the hall. Plagued by the smell of ginger still and the searing jolts of pain shooting through her body. Thinking about specters and souls. The afterlife, and she reaches for her coffee mug and her lip burns when she sips from it and she curses at it and sucks on it awhile after she swallows, then raises the mug back to her mouth and sips and curses again.

When Gus returns from the pharmacy, Finest sits in front of the television, handcuffed to the leg of the sofa. Swaddled in sweat, humidity and the sump of his own urine. He smells him as soon as he walks through the door. The ammonia in his urine cutting into the body filth making itself at home already in the baseboards and walls of the room, and sees him, his cane banging and bouncing on the floor between his legs like a pogo stick. But for the setting and the cloak of stench wrapped around him and the hand-cuffs, he could almost be a circus clown sitting there in his oversized suit and unlaced shoes. The hair on his face gray and matted. Painted around his mouth in an exaggerated frown.

Gus drops Mabel's medicine on the coffee table and goes to him. Fumbles in his pants pocket for his keys and releases the handcuffs. Finest rises to his feet and stands there. Star-ing and blinking at the television set. His crotch and the seat of his pants and the cushion where he sat wet with urine, and Gus stands to the side of him. Inhaling the fumes of baked-on urine and filth, and he looks at him. Blinking. Sweat streaming down the side of his face from his temple. Teem-ing on his forehead. Spilling from the corners of his eyes as if he were crying. Gus takes his handkerchief and dries off his face for him and stands there awhile. Staring. Unable to move. He stares at the handcuffs. Pink and furry. Dangling from his fingers. Skeleton keys still wedged inside the lock. He stares at the painkillers Doc Rawlins prescribed for Mabel tossed in a hurry on the coffee table, at the walls closing in and the room. Spinning around him like a carnival ride where the floor drops out, and he sticks out his arms away from his body as he does on the ride and when the floor comes back, finally, he stays like that. Arms and hands out in front, bracing himself against the urge to run. To run anywhere but here, and when everything stops moving, he lowers his arms and turns back to Finest and dries his face again.

"I'm sorry, Superman," he says.

Finest bangs on the floor with his cane.

"Okay. Okay. Here we go."

He picks up the pain killers and takes Finest by the arm and leads him into the bathroom. The moisture in the air stained with plumes of ammonia and body filth. Dutchmen screaming across the sky overhead.


HE WAITED FOR her. He stood back from the road amid the gaunt trunks and limbs of the river birches. The walnut and cedar, and he reached across his chest, inside his overcoat, into his service jacket and took out his tobacco pouch and he rolled and smoked a cigarette, then rolled and smoked another and he stood there in the shadows. Smoking in his uniform. Under the moonlight. Cheeks hollowed and starved for warmth like the trees. His tie loosened and his collar undone and he smoked and he stood there and he watched for her and he waited. His cap garrisoned to the side to conceal the lump on his head.

He thought it would make him normal. Going to war. Thought that if he fought and shed blood for his country and came back a hero, they would look past everything else and see only the uniform. But it was the same over there as it was here and he knew now that there was no normal. That for him, normal would never be.

When he saw her he put out his cigarette and stepped from the shadows onto the shoulder of the deserted roadway and spoke to her.

"Finest!" she said and she stopped and she brought her hand to her chest and her breath caught in her throat and she held it there a moment, then let it out and started walking again.

"You startled me," she told him.

On her hands she wore a pair of black leather gloves, and in the one not clutching her chest she gripped the handle of her suitcase. A handbag, alligator like the suitcase, hung from her shoulder.

He cleared his throat and asked if he could carry it for her. The bag, and she looked at him a moment, then gave it to him and he let her pass ahead of him, then went around and walked on the other side of her. Nearest the road.

"What were you doing out here all by yourself?" she said to him.

"Saw the bus comin' in," he said.

They walked.

"You stood out here in this cold all this time, just to wait on me, Finest?"

The suitcase swung between them.

"Yeah," he said.

Belle was silent.

"What if I hadn't been on it?"

His face scrunched up and he shrugged his shoulders and smiled at her.

Belle tightened her scarf around her neck, then drew the mink shawl collar on her coat about her head so that it covered her ears, and they walked that way for awhile. The suitcase swinging. Quiet. The heels on her shoes and the soles of his boots against the gravel and the wind baying the only noises, and she looked up ahead of them at the moon. Hanging low and sated in the clear night sky. The road curving. Flanked by emaciated shadows. Disappearing into darkness, and Finest looked at the gravel kicking up under their feet and at their breath clotting in front of their faces like the smoke from wounds cauterized with the tip of a hot poker as they walked, and after awhile she let out a sigh that barely passed the opening in her lips before floating away on the wind. The lost balloon of something already determined, and she nearly had to holler to be heard over the howling and rumbling of it when she turned to him and said, "Have you anything in that coat of yours to drink, Mr. Coon?"

Finest scrunched up his face and cleared his throat and switched the suitcase from one hand to the other, then reached inside his overcoat into his service jacket again and handed her the bottle.

Belle unscrewed the cap and wiped off the mouth and drank from it. Swallowed, then drank again and gave it back to him.

They walked.

"Let's have a cigarette," she said and she slipped her arm through his and sought out his hand in the pocket of his overcoat and she cradled it there inside his pocket as she led him from the gravel of the road into the stalks of wild grass. Dead and flattened on the ground. Worn by deer hooves and the tracks of the men who hunted them, onto a trail which led to another trail that wound its way into the drawn and pallid woods, and at the end of it the trail dropped them off at the mouth of an old covered bridge. Perched like a giant bird feeder above the water rushing over the rocks and sticks below. Ice-capped and dammed by beavers in the fork of the river, and they walked to it and stopped under the middle of it.

"Hog say Tecumseh built this bridge," said Finest.

He put down the suitcase and took out his pouch and rolled a cigarette and for awhile the air smelled of fresh tobacco spiced with ginger.

Belle leaned against the lattice work and looked at him.

"Tecumseh?"

He cleared his throat.

"Mmm hmm. The Indian chief."

"Oh, I know who Tecumseh is," she said. "I just never figured him for a bridge builder. Being so busy with Custer and all."

Finest shrugged his shoulders.

"That's what he say," and his scars twitched as he wet the seal on his cigarette and blew on it.

Belle watched him. Her Chesterfield in her hand between her fingers. Waiting for him to light it.

"How do you ever smoke those things?" she said to him. "All those little pieces getting stuck on your tongue? Caught in your teeth?"

Finest lit her cigarette and scrunched up his face again, then lit his own and she stared at him. Standing there. Smoking. His field uniform worn and torn in spots. Sullied as if he were taking a break from a battle already lost.

She stared at his nose. Smashed into his face like a mound of soft clay punched flat with the knuckles on a fist. His moustache and his lip squished up against the leveled bridge of his nose, at his chin welded into his mouth and jawbones like metals with no business being fused, and she stared at his scars. Twitching.

"Do they hurt?" she said.

Finest shook his head.

"Not no more. Don't feel nothin' no more. Get tight sometimes. Jump on me."

"So you can tell then when they twitch?"

He nodded. "Feel it in my lip. Like somebody pinchin' or tuggin' on it. And my eyes blink."

She stubbed out her Chesterfield then took off one of her gloves and pushed it into her coat pocket.

"May I touch them?" she said.

He stood there and blinked at her and she reached up and traced the side of his jumping face with her fingers. His neck. And when she finished and drew her hand away, he opened his overcoat and his service jacket and pulled back the collar on his shirt and revealed the crude leather patches of overgrown skin twitching on his collarbone and shoulder.

She touched them and he blinked at her.

"Nothing?" she said.

He shook his head.

She pulled her glove back on and felt inside her handbag for another Chesterfield. Stuck it between her lips and folded her coat around herself and looked at his hands. Scarred and bony as he lit it for her.

"What did he do to you?" she said to him.

Finest cleared his throat and turned away from her toward the diamond cutouts in the lattice work on the bridge wall behind her and rolled another cigarette. He felt in his pocket for his matches and cupped his hands over the cigarette and lit it.

"When you leave here all the time?" he said to her. "Where you go?"

She looked at him and smoked.

"Depends," she said.

"Depend on what?"

"A lot of things, I guess."

"What kinda things?"

She shrugged her shoulders and exhaled.

"I don't know. Work mostly."

He looked at her.

"Wherever I can make the most money in the shortest amount of time. Cleveland. New York. Atlanta. Charlotte."

He drew on his cigarette and his eyes blinked at her as he thought about what she said.

"Why you always walk?"

She laughed and blew a small gust of smoke and crystallized ginger breath into his face, then shook her head.

"You mean back and forth to the bus stop?"

He nodded.

She stubbed out her Chesterfield on the ledge beside her and pulled her shawl about her.

"I don't know, Finest," she said. "To clear it all out, I guess. To forget."

"Forget what?"

She stared at him. Into his eyes. The scars and disfigurement, as if she were staring into herself.

"What I've done. Where I've been."

"For work?"

"Work. Life. Bad. Good. All of it."

"Why you don't wanna remember the good part?"

She turned away from him and looked through the mouth of the bridge all the way up the trail into the dark and shadows beyond, then faced him again. The river rushing over the rocks below.

"I think I just need it to be clean," she said. "Somehow the walking from one to the other separates it. Puts it behind me so I can be okay with it if I never see it again."

She looked at him.

"Whenever it should come to that," she said. "So I can be ready for it."

A branch snapped on a tree and fell into the brush somewhere in the woods. They turned toward the sound of it and they stood there awhile. Staring into the darkness. Listening to the river rush.

Finest cleared his throat and pulled out the bottle and drank from it, then passed it to Belle who drank and passed it back.

"He be always on me," he said. "Chewin' on me."

He stared into the darkness.

Belle pulled her coat around her and stuck her hands inside her pockets and looked at him and listened.

"Tellin' me how ugly I am all the time."

He drank from the bottle again.

"Say it be my ugly killed my mama. Say my punishment be to take her place. Make me dress up in her clothes and stand there. Watchin' me. Touchin' hisself."

Belle waited awhile before she spoke.

"Did he ever touch you?"

He glared into the dark toward the place where they heard the branch fall. He was silent. His eyes blinked and filled with water.

She pulled her hands from her pockets and reached for him…

"Just didn't want him chewin' on me no more," he said.

…and made him face her.

"Every time I look up," he said.

He blinked at the cutouts.

"Starin' at me like that.

She took the bottle from his hands and set it beside her on the ledge…

"Even when I be in my own clothes."

…and pulled him to her…

"Didn't wanna be stared at no more."

…and put his arms around her…

"Tired a bein' stared at all the time."

…and she held him there and took his head in her hands and she kissed him.

"Everybody. Always starin'."

She kissed his chin. She kissed his mouth. His nose. The water filling up in his eyes. She kissed his cheeks and the lump on his head. The scars twitching and jumping on the side of his face and neck and when he tried to pull away. When she parted his overcoat and service jacket and shirt collar with her hands and pressed her lips to the divot between his collarbone and his shoulder, she shushed him and held him there and rocked him while he wept. Convulsing in her arms, and the river rushed and she shushed and the bottle rattled on the ledge beside her where she'd placed it, and when it fell to the floor and shattered about their feet and the fetor of alcohol engulfed them like flames in a fire, he stiffened against her and lifted her onto the lattice work, into one of the cutouts, and pushed her skirt back over her hips and the river rushed and the fire raged and she locked her legs around him and pulled him to her and they held each other as he wept and drove her into the lattice work and she kissed him and told him he was beautiful. He was beautiful. The river rushing over the rocks below. The low rumble of wind. Breath clotting in front of their faces.


THE DOG APPEARS while he is bathing him. Gus sees it when he glances through the open window. After he puts down the washrag and takes a break and stands for awhile before attempting to shave his beard. From the clearing where the cemetery used to be. The sugar maple and the rest of the woods. The dog half trots into the yard. Sniffs around the empty garbage cans on the side of the house, then lies down and crosses his legs in the grass. A rangy sort of mutt, with his tail wagging sort of as if he could take life or leave it. Lean and tired and hungry. The kind nobody would miss. Gus stands there awhile and watches him. Lying there. Panting in the grass. Taking in the piles of rubble which surround them now on all sides of the house save the clearing from which the dog trotted, then he turns back and he looks at Finest, who sits on the shower seat naked in the bathtub. Ankle deep in blackened water. Handcuffed to the safety rail. From the shower nozzle above his head clean water sprays down and rinses the soap from his neck and back and he sits there with his legs closed together in front of him. Facing the tiled wall over the shallow end of the tub. His free hand and forearm tensed across his lap. Hiding his privates. Steam sweats down the faces of the walls and the mirrors scented with flowers. Liquid roses and lavender leaves from the bath balls he dusted off from the cupboard below the sink teased with the stench leftover from Finest's clothes piled up on the floor in the corner between the window and the toilet next to the cane.

Gus turns off the shower and unplugs the stopper and drains and rinses the soot from the bottom of the tub. Then sits on the edge of it with the scissors in his hand and looks at him.

The gash over his eye made out better than the rest of the scars. It takes him awhile to find it. Camouflaged the way it is by his eyebrow, and he sits there on the edge of the tub in his undershirt. The kind with no sleeves like wife beaters wear, with his trousers rolled up past his calves to his kneecaps. Staring at it. Barefoot. He stares at his lump. At the worn sheaths of calfskin knit like patchwork over his collarbone and shoulder. The outlines of bones drawn through the trace of his skin sheer like fabric. Clumsy replicas of the originals. His chest sunken.

"Ready for round two, Superman?" he says to him.

Finest blinks and stares at the sweating tiles on the wall.

Gus glances at the window, then straddles his legs around the shower seat and braces his feet flat on the porcelain and leans in and grabs the tail of Finest's beard and snips it and drops it into the bathtub.

"I'm like that ol' dog out there, Superman," he says.

Finest blinks.

"Layin' up lookin' for redemption from a world that's been demolished."

He grabs another knot of Finest's beard and cuts it into the tub.

"Think an ol' dog like that would have enough sense to look up and see there's nothing left to it anymore but ruin. Nothin' for him here and move on."

He cuts off another clump and another after that, then tilts Finest's head back and clips away the dreadlocked mass rooted beneath his chin.

"But ol' dog's just out there kickin' it," he says. "Lyin' around starin' at all that shit in front of him with his legs crossed. Legs crossed! Pantin'. Like he's waitin' for somethin' to happen. Expectin' it. For her to rise up out of those woods we left her in, cradling wine and bread and forgiveness in her arms like grocery bags from a twenty-four-hour market. Salvation and blessings and resurrection, showing us the way home."

He snips and looks out at the rubble.

Finest blinks.

"'Cause this sure is hell ain't it."

He wipes off the scissors, then makes another pass around his face.

He came back thinking he could bury her proper. Tell Mabel what really happened, dig her up and give her a proper funeral. Give them all a little peace for whatever time they had left. Finally let them sleep at night. Didn't quite work out that way, did it, Junior?

"Shoulda stayed gone, Superman," he says to him. "This late in the game. Shoulda stayed on the bench."

When he shears the hair close enough to where he can see skin showing through but not yet stubble and the ill-advised fusion of mouth and chin to bone, he stops and he looks at him.

Finest stares at the wall.

"Least you got an excuse," says Gus.

He puts down the scissors and fills a bowl with lukewarm water and reaches on the back of the toilet for the package of disposable razors he purchased at Caleb's and opens it. His undershirt and trousers speckled gray with Finest's beard hair.

He starts under his chin back by his throat against the grain and he holds the skin taught with his thumb and forefinger spread apart on either side of his neck.

Finest coughs a little as he does so and he loosens his grip.

He pulls the handle forward on the razor and swivels the head up and over the absence of chin up to his lip.

Finest blinks and flinches and his scars, visible now, jump and twitch on his face.

Gus douses the razor and taps it and starts another row.

"Knew this lady once," he says to him. "When I was out in LA. Old lady. Age we are now, probably. Used to see her sitting at the bus stop around the corner from where I was staying. Never got on it though. Just sat there. On the bench with a suitcase by her feet, letting the day pass. Suitcase was old as she was. Every time I saw her she had a smile on her face and no matter what time of day it was or day of the week, save the suitcase she was dressed like she was going to church. Wore one of those turban hats like the Muslims and Indians wear. Purple with a matching purple skirt suit and a scarf around her neck tucked between the lapels. Camisole sometimes. Said her name was Martha. Whenever I passed by her she'd look up and smile at me. Say hello and ask me my name. Who my people were. Never remembered that we'd been over that already. Sometimes four or five times on the very same day. Didn't matter. She always asked and I always answered and she never seemed to care one way or the other what shape I was in or whether I made any sense when I did so. Sweet old lady," he says and douses and starts another row. "Somebody's grandmother, I figured. So I started calling her Granny. How you doin' today, Granny? I'd say to her. *I'm just fine, sweetheart,* she'd say. Or some-times *Fair to middlin'* when she looked like she was in pain and *Scratchin' like a dog with two sets of fleas* when her skin broke out in hives or reddened with rashes. One day I asked her how come she just sat there and never got on the bus when it came. She patted her suitcase beside her and told me she was waitin'. Waitin' on what? I asked her."

He disposes of the razor and reaches for another and looks at him.

Finest blinks as if waiting for the answer.

"*The Lord, sweetheart!* she told me." Gus shakes his head and glances through the window and laughs at the memory of it. "Just sittin' there waitin' on the Lord."

When nothing remains but bristles on his face, he throws away the second blade and drapes a hot towel over his head and leaves it there a moment while he empties and rinses out the bowl of lukewarm water. From the back of the toi-let basin he picks up a can of shaving cream and sprays some into his hand and spreads it over the stubble field of Finest's face.

"Last time I saw her," says Gus. "After she asked about my people again, she told me she was going away soon and wanted to know if I was acquainted with Jesus."

He stops and looks at the window, then douses the razor and taps it on the rim of the bowl. "No, ma'am, I told her. I didn't believe I was. She smiled at me and reached out and held my hands in hers and told me when she got to where she was going she would tell Him about me and try to arrange a meeting."

When he finishes he removes the little pieces of toilet paper where he nicked him from Finest's neck then wipes off his face with the towel and rises and steps back from the tub and takes a look at him. It's him alright.

Finest sits there and blinks at the wall.

"What do you think, Superman?"

Finest blinks.

"Think there's someone up there watching over everything? Waiting at the end of the line to bring us home?"

He brushes off his undershirt and rolls down his pant legs, then rubs some lotion over the familiar angry and contorted face. Sagging a little now. Age-softened and weary more so than angry. But unmistakable still. Even to the fingers of the blind.

He unlocks the handcuffs and helps him to his feet, into his shoes and the pajamas Luke brought over, then hands him his hat and cane and leads him into the sitting room. Shoes flopping around on his feet as they walk, and he sits him on the sofa in front of the television and locks him down again.

When he finishes cleaning the bathroom and throwing Finest's clothes into a garbage bag, he sticks his head in the door and checks on Mabel, who is sound asleep and snoring. The half-bottle of whiskey empty on the nightstand next to the coffee mug. The bottle of pills.

He crosses to the window and looks out into the yard. The dog is gone. Smart boy, he thinks. He stands there and listens for awhile. The television in the other room. Cicadas chirping. Grasshoppers. Silence otherwise save Mabel's snoring.

He closes the door behind him when he leaves, then walks down the hall into the kitchen and stops in front of the telephone and looks around and listens again, then lifts up the receiver and dials.

# 1943

"None of 'em is?" says Luke.

"Nope," says Gus.

Finest is silent.

They enter through the back from the porch and sidle along the wall with their hats in their hands and settle into the corner between the window that looks out onto the shed and the wall with the picture shelf that never has any pictures on it. Opposite the doorway between the dining room and the kitchen and the new mahogany china cabinet Belle lugged home after the snow thawed in the bed of a pickup truck driven by somebody named Gooch. The doors to the cabinet sealed shut with masking tape still. Lattice work cut across the glass like diamonds.

"Not one?" says Luke.

"Nope," says Gus.

The others arrived sometime later. One or two at a time over a period of hours. As if they were homing pigeons come to roost with messages ferried over the ages. Flight weary and hungry, in need of something to drink. A staggered caravan of handed-down Packards and Chevys. Hudsons and Fords piloted by women who looked and dressed and lived as men. Hard men with lines in their faces and age smoked into their lungs even though they were young still, who worked in munitions factories and limestone quarries. Steel mills, and answered to names like Tre and Hamp. Peachfuzz and Coop. Who brought wives and girlfriends with them who rode alongside in the passenger seats. All done up. Looking as if in another place and time they would have been movie stars.

"The one with the cigarette behind his ear?"

"Nope," says Gus. They stand there awhile and they watch them, these other men about them. As hardened and postured by life as they, and Luke turns his hat around in his hands by the brim as if it is a steering wheel on a car and he grins and whistles and shakes his head as one of them holds his hand out and asks his wife to dance with him and they move together in a circle in front of the three of them no wider than their feet. Cheeks touching. Hands rubbing on backs of necks and asses. Eyes closed in the middle of the hardwood floor. Dark against the grain. Like shadows shifting in sand. The curtains closed.

"Dancin' right there! In the fedora with his shirt sleeves rolled up!"

"Nope," says Gus, and Luke whistles again. The pitch of it gathered into the folds of the voices talking and the laughter. Easy tucked between the scratches of music issuing from the sound box on the gramophone. Fats and Billie. Ella and Louis. Bessie. Then Ma comes on and somebody quiets the room and calls out a toast and hollers, "To my big black bottom!" and someone else hollers back, "To your jive black ass!" and they raise their glasses and drink to one another and go back to talking about defense work and Hitler again.

"And the white lady?" says Luke. "Next to your sister? She ain't white?"

Gus shakes his head.

Across the room from them on the sofa, Belle and Mabel are talking and laughing with the one they call Gooch. Finest crosses his legs and leans back on the wall with a toothpick in his mouth and twitches and stares at them, at Gooch. Rocking slightly in the rocking chair by the end of the sofa in a chocolate twill suit. His hair slicked back and his collar starched. Shoes polished and buffed to the shine, and he sits there and laughs with them. His hand every so often stroking his moustache. The scar across his throat.

"And she pays you all to let her sleep in the shed out back? Your daddy's old work shed?"

"Plus board," says Gus and he stares into the room.

Luke turns around and looks behind him as if he is looking for a place to spit. "Well I'll be a goddamn lie!" he says. "Good thing Daniel ain't here. Daniel'd be liable to blow a gasket about now. Bust a vein or somethin'. Hell a artery, he was seein' what I'm seein' right now." He looks down at his hat in his hands and whistles again and stares at the floor awhile, then looks back at his hands. "A goddamn lie," he says.

The day before they touched down, Mabel and Belle spent the whole day cooking and the day before that soaking and scrubbing clean piece by piece the insides of pig intestines for Finest's going away party, and when the first cars began to roll into the driveway and park behind the pickup, beneath the aromas of the half pound of butter stirred into the macaroni and cheese sauce and the fatback in the green beans and the black eyed peas, the lard in the biscuits, the smell of hog shit still lingered slightly. So Mabel cut up a potato and dropped it into the pan and Belle set out some baking soda and lemons in a bowl, and from the first to the last who was forced to park in the yard because the driveway was full. Up and down the length of Hope Street the curtains parted in the windows, and not long after the curtains parted doors swung open and glances were exchanged, and after the glances were exchanged the doorbell started ringing and never stopped. Neighbors they hadn't seen since they buried their father, even though they lived just across the street. The Mill Worker's Widow, standing there on the other side of the door. Craning her neck and peering over Mabel's shoulder like a turkey, squawking about how she'd been meaning to come by but time just kept getting away from her. And Puddin Sutton. The Colonel's wife. Precious Pettiford's sister, talking her way in and introducing herself to everybody. Shaking their hands and pointing toward the window. Telling them if they needed anything she was just in the house on the corner. The one with the flag waving in the yard. And Althea Marston. Junkman's woman. Leaning against the wall by the empty picture shelf. Rocking her leg back and forth like a school girl, having a drink with one of them.

Finest and Gus and Luke stand there and look at each other and take it all in. Like sentient castoffs in a mannequin factory. Old and ill-formed molds discarded to walls and corners. Eyes wide in bas-relief. Staring out at their replacements.

From across the room Belle looks up and sees them standing there and pats Mabel's knee and points to them and puts her drink down and the world stops as she rises and crosses the floor and stands in front of them. Smiling.

"You must be Luke," she says, and she looks at him perhaps a little longer than she ought and his face reddens when she holds her hand out to him and waits for him to take it. "I'm Belle," she says to him, then turns to Gus and Finest.

"How did you all sneak in here without my seeing you? And why are you standing way back here in the corner?" Before they can answer she herds them into the middle of the floor and presents them to the room like debutantes at a coming out.

The others nod their heads and raise their glasses to them. A few offer names and handshakes in turn.

"Finest leaves for boot camp tomorrow," she says.

They look at him a moment, at his face. His scars. Twitching. And they raise their glasses again, then look at the white man standing next to him, at Gus.

"Germany or Japan?" says one.

Finest blinks and shrugs his shoulders.

"Wouldn't let 'em send me no place but France," says another.

"Negro, what you know about France?"

"All I need to know."

"You speak French?"

"I speak French kiss."

Groans of "Negro!" and "Please!" echo about the room.

Gooch sits there and stares at him, at Finest, and traces his scar with his thumb.

"You know you not gonna see no action," he says.

Finest clears his throat and turns to him and blinks.

"Don't start now, Gooch!" somebody hollers.

"I'm just sayin' the way it is. Just like last time."

"It's a party, Gooch!"

"You really think they about to give a black man some bullets and a gun and let him go around the world takin' out white folks?"

"Gooch!"

"Naw. Gooch is right. Got a Christmas card from a cousin a mine from Detroit got called up last April. Says for the first six months they had him marchin' through swamps so deep in Louisiana he thought the war was bein' fought on the Bayou. Now they got him in India."

"India?"

"Hangin' off the side of a mountain someplace. Buildin' a road through a jungle."

"Wait now. Doin' what?"

"Buildin' a road."

The room quiets a moment.

"India cain't build its own roads?"

Gooch turns from Finest and looks at Gus.

Gus looks back at him.

"You goin', too?" he says.

Gus shakes his head and Belle announces that "Gus is going to college," and they go on this way for awhile talking about wars and who has the right to fight in them and why would they want to when they got a war going on right here to fight at home? And Belle tells Finest he should be proud for stepping up and standing for what he believes in, then Luke interrupts and informs everybody that he's objecting and they turn to him and look at him a moment as if he's only just entered the room, then back to each other and laugh and Mabel and Belle and a few of the others set the food on the table and tell everyone to grab a plate and sit wherever they can find a seat, and on the other side of the curtains closed around them the day dims down to half-light and they sit there together and they eat and drink and think about war and fighting, and when they finish they wash up their dishes and relight their cigarettes and smoke and drink some more and dance. Easy with each other and wary all at the same time.

NOBODY SEES GOOCH leave and none of them hears Sister Tremble enter. She stands there just inside the door. Wrapped inside her coat with her scarf tied around her head like a rain bonnet. Looking down at the floor with her shoulders hunched. Face hidden as if she were caught without an umbrella in an unexpected downpour. Back turned toward them all against the wind of it. To block it.

Mabel is the first to see her there. Small and hunched. Feet drawn together. Rooted to a single spot on the doormat. Like some lost and disoriented gnome. Shivering a little as if wet through with water. Afraid to come into the room for fear of ruining the rugs. Dulling the shine on the floor.

"Sister Tremble?" says Mabel.

The rest of them turn around and look at her...

"You alright?"

...and wrest their conversations and step back and make some space around her and she stands there. Back turned to them. Hunched still, and stares at the floor.

Mabel rises and goes to her and whispers into her ear, then leads her by the arm with her face still hidden back to the sofa and somebody turns off the music box as she does so and for the first time all day it is quiet in the house save the clink of ice cubes in glasses, and they stand there awhile and they stare at her and drink.

Mabel and Belle sit beside her and grab hold of her hands like bookends on the sofa, and Finest and Gus and the others gather around in front of them.

"Sister?" says Belle, and when she lifts her head and raises her eyes to look at them, they steel themselves. Minds against hearts. Eyes against the ruin and devastation they expect to witness, but when she looks up and shows them her face they see nothing. No bruising. No cigarette holes. No cuts. They see no rips nor tears in her clothing nor welts or rope burns around her wrists. Her neck. No blemish or any other discernible marker of any kind to explain why only a few minutes before she stood inside the door with her head ducked under and her shoulders hunched as if it were pouring down rain from the ceiling. None save the light. Gone from her eyes like stars. Streaking across the blackened sky before dying. The absence of it a pall over all that remains there and Belle and Mabel look at her, at the light fleeing her eyes faster than dying comets, and Belle whispers something to her that The Sister doesn't seem to hear and she strokes and pats the back of her hand, then looks up and apologizes to everybody and announces that "The party's over." And after asking Gus and Finest to see them all to the door, from the sofa they lead her out back to the shed and they sit there with her on the bed and stay there with her awhile and Belle looks at her, at her eyes. Vacant and black. And she reaches inside the drawer of the nightstand and lights two cigarettes and hands one to her. She knows those eyes. As well as she knows the monster that steals the light and turns them dark like that. She sees them everyday in the mirror. Black bottomless holes where color and light used to be. Life.

Sister Tremble takes the cigarette from her and inhales and exhales and they sit there together. The two of them. Smoking and staring at nothing while Mabel adds a log to the fire.

In the morning before they wake she is dressed and gone, and when they see her next she will go on as if she had never been there at all and if they should mention it to her in passing she will look at them as if she has no idea what they are talking about and she will strike from all recall, all conversation and reference to it and it will lie there. Pushed down in the recesses. Dormant. Piled atop the other nightmares until there is no more room.

Mabel opens the drapes and gathers the glasses and beer bottles and carries them into the kitchen, then disappears and returns again with the ashtrays and crumpled up cigarette packets and empties them into the garbage pail.

Belle stands at the stove. Warming the milk for the coffee. Staring through the window into the sober blue morning.

"Is Gooch still sleeping?" she says.

"Gooch?"

"On the sofa."

"Gooch gone," says Mabel. "Everybody gone. Finest. Gus, too."

"Then what's his truck still doing here?"

"Who's truck?"

"Gooch."

Mabel looks out the window and shrugs her shoulders.

"Maybe he slept out there," she says and she vanishes into the sitting room again.

Belle turns the fire down under the milk and hollers over her shoulder as she unties her apron and goes to the door.

"Why would he do that?" she says. "When he's been sleeping on the sofa all this time?" And when she opens it and the chimes ring on the back and she sees him there, face down on the doorstep, she stops and she looks at him and smiles a little and shakes her head as if she's not quite sure what it is she's looking at, and she stands there a moment and waits a bit, then screams and hollers into her hands as if someone has just come up and told her.

His eye is swollen shut. His mouth pried open and drowned with his nose in a pool of his own blood and vomit. His suit is ripped at the seams. He reeks of cigarette smoke. Low-grade whiskey and cheap perfume.

When Mabel comes running, Belle is already on the stoop on her knees with him. Leaning over his head with her ear to his mouth. Listening.

"Is he breathin'?"

"Barely," she says. "We need to get his binder off and make sure nothing's broken."

They lift him by the arms and the ankles and as they do so she glances around the yard at the cemetery. The curtains closing in the windows next door, and they drag and carry him inside the house and lay him on the sofa.

"Shit!" cries Belle. "Not here! Not here! Not here!" and Mabel runs to the kitchen and wraps up an icepack and grabs the scissors and a wet rag to wash his face with, and when she returns she takes his shoes off and puts a pillow under his feet and she sits there with him, holding the icepack to the side of his head and wiping his face a little with the rag and she watches as Belle takes off his clothes and with the scissors cuts away his undershirt and something that looks like a girdle or waist nipper from around his chest, and she sits there and she looks at him, at his chest. Bare and rising up and down in front of her. Belle pressing around the muscles in his abdomen with her fingers. Kneading for broken bones.

TODAY BEATRICE SITS in her chair. Watching the leaves sprout on the crown of the sugar maple tree. A glass of water sits on the tea table in front of her. Full. Undisturbed. The pine siskins are back. Yesterday a red-tailed hawk rode the sky.

Belle opens the door and stands there and stares at her before entering, at her head resting against the back of the green velvet chair. Facing the window in the center of the room. She holds onto the door knob and bends and removes her shoes, then crosses to the bed and stops just beyond Beatrice's line of vision and sits there awhile and takes off her hat and looks at her and drinks her in like water. Listening for footsteps or floorboards moaning on the stairway. A hasp on her breath.

Such cautions are unnecessary, she knows. The removal of shoes and keeping from sight. Surveillance of breathing patterns. On most days Beatrice is sleeping when she arrives, and even when she is awake and turns from the window and stares at her, she never sees her. Still, as soon as she enters Belle catches the door behind her before it closes and holds it there by the handle, open just enough to let a splinter of light snag through and she repeats this ritual of bending and removing and hiding beyond lines of vision in the manner of the penitent gesturing the sign of the cross upon entering the confessional. Conciliatory. As if the action of it, the motion of crossing: forehead to chest to shoulder to shoulder. Bending and removing. The gesture itself rather than the devotion behind it is enough to confess the faith. Ward off evil and renew the baptism. Accept one's share in the suffering. Without it the moment she is entering might never receive her. The walls and the floorboards. The bed. The woman in the chair. All of it might collapse and vanish as if it never existed to begin with. The photograph in her pocket. Dissolving in her hand. Dispelling the moments before it and after as myth. Rumor not to be believed, and the little hold she has been able to claim. The thread that has weathered on in spite of itself all these years will fray past the point of breaking and there will be nothing left of it for her to hold. So she bends and she removes and she hides and she sits there and drinks her in and she listens, and when she is convinced no footsteps approach on either staircase and that her presence in the house has gone again unnoticed from the bed, she rises and crosses to her.

She's awake.

Belle sits in the chair on the other side of the table and draws her legs toward her and her feet behind her and lets her head fall against the seatback, against the velvet, so that she is curled up like a ball between the armrests, and faces her. From behind by the door, the chair she is in looks empty still as if it is just Beatrice sitting there. Alone. Staring through the window at the sugar maple. The pine siskins. The sky. And she sits there with her. Quiet. Cleansed from knowledge and sight by a sea of green velvet, and she lets her head splash into it and she closes her eyes and sucks her breath in and holds it there and sinks for a moment beneath the surface of it and floats there awhile immersed and born anew, and then she breathes again and she looks at her and rides the swells of lavender about her.

Sara has changed her hair. It is parted now. Deep on the side and rolled back soft off her face, curled under her neck on her shoulders. Like Bette Davis in *The Letter*. The doctor comes everyday now. Constant vigil no longer required. Only during the hour before to prepare for his coming and the one after should she react to the injection and convulse and throw fits at his leaving. Otherwise a checking on now and then is all, and again when it is time to sleep and wake in the morning.

The hours she sits alone without interruption are the hours when Sara retreats to the kitchen to get supper ready, and it is during this time, before the sun retires and the half-light descends with the frenzied shadows of bats swooped from caves after six months of sleeping. The moon slow in waxing to light the stage nocturnal. It is during this time at those hours when the sun's rays have not yet waned and Beuford and Luke are out in the fields still or gone in the truck to town, that Belle slips into the stairwell and sneaks up to the attic and sits here with her. Everyday save when she's working, since Gooch got up from the sofa and bathed and dressed and sat at the table in his undershirt and washed down a plate of syrup with milk and a couple of Mabel's biscuits for breakfast, then climbed in his truck and drove back to Cleveland. Since Finest left for the war and even before that, when Hog shipped out and Beuford needed Finest back on the farm again and the doctor started coming with his daily injections and Finest went back out to the stalls full time and the fields and started whispering to the souls of swine again.

In all these moments and hours they have passed together in this room in front of this window, Beatrice has never spoken. Nor has she ever looked at Belle and wondered who she was. Noticed that they share the same jaw line and dimple under the chin. The same collarbone and hands. On the days when her eyes are open, she looks through the window at the crown on the sugar maple tree. The sky and nothing else.

She has a tick. A small one. A quivering in the lips that could be mistaken for a smile or the promise of one that never comes, and when she sits in the chair she likes to have her feet crossed out in front of her at her ankles. On the divan: Furled behind her legs up by her thighs. Belle sits here with her until the light begins to fade and she can smell the ham or the potatoes in the pot roast sifting through the cracks in the floorboards. The greens on the burner. Cabbage and sausage boiling, and it is almost time for Beuford to come in and Luke from the fields or the barn and Sara to come back and take her down to supper. She sits here and she stares at her and she does not think about the fact that after conceiving of her she gave her away, nor what might have been had she decided to keep her. In these hours before the light fades, when the house is empty and she has her all to herself, she sits here with her and she looks at her and she breathes her in and she does not think. She does not think about anything.

"Got my deferment," says Luke.

By the time she starts at the sound of his voice and reaches for her things and jumps to her feet he is already standing in front of her, silhouetted against the window. Swaying a little on the other side of the table. Hat twirling in his hands like a windmill on a windless day. Slow if moving at all.

"But I still got to go," he says, and backlit by the sun the way he is and swaying, she is unable to see his face clear or his mouth move and his words fall flat and searching as if they are being fed to him as lines from a hideous offing in the wings somewhere attempting to woo her in a deranged and perverted staging of Cyrano, and she looks at him, at the shadow of him, faceless and swaying in the sunlight flooding the room, at Beatrice, and she steadies herself on the chair back and she slides and eases her feet into her shoes and she stands there. Like mother like daughter. Calculating in her head the distance in footsteps to the door behind them which is closed now and she stares at him. Swaying there. Wondering why she never heard the hinges creak or the latch catch. The soles of his boots against the hardwood. Whether or not she can make it that far. Onto the landing and forty-five more steps down to the stairwell before he overtakes her.

He smells of horse manure and straw and beer chased with whiskey and the gentle swells of lavender about them turn rank and bitter. The shadow of his face stares at her, at the pocketbook in her hands, down at her shoes, then lifts and sways and stares for awhile at his mother, who sits and stares through the window still.

"Deferment?" says Belle.

He nods.

"For my objection."

"Objection?"

"To the war."

He steps forward a bit in from the light and his hair falls limp and greasy in front of his face and she can see him now. The cut of his jaw. The dimple under his chin, and he grips the brim of his hat and he looks at her and his eyebrows bunch and gather when he frowns.

"I can object, they said. But I still got to go. Said I'd be what they call a non-combatant. A medic or driver or somethin'. Said the only way I can keep from goin' at all is if I volunteer to live in some lab somewhere and let 'em experiment on me."

He raises his fist to his mouth and turns back to his mother again and belches.

"Well, I ain't bein' no guinea pig for nobody," he says and he bunches his eyebrows and runs his hand over his mouth and the stubble on his face that looks more like bruising, as if he's been on the losing end of a fist fight rather than beard growth, and he stands there and his eyes dart and skirt the room like the eyes of wild horses trapped and corralled in barbed wire.

Belle watches him and steps and rests her hands and her pocketbook on the seatback so that the chair she was sitting in is between them now and she stands there on the other side of the chair a step closer to the door and she glances at the light drawing through the window again. The sugar maple and the pine siskins. Feeding on the wooly aphids on the buds of newborn sugar maple leaves.

"I don't know," she says to him. "Being a driver doesn't seem so bad. And a medic sounds kind of noble." She hedges a little more toward the door and stops and smiles at him when he steps forward again and stares at her. "Maybe it will all be over soon and you won't have to go for very long."

He belches and turns away from her and looks around the room and stands there awhile. Holding his hat and stroking his stubble as if he is an explorer come upon the ruin of something. He looks at the bed his mother sleeps in. The divan where she sits when she tires of the chair. He looks at the bureau where her clothes are kept and the pot on the floor next to the bed in case she wakes in the night and has to relieve herself when the door is locked and Sara is sleeping, and he looks at his mother again, her mouth quivering as if she might smile, and he stands there awhile and he waits for it, the smile, then bunches up his eyebrows again and turns back to his sister when it fails to come.

"What's the point of goin' to war?" he says. "If you ain't gonna fight? It ain't objectin' if you still got to go and take part in it."

Belle nods at him in agreement and slides another foot toward the door.

"Think if the Nazis or the Japs catch me in my uniform they'll care whether I was drivin' a truck or fightin'?

"No," she says and she shakes her head. "I suppose they wouldn't."

"Might as well paint a bull's-eye on my back and drop me behind enemy lines."

He sways and looks at her and catches her moving and steps around the chairs and table, around Beatrice, and blocks her path.

"If I got to go no matter what," he says, "I might as well go on and fight, right?" And he stands there and faces her and grips the brim of his hat tighter and turns it in his hands. Dirty and callused, and he stands there and he sways a little and he stares at her, then looks around at the ruin again.

"You look like her some," he says.

She looks at him.

"Daniel always swore you were real. Said it was the only thing they ever said about her they were too scared to say to our faces. That one and the one about Daniel."

She stands there.

"Been watchin' ya," he says and he raises his fist to his mouth as if he might belch, then wipes his forehead with his shirt sleeve when nothing comes out. "Comin' and goin' the way you do. Took me awhile to figure it out. Then I remembered the party."

"The party?" she says.

"For Finest."

She nods.

"Weesfree said you were a Negro."

He looks at her and she shifts her weight from one foot to the other and stands there.

"I can see it now," he says. "Now that I look at ya. Everything's just a little off, ain't it? Not quite right?"

Beatrice slumps and nods off in her chair.

He looks at her, then back at Belle.

"Daniel said sure as he was breathin' you were gonna come back here one day and try to lay claim to somethin'." He lowers his eyes a bit. "He also said you were a he," and his face reddens some.

"You ain't no he," he says. "Guess there's been a lot a that happenin' around here lately."

She looks at him.

"That what you're doin' here?" he says. "Tryin' to lay claim to somethin'?"

She shakes her head.

"What then?" and he moves a step closer to her.

Belle steps back and looks around the room. At Beatrice.

"At first I just wanted to know. You know?"

"Know what?"

She shrugs her shoulders. "Her," she says and nods at her. "If I had any brothers or sisters. My father." She looks at him. "Then when I saw her..." and she glances at Beatrice again. "How she was. I don't know. I just wanted to be near her. Feel her, I guess."

He looks at her awhile and the light begins to fade and the sky changes from a kind of blue into a kind of red. Pink almost. Like his face. And the smell of biscuits and gravy and pan fried chicken rises around them through the floorboards and a pink and red swell washes over the ruin of the room.

"She ever talk to you?" he says.

Belle shakes her head no.

"Ain't said a word to me my whole life," he says and his voice takes on a kind of pleading quality to it. Halfhearted and resigned as if begging for a mercy long ago denied. "Not even my name," he says and he stands there and stares at her, at Beatrice nodded off in her chair, and says, "My daddy told me he let God name me. Closed his eyes and turned to a page in the Bible and put his finger down on it and it landed on Luke."

He looks at her and laughs a little and sways.

"Wonder if it had landed on Esther if he'd have asked for a do-over?"

"Luke," says Belle.

"When I was little," he says, "I used to try and talk to her. Tell her things. 'Bout school. Somethin' funny Daniel said. The farm. Whatever I could think of. Figured if I followed her around enough and talked long enough. Nothin' else she'd at least get tired of hearin' my trap yappin' and tell me to Shut the hell up! Like Daniel always does."

He laughs again.

"She never even blinked at me."

Belle starts to speak, but he shakes his head and stops her.

"You can't come here no more," he says to her.

"I know."

"It's like diggin' up the dead or somethin'."

"I know."

"No good to it."

He looks at her.

"'Specially if Daddy or Daniel finds out."

She nods her head at him and glances at Beatrice and the room smells like lavender water and horse manure. Whiskey and beer and chicken and biscuits, and they stand there together. Washed in a swell of pink and red light and they stare at their mother, and after awhile Belle stiffens and turns to leave and Luke steps back to let her pass, and when she reaches the door, before she opens it, she stops and turns to him.

"Luke," she says.

He looks at her.

"Do you know who my father is?"

WHEN SHE SEES his truck in the driveway she thinks something's wrong, and when she enters and sees them sitting there together at the table, she knows it is. It is dark. Geese honk by overhead north across the sky. Like fighter squadrons in victory formation returning home to Canada. The lamps are off in every room in the house save the kitchen.

Gooch sits in the chair across from the door while Mabel faces the sink. Coffee mugs between them. Hands cupped around the mugs as if for warmth. Fidgeting. Eyes lowered and staring at the table. Glancing at each other now and then and smiling from time to time. Looking back down and laughing a little more and looking up again.

She has interrupted something. When the chimes ring and the door opens, Mabel turns and looks at her as if she had no idea a door existed there let alone the possibility of somebody walking through it. Chimes ringing, no less. And when she sees who it is she hops up from the table and reties her apron and turns her back to her and checks on the soup beans simmering on the stove. The cornbread in the frying pan.

Gooch just sits there in his shirt sleeves and suspenders and picks up his coffee mug and sips from it and grins at her and looks at his wristwatch.

"Beginnin' to wonder if you was ever comin' back," he says. "Good thing Mae was around." And he turns away from her and looks at Mabel at the stove awhile, then looks back.

Belle puts her pocketbook down and glances at the mugs on the table and takes off her hat and her coat and fluffs her hair and smiles at him.

"Little late in the day for coffee, isn't it?" she says.

Gooch nods at her and laughs a little. "Maybe if it was coffee," he says.

"Early then for the other perhaps."

"Depends on what you callin' early."

He watches her as she drapes her coat over the back of the chair and he puts his mug down and stands and steps away from the table, and she walks to him and they kiss and hug each other. And after stepping back and looking at him awhile she crosses to the stove and wraps her arms around Mabel and kisses her shoulder.

Both smell like whiskey.

She stands there a moment and puts her hand in the middle of Mabel's back and rubs it a little and leans over the soup beans and breathes in the aroma.

"Mmm!" she says. "I'm starving."

Mabel looks at her.

"You alright?" says Belle.

Mabel nods her head and glances at Gooch, then turns off the fire and picks up a knife and cuts the cornbread into pie wedges in the skillet.

Belle reaches into the cupboard and takes down the bowls and bread plates, spoons and butter knives from the drawer, and sets them on the table. Another squadron of geese honks by then dies away and goes silent. She sits and lights a cigarette and shakes out the match and looks at them.

"You look well," she says to Gooch.

He strokes his moustache and smiles at her.

"Your eye looks great!"

He raises his mug to her and nods his head at Mabel. "That's you all's doing," he says.

She drags on her cigarette and glances at the coffee mugs. "Are you sharing what's in those mugs? Or is there only enough for the two of you?" And she smiles at him and Gooch gets up and takes down another mug and fills it a quarter full with whiskey and she takes it from him and raises the mug to Gooch and to Mabel at the stove and says "To Family" and swallows and drinks from it.

Mabel dishes the beans into the bowls and brings the pan of cornbread over along with a stick of butter and joins them at the table.

"No Gus?" says Belle.

Mabel shakes her head. "School," she says and reaches for a wedge of cornbread.

"Where did you find real butter?"

"Gooch brought it."

He grins at her and shrugs his shoulders a little and they butter their bread and look at him and laugh, then look at each other and shake their heads and laugh again.

Belle takes a mouthful of soup beans and closes her eyes and sits there a minute. Chews and swallows and takes another bite and says, "Mabel, you outdid yourself this time." And Gooch nods in agreement and butters a piece of cornbread and eats it and nods again and they go on this way for awhile. Chewing and nodding and swallowing. The three of them. Eyes closed. Faces sweating and glowing with reverence. Spoons clanging against the bottoms of bowls and souls like clappers against cracked and muted liberty bells and dampened tolls of freedom. Geese quiet. Knives against plates.

"When do you have to be back?" asks Belle.

"Wanted to talk to you about that," says Gooch.

"Okay."

"I was thinking maybe I might stick around awhile."

They look at him.

"How long awhile?" says Belle.

Gooch shrugs his shoulders.

"Little while. Month maybe. Longer, you all okay with it."

She chews and swallows and looks at him, at Mabel.

"Something happen in Cleveland?"

He turns up his mouth and shakes his head at her.

"Nothin' I need to run from."

"What happened?"

"I said I ain't runnin' from nothin'."

She sits there and looks at him, then turns back to her bowl and finishes eating. Pushes her plate away and lights a cigarette.

"You okay with it?" he says to her.

"Not my house to say," she says.

Gooch turns to Mabel.

Belle watches her and smokes.

Mabel looks down at her mug.

"Little while be alright, I guess," she says.

In the morning when she finds the gun in his truck, she looks for him on the sofa, and when he is not on the sofa she walks to the end of the hall and listens at Mabel's door awhile, then returns to the shed and sits there in the dark and waits for him, for the sun to rise. Thinking about the smell of lavender and velvet. Pine siskins.

When he knocks on the door and enters, crows caw and the sun has been visible less than an hour. The coffee mug is in his hand and a stocking cap creases his forehead. His shirt hangs open and his sleeves are rolled to his elbows. His suspenders hang down by his sides.

She sits on the bed and points the gun at him.

He closes the door behind him and stands there. Sips from the mug and looks at her.

"Why are you here?" she says to him.

He glances through the window at the house, then back at the gun and smiles at her.

"You went through my stuff," he says.

"Why are you here?"

Again, he glances at the house. "Oh. You all out about that?" he says. "You know how I am, Bellie. All you got to do is say the word. Just say the word, and I'll give 'em all up for you."

"What happened in Cleveland?"

He drinks from the mug.

"Cleveland ain't shit," he says. "Tradition the only place I gotta worry about."

She looks at his eye. The scar raised on his neck.

"So that's it," she says to him.

He grins at her and shrugs his shoulders. "Can't keep lettin' 'em get away with it, Bellie," he says to her. "Can't do it no more."

"So what? You put a bullet in somebody's brain and let 'em lynch you instead?"

He drinks and shrugs his shoulders.

She watches him awhile, then nods and smiles a little and puts the gun down and lights a cigarette.

"You want to kill yourself," she says to him, "go ahead." She exhales and shakes out the match. "You just can't do it here. This," she says. "All this," and she looks at the house. "This is mine. So go on. Kill yourself if you want to. Just don't do it here."

"You tellin' me to leave?" he says.

She looks at him.

By the time she finishes her cigarette and stubs it out in the ashtray he is gone.

# may 10, 2007

The dog is back. On the porch this time. in the shade out of the sun. Legs crossed again. Tongue hanging out of his mouth as if he's just laid up to rest after running a great distance, and when Sojourner walks up the walkway and climbs the steps to the porch and sees him there and fits her key in the lock, he watches her and wags his tail a little and pants. She looks at him, at the rubble around them. The work crews loading the trucks to haul it all away. And she wonders if he belongs to one of them.

The house smells of maple syrup when she enters. Maple syrup, pancakes and sausage patties. The day bogged down in moisture still. The warblers have returned and the thrushes. The windows are open. No breeze stirs the trees.

Finest sits on the sofa in front of the television in his pajamas. His hat and his shoes. Blinking at the screen. Listening to the birdsong playing in stereo outside the window accompanied by the voiceover from an episode of Snapped about a woman in Texas who used a kitchen knife to cut off the arms of her eleven-month-old baby. His hands clasped at attention on the handle of his cane.

In the kitchen, when he hears the front door open, Gus counts the last of the bills from the silverware drawer, stuffs them back under the tray and eases the drawer closed as she calls to him.

"Auntie Mabel! Uncle Gus!"

He takes out his handkerchief, wipes his face and hands and enters the sitting room to greet her.

The picture in his pocket doesn't begin to tell the half of it. She sets down her suitcase and stands there. Keys still in her hands. Staring at Finest, at the handcuffs. Pink around his ankle. Attached to the leg of the couch.

Gus crosses to her as she pushes the door closed and she turns to him and holds out her hand.

"Uncle Gus?"

He nods a little and smiles as though he's been caught at something. "Gus," he says to her. "Just Gus," and he looks at her and studies her a moment as if she is a vision of some kind from the realms of the unreal. A visitation projected from both past and future come to the present to forgive him, and he stands there, staring at her. Mouth open. Shaking her hand.

Sojourner pulls her hand away and puts her keys back in her purse, then looks at him, at Finest. Laces missing from his shoes. His cane. His hat, and she looks at his scars. Twitching, at the jumbled mess of features confusing his face and at his handcuffs again.

Finest stares at the television and blinks.

"Where is Auntie Mabel?" she says.

"In the bed still," says Gus. "I was just about to go check on her."

Outside the warning signals beep on the trucks as they back up to the piles of rubble to haul it away, and they stand there awhile. The two of them. Listening to it. The beeping. Staring at Finest. The smell of sausage grease, pancakes and maple syrup filling their lungs.

"You remember him?" says Gus.

Sojourner nods. "What's wrong with him?"

"Doctor says it's some kind of dementia."

"Dementia?"

"Mmm hmm. Something to do with the veins."

"And he prescribed handcuffs for it?"

Gus looks at her, at the handcuffs, then down at the floor.

"He wanders," he says. "Moves things."

"Moves things?"

"Furniture and stuff. Bookcases. Tables. Hard to believe until you see it. They got a name for it."

He thinks a moment.

"Sunset something," he says.

"Sundowners Syndrome?"

He nods. "Sundowners, that's it."

"So he has Alzheimer's?"

He shakes his head. "Somethin' else. Doctor says…"

"I know," she says and raises her hand to stop him. "Something to do with the veins."

She turns to him and looks at him and suddenly it is as though he is standing in one of those body-scan machines they're installing in all the airports.

"Uncle Gus?"

"Hmm?"

"Why is he here?"

He looks at her. "It's a long story," he says.

Sojourner nods and picks up her suitcase and carries it to the back porch door.

Gus follows her.

She puts down the suitcase and faces him.

"And why are you here, Uncle Gus? Let me guess," she says. "Another long story."

"Beg your pardon?" he says.

"What do you want here? Auntie Mabel doesn't have any money. All those years of cleaning people's houses under the table didn't yield much Social Security." She looks at the cracked and yellowed walls and ceiling. "And anything she had of any value, mainly this house, has long lost it. So why are you here?"

She waits for him to answer.

"Just wanted to come home," he says.

"After all these years you just wanted to come home?"

He looks around the house. At the china cabinet. The rocking chair. The picture shelf. Finest. "Yeah," he says to her.

"I think I want to see Auntie Mabel now."

When they enter the bedroom, she is sitting up. Propped against the pillows. Asleep. The mug in her hand threatening to slip from her fingers and fall to the floor. Its contents spilled across the bedspread.

Sojourner sees the mug and crosses to the bed and rescues it before it falls from Mabel's grasp and shatters.

Gus follows and stops behind her.

She sniffs the empty mug and sets it on the table, then picks up the pill bottle and reads the label.

"Who's Doctor Rawlins?"

"Luke brought him over," says Gus. "From town."

"Luke?"

"Simler," he says.

She nods and stares at him. "And you let her take these with alcohol?"

"I…"

"This is oxycodone!" she scolds and stands there and stares at him, then turns to Mabel.

"Auntie Mabel," she whispers.

They look at her.

"Auntie Mabel, wake-up."

They wait.

"How many pills did you give her?" she asks him.

"Just the one!" says Gus. "Like it says on the bottle."

"Auntie Mabel!"

Mabel stirs and opens her eyes and looks at her awhile and closes them again…

"Auntie Mabel."

…and turns back over…

"Auntie Mabel, quit fooling."

…and pretends to snore.

"Come on, Auntie Mabel. Stop."

Mabel rolls over and looks at her again, then looks over at Gus and licks her lips and clears her throat.

"How'd you find the number?" she says to him.

Gus looks at Sojourner, then back at Mabel.

"Only one you had written down."

She nods. "Well," she says and feels around the bed for her mug. "Everybody's here now, may as well go on and start the party."

"Looking for this?" says Sojourner. She holds up the coffee mug.

"Auntie Mabel," she says. "We talked about this. Either you stop drinking or we sell the house and you come to live with me in California."

Mabel closes her eyes again.

"We had a deal. Remember? And now look what's happened."

"California ain't shit," says Mabel and her eyelids flutter a bit and her mouth quivers as if she might smile.

Sojourner picks up the bottle and shows it to her. "This is the last time, Auntie Mabel. Auntie Mabel, look at me."

Mabel lies there.

"There's no time for this, Auntie Mabel. We have to make arrangements."

Still, she lies there.

"Fine," says Sojourner and she rises from the bed. "I'm going through the house," she says to her. "And pouring out every bottle I find. You can't drink like this anymore. You're too old. And we're both too old to keep up all this silliness."

"Old ain't shit," says Mabel.

Sojourner shakes her head and takes the bottle and leaves the room, then returns with a glass of water.

"You get thirsty," she says, setting it on the table. "You'll have to settle for this."

Gus and Mabel stare at her, at each other, then back at Sojourner.

Sojourner sits.

"First thing tomorrow," she says, "I'm calling Mr. Dixon."

Mabel looks up and sniffs at her. "When did you start smokin' again?" she says.

"What?" says Sojourner.

"Smell like you smokin' a cigarette. And ginger. You been makin' curry or somethin'?"

"Auntie Mabel, you know I don't smoke."

Mabel coughs and waves her hand in front of her face.

"Whoever it is got to put it out," she says and she coughs again. "Makin' me sick."

Sojourner turns and looks at Gus.

He shrugs his shoulders and shakes his head.

"Auntie Mabel," she says to her. "Nobody's smoking."

They look at her, at each other, as the coughing continues. Sojourner reaches over and hands her the glass of water.

"Here," she says. "Drink this."

Mabel takes the water and sips from it and swallows.

"Better now?" says Sojourner.

Mabel looks at her.

"Auntie Mabel, we have to talk about California."

Mabel sips and swallows. "Nothin' to talk about California," she says and she coughs a little.

Sojourner sighs. "Auntie Mabel."

"Ain't goin'," says Mabel. "Ain't goin' nowhere. 'Cept in the ground when it's time."

"Auntie Mabel, don't talk like that."

Sojourner looks at her and puts her hand on her arm. "You can't stay here anymore, Auntie Mabel. Not with the drinking. Not by yourself."

She looks back at Gus.

"None of you can. I'm sorry," she says to them. "But it's just not safe. And Mr. Coon needs to be in a facility."

The trucks have quieted. The workmen off on their lunch break. Even the dog has gone. For good this time, hopes Gus.

THE NIGHT GOOCH came back Mabel was unable to sleep, and as she lay in bed staring at the shadows of the tulip poplar branches, bending and twisting like fingers broken across the ceiling, she couldn't stop thinking about him.

She thought about his hands. Weathered and cracked as if they spent the whole of their lives working and sleeping outside. The way they shook a little whenever he lit his cigarette or took a drink of something, even a glass of water. She thought about the way he cocked his head to the side and back a little and smiled when he spoke to her. About the way she dropped things around him and went cold and numb in spots and warm in others whenever he entered a room she was in. She thought about the scar on his neck and wondered how he got it. His moustache. About the moment she saw him lying there on the doorstep that morning. When they dragged him into the house and heaved him onto the sofa and Belle cut off the thing she called a binder but looked more like a girdle or waist nipper. Hospital bandage, maybe. That under all that weathering and callus something soft was hidden and it was this softness buried beneath all that hardness, that contradiction in him that drew her to him. He was the opposite of Belle, whose warmth and tenderness she knew even then lured you to a hard place you would never be able to leave and yet never be allowed to enter, and she was lying there thinking about all that. Bindings and calluses, hard places and contradictions, when her door swung open and he was standing there suddenly and closing it behind him and leaning back against it in his undershirt. Head cocked. Grinning at her.

He was from Pendleton, he told her. South Carolina. His father disappeared on his way home from work one day when he was two months old and he had no memory of him. He had not seen his mother since he was seven. After his brother was castrated and hanged for having marital relations with a white girl from Laurens County. It was no longer safe for him there. She was sending him to Chicago, she said. North to live with his aunt and uncle. The same uncle who always looked at him funny and liked to sit him on his lap and bounce him on his knee all the time whenever they came to Pendleton to visit. The night before he was scheduled to leave, after his mother went to bed, he cut off his hair, disguised himself in his dead brother's clothes and ran. The money he removed from her pocketbook, he reasoned, she was planning to give him anyway and, save a family or two who took him in from time to time, he'd been on his own ever since.

In turn she told him the things she never told to anybody. Not even Belle. About her mother. How she had taken sick and died. About Gus, and Sister Tremble and The Pastor driving them up to a red brick building in Cincinnati to wave to a window. About Finest and the fire. His face, and about the pills she crushed up into a glass of creek water and fed to her father to make him go ahead and die already. And when he reached across the blanket and put his hand on her knee and started rubbing it with his callus, she was more surprised that she had told him all that and that her body parts had finally settled on a single temperature than she was that he was touching her, and though she had never kissed anybody before and was unsure how to go about it, putting her mouth on his was exactly what she wanted to do just then. And as he sat there scraping the skin on her kneecap with the calluses on his fingers, talking about Pendleton and lynchings, she pressed her lips to the corner of his mouth and held them there and breathed. He smelled of sweat, cologne, cigarettes and whiskey and hair grease, and when he turned and kissed her back and searched inside her mouth for her tongue, she panicked a little and jerked away from him.

Half an hour later they were naked together, save the binder, his undershirt and shorts, and at first their love-making fared about the same as their first kiss. The bed was narrow and the hinges squeaked and she stopped him several times and pushed him away and shushed him and asked if he could slide his elbow over a bit. His knee to the side a little. And she worried that they might wake Gus Junior in the adjoining room, and at one point she thought she heard noises inside the house. Someone outside the door. Standing in the hall. Listening to them, and he kissed her again and this time she kissed him back and he whispered to her and told her there was no one, and then he asked her if it was okay what they were doing and she looked at him a moment and thought about this new road she was on and nodded and they lay there together and kissed and touched and tasted each other and after awhile she could think of nothing save how thick the air had become. Warm and damp. Difficult to breathe, and sweat beads trickled from her neck onto her chest, into her armpits, down her sides. Hinges squeaking on the bed frame. The headboard. Her breath.

In the morning when they woke she made coffee, then returned to the room to clean up the mess they had made, and when she carried the empty bottle and mugs back into the kitchen he was gone and so was his truck, and Belle was standing there in his place in front of the stove cooking bacon and eggs. The table set for two.

Belle looked at her, at the bottle and the mugs in her hands, then back to the stove and turned the bacon.

"Gus never made it home last night," she said. "I think maybe he's found himself a little girlfriend or something."

Mabel set the mugs in the sink and threw away the bottle and watched her. The bacon sizzling in the pan, then stared through the window at the driveway where the truck had been parked.

"Hungry?" said Belle. "I never have been any good at biscuits," and she nodded toward the stove at the hard black discs stuck to the baking tray. "Gooch went back to Cleveland," she said. "Something he remembered he had to do."

Mabel's mouth went dry.

"He comin' back?" she asked.

Belle looked at the stove and shook her head.

Mabel stood there awhile and nodded. Nodded and swallowed and looked around the room and through the window one last time, at Belle, at the bacon sizzling. The grease. Popping out of the pan. She had been claimed and she stood there awhile nodding and swallowing and thinking about what that meant. Lovemaking was not the word. What she had done with Gooch. They had not loved each other in the night. They had salved each other. Tended to one another's wounds. It was Belle they loved. Always would be. So it wasn't love that got sent away when the claiming happened. Love was still here. It was the ointment against it that was gone. The soothing of the wound. And she stood there, staring and swallowing, and after awhile she put on her apron and went to the basin and washed her hands and after she dried them she reached into the cupboard for the flour and the sifter. The mixing bowl and the lard.

FROM THE KITCHEN they hear yelling coming from Mabel's bedroom. Muffled and angry. Gus checks on Finest in front of the television, then follows Sojourner down the hall.

She is dreaming. Arguing with someone in her sleep.

Sojourner touches her shoulder and whispers to her.

"Auntie Mabel?"

Mabel opens her eyes.

Gus stands there and stares at her and wipes his face with his handkerchief.

"You were dreaming," says Sojourner. "Sounded like you were fighting with someone."

"Why?" says Mabel.

Sojourner looks at her.

"Auntie Mabel?"

"Why?" she demands. "Why did you have to come back?"

Gus and Sojourner stare at her.

"Why couldn't you just stay gone? Finest?" says Mabel. "Anybody but Finest!"

Sweat pours down her face from her forehead and she shivers a little and her voice shakes and sounds as if it is coming from somewhere else. Someplace distant and scared.

"I think she's still sleeping," says Sojourner. "Get me a towel from the linen closet."

Gus leaves and returns with the towel.

Mabel flinches and pulls away as Sojourner tries to wipe her face with it.

She waits for her to calm, then tries again.

"It's okay, Auntie Mabel," she says to her.

Mabel looks at her.

"It's me, Sojourner."

She stares at her and blinks.

"It's okay," says Sojourner.

Mabel stares at her, at Gus at the room. The window and the day taking shape beyond it, and she licks her lips a little.

Sojourner picks up the glass of water from the night-stand and hands it to her.

"You were dreaming," she says to her.

Mabel drinks.

"Do you remember?"

She looks at them awhile, at the window, then shakes her head.

The engines and the beeping on the trucks start up again. Voices holler in the background over the din of it. Inside the house it smells like rain.

# 1946

Belle gets out of bed and puts on her shoes and walks into the hall, into the kitchen, to the door and opens it and the chimes ring as she leaves and closes it behind her. She has given over to wandering. At night mostly, in the small hours when she is unable to sleep and the world lies deep in dreams and slumber. Whispers to itself in the hollows of decimated landscapes in the dark and quiet of basements and low-lit rooms, at tables in kitchens and bars and other small-hour spaces over cigarettes and bourbon. Cherry rhubarb pie. And often when she returns she has no idea where she's been nor how long she's been gone. What she did or said or thought while there. Heard and saw. Smelled. Tasted. Most of the time she has no memory of leaving the house at all, let alone the route she followed to return to it, and she stands there awhile in the middle of the floor in the middle of her room in her gown. Barefoot with her coat on, or shoes on her feet but no coat. A hat and pair of gloves or a scarf all by itself, but never all or a combination of accessories at once, and she stands there. Staring at herself, at the bed. The room, as if she is just coming out of something. A somnambulant aroused save that she was awake already and recalls the frost on the ground beneath her feet. Air on her face. Dirt and gravel between her toes. Knows that she has been out walking.

Tonight she starts out north. Wind chills her neck and her arms and blows through the folds in her nightgown. She crosses the yard and stops at the edge of the road and turns and looks around her and listens, then glances back at the house. All of Hope Street is dark. Mute and cold. Extinguished as if life gave up living on it finally and snuffed itself out like a candle. Even the cook stoves have expired. The only smells present of the earth and the river carried through on the wind. In the treetops on the verge of a clearing somewhere raccoons mate beneath the moonlight and claw each other and screech and squeal through the darkness like the souls of babes murdered and sacrificed in Hades, and after awhile it is quiet again save the crunch of her shoes on the roadway. When she reaches the Colonel's house with the flagpole in the yard on the corner of Justice, she turns west toward Prosper and passes by the old Coon property, then stops just beyond it and turns around and wraps her arms around herself and stands there and stares at it.

Weeds and untamed grass hide most of the foundation. From the road a leftover piece of corner wall and two or three stairs escalating up from the ground into nowhere, weather-burned and charred still, is all that is visible. No one has gone near it since the fire. Many bow their heads and say a prayer when they pass. Even kids stay clear of it, and though interest piques now and again regarding its purchase, it dies soon after the lending of its story. The man who used to live there was murdered, prospective buyers were told. Set on fire by his son in the middle of the night while he was sleeping.

Belle stands there. Staring at it. The wall and the stairs ethereal in the moonlight, viewed through the weeds and grass as if through an aqueous veil, and watered down below its murky surface she can almost see the fire. Raging still, and the smoke billowing. Black into the night. Breathe in the fumes from the gasoline. The searing of flesh and bone. And after awhile she turns from it and wanders on.

At Prosper she heads south again. In Doc Agee's house a lamp burns dull behind the curtain drawn in the front window, and on her left she passes the new schoolhouse and the Liberty Bell replica in place of the usual school bell The Pastor insisted on adding to its design.

By the time she climbs the hill and recognizes the inside of the church, she is already down the aisle way past the pews and the pulpit, through the stage and rear door exits, into the parsonage and running. Called like a child by the flute of a piper to the screaming and the yelling. Dishes shattering in the kitchen, and by the time she realizes the butcher knife is in her hand and hears herself yell "Let her go or I'll kill you!" she has already cut him once across the face and is raising the blade to cut him a second time, when Sister Tremble looks up and hollers "No!" and she stops. Blade suspended at its height. And The Sister stares at her and The Pastor stumbles back against the countertop and squeals and moans and curses and clutches his cheek with his hands. Blood seeping through between his fingers. Sister Tremble cowering against the wall in the corner. Mouth bludgeoned and sobbing. Arms bruised. Held in front of her face still. Her head. Attempting to block the next blow.

The three of them stand there and stare at each other. Sister Tremble and The Pastor at Belle as if they are seeing a ghost, a wraith risen up through the grates of hell. Hair all over her head and pale. Wasted. Hovering above the damned with a butcher knife in hand. Raised and stained with blood. Eyes burning wild with fire. And they cower there and stare at her and for a time the room is still and calm. Motionless, as if it were stricken by some kind of narcoleptic fit and nodded off for a moment in the middle of all the excitement and is just coming to, trying to understand what's happened.

The Pastor pulls his hand from his face and sees the blood and yells at her and takes a step toward her and Sister Tremble hollers "No!" again as Belle cocks the knife back to stave him off and he stops and stands there and looks at her, at his hand.

"You stupid bitch!" he says to her and he clutches at his face again. "You stupid heathen hussy bitch! I know who you are. You that devil Weesfree brought into the world."

Sister Tremble brings her arms down from her face and goes to him, but The Pastor throws her off and glares at her.

"Mark my words, Satan!" he says to Belle. "The Lord is going to take you down for this!" Then turns and marches from the room.

"Lucious!" The Sister cries after him. "Lucious, please!" And she grabs herself with her arms and crumbles to the floor in the spot where he stood, and Belle puts the knife down and kneels beside her and wraps her arms around her and holds her and The Sister cries. Vacant tears through vacant eyes, and tries to push her away, but Belle holds on.

"Why?" she sobs at her. "Why did you do that? You shouldn't have come here and done that!"

Belle looks at her.

"Why?" she insists.

"He was hurting you."

"You shouldn't have done that! You had no cause!"

"Sister, he bloodied your mouth."

Sister Tremble stops pushing and sobs and shakes against her.

"It's not his fault," she says.

Belle looks at her.

"Lucious is a good man."

Belle stares at her mouth, at her arms. The dishes and glass shards about them.

The Sister speaks to the floor. "I pray," she says. "Every-day. Seems like all I do is pray for the Lord to come and show me what I'm doing wrong. It's not his fault." She shakes her head and smiles a little as if she is surprised. "I

can't have children and I don't know how to please him otherwise. I try. But nothing is ever good enough. I sit there
sometimes. In the pews in the sanctuary after everyone has
gone, I sit there and I beg of Him. Plead with Him to tell
me what it is. So I can right it."

Belle stands and wets a rag and hands it to her and The
Sister takes it and holds it to her mouth as if in prayer and
squeezes her eyes shut. "Show me, oh Lord! Tell me, Jesus!
Teach me how I can right this! Please let me right it, oh
Lord!" She lowers her hands and the rag and her voice qui-
ets and she opens her eyes and speaks to the floor again.
"But He never does," she says. "No matter what I do. What
I promise.

"I know I don't deserve it. His mercy. I know it is selfish
of me. Unchristian to ask for more than He's already given.
A good man who provides a good home. To ask the relief
of a burden. I know I am being ungrateful. But I just wish I
could know. Know what it is I've done."

"You haven't done anything," says Belle.

Sister Tremble shakes her head and blows her nose on
the rag and wipes her mouth with it and looks at the blood.
"Even if He won't allow me to right it. If He would just let
me know."

In the distance footsteps fade away down a hall to a door
that slams closed at the end of it. Belle looks up toward the
sound and listens, then back at Sister Tremble.

"I'll never forget the way his face changed," she says.
"When Doc Agee told us. The way his mouth stilled and his
eyes hardened. Like watching steel get hot, then cool back

down. I even got her to give me some of those roots. Popular with the Indians. That are supposed to help with these kinds of things, and I ate them behind his back. But all they managed to do was turn my stomach and make him grow colder. So you see," she says and she looks at her and blows her nose again. "It's me. Not him," and she nods her head. "There is something wrong inside *me*. Something living there that does not belong. Some kind of demon spoiling me that has turned him cold." And she puts her hands on the floor and crawls and pushes to her feet and straightens herself a bit, and she stands there and looks around the room and after awhile she begins to clean. "Please leave here," she says to her. "Please. Leave here and don't ever come back."

When she returns to the house the sun is up and Mabel is at the table in the kitchen with Sojourner. Belle closes the door and the chimes ring and she stops and both look up and stare at her. Standing there in her nightgown. Hair tossed over her head, inside the doorsill, and Sojourner burps a little and stretches her arm and sticks her hand in the air and turns it on her wrist and opens and closes it and grips her fingers together and for a moment it looks as if she is smiling at her and waving.

HOG WALKS THROUGH the door to Sim's Liquor then walks back out into the alley and hands Finest the bottle.

"Thanks," says Finest and he coughs a little and lowers his head and clears his throat.

Hog looks at him, then back toward the street and spits.

"What the hell happened to you, Coon? You smell like shit."

Finest stands there and looks at the ground and uncaps the bottle.

"You know I could have you arrested for lettin' your OD's go like that?"

Finest looks at his ragged service uniform like he's just now seeing it and nods, then holds out the bottle and offers him the first taste.

Hog stares at him, at the bottle, then snatches it from him and looks toward the street again and drinks from it, then hands it back. He wipes his mouth on his coat sleeve, then turns up his collar to leave.

"Happy birthday, Coon," he says and he walks back into the street.

Finest watches him go, then rubs the mouth of the bottle dry with his hand and drinks and swallows and drinks again, then screws on the cap and hides it inside his jacket and steps out onto the sidewalk across from Crawford's Funeral Parlor.

Rationing has ended and discarded coupons litter the street which is crowded with Christmas shoppers and cars and interstate buses and soldiers returning greeted by wives with jobs and children who no longer recognize them, and they stand there, some of them. Staring. Shell-shocked at the familiarity of things in all that has changed. When he sees her on the other side of the street, he turns his back a little and waits for her to pass, then crosses the street and falls in behind her and follows her from a distance.

She is dressed as if she is out for a Sunday drive with the top down, and she strolls and stops in front of the holiday window displays, unhurried as if she is shopping. East past the manicured lawn of the Funeral Parlor and the receding storefront of Eaton's Hardware Store and Caleb's. In the plate glass panels of the Five and Dime and Lotte's Dress Shop, he can see her reflection, and at the Dairy Corner. Windows shuttered against the waxen months of winter and the damp and cold of a day trying to decide if it should snow or rain or both, she turns north onto Spruce Street.

The air smells of fireplaces and bus exhaust and The Missionary Ladies and Ladies Auxiliary sit at tables set up on opposite sidewalks selling cakes and pies, homemade cookies and hot apple cider. The lights are hung. Stars and stripes and snowflakes strung along the telephone lines above his head like garlands the length of Main Street. At night when the bulbs are lit the glare they give off rivals the sun.

From the Dairy Corner she walks two more blocks past Phoebe's Diner and Ray's Barbershop and people stare at him and move away and shake their heads at him as they pass. When she reaches the corner of Dogwood Street, she disappears into a white clapboard house with a sleeping porch on the second story and a sign in the yard that reads Law Offices.

Finest wraps himself inside his jacket and leans and sits against the trunk of an old sycamore tree on the other side of Spruce Street and reaches into his pocket and smokes and drinks and waits for her. Cars brake and slow when they see him there. The occupants inside staring and pointing through the windows as they pass.

His OD's are soiled beyond recognition. The service jacket torn and the pants defecated on. His overcoat and dress shirt along with his tie and hat are gone. His chest is exposed. His arms bare and shivering a little inside his jacket. The moss of hair on his lump and head thickened and matted, and beard growth hides much of his face. All save the scars.

From the north on Spruce Street a woman and little girl approach on the sidewalk.

He puts the bottle away as they stop and cross to the other side of the road. The girl clinging tight to the woman's hand and staring at him over her shoulder.

A Packard drives by and blocks them from view. Four door. The new Clipper. And it honks and after it passes he drags on his cigarette and watches them, the woman and the girl, and he looks around the corner at the streets intersecting and the branches on the trees creaking, at the clapboard and surrounding houses. Not as a soldier who goes off to war and returns to discover everything changed, but as one who returns to find the world the same. Exactly the same as when he left and is forced to keep on fighting.

When she emerges from the clapboard house Sheriff Newsome has him in handcuffs. They wait for her at the curb.

Finest stares at the ground.

The sheriff looks at the house and the sign in the yard.

"Can't have him hangin' around in town like this, Belle."

She looks at him, at Finest...

"Says he was waitin' on you. That right?"

…at the rips in his service jacket, at the handcuffs. His pants.

"If it is and you take him back over The Bone with you, I'll let him go this time. Otherwise I gotta lock him up."

The sheriff turns from the sign and looks at her.

"Was he waitin' on you? Like he says?"

He waits for her to answer.

She nods finally and he unlocks the handcuffs and turns Finest loose.

"Found this on him," he says and he holds up the bottle and looks at him. "Think I'll hang on to it," and sticks it in his pocket. "Imagine it's better off down my throat than his."

When he pulls away from the curb they turn and walk down Dogwood together, toward the primary school to Maple and double back south toward The Bone.

Belle reaches into her purse and lights a cigarette.

Finest walks to the side and behind her a little. Silent.

"You have to stop following me," she says to him.

He walks and rubs his wrists while she smokes.

"You have to cut this out now and clean yourself up. Handle your business."

He coughs and clears his throat and runs a little to keep up with her.

"You know what they did to me over there?"

"Same as you've gotten your whole life, I imagine."

She stops and looks at him. "Same as you'll get until it's through. That's how it works, Finest. We get what we get and we handle it or we don't."

He looks at her, then glances back at the clapboard.

"That him?" he says. "Or work?"

"Is that him what, Finest?"

"The house back there. The lawyer."

She walks.

"I need to know," he says and follows.

On the other side of the primary school they cross Mulberry Street. The stars and stripes again and the snowflakes strung above the intersection of Main Street. A block away at the corner of Elm and Main the sheriff's car is stopped at the curb with the sheriff standing on the sidewalk talking to Hog Simler.

She glances at them and blows the smoke from her mouth into a wispy veil and says, "There's nothing to know, Finest. You have to stop this."

He clears his throat.

"She's mine, it's my right," he says.

"She's not anybody's, Finest," she says to him. "Nobody's. Not even mine."

He looks at her.

When they arrive at Oak they make a quick jog to the right and another to the left and turn onto The Bone.

She turns and faces him.

"I can't take care of you in this, Finest. I'm barely taking care of myself these days."

He blinks at her and twitches.

"We can cross The Bone together," she says. "But as soon as we get to Justice, that's it. No more."

She drags on her cigarette and drops the butt on the ground and grinds it out beneath the sole of her shoe.

Finest watches the ball of her foot twist back and forth on the roadway. His scars twitch as he follows her down onto The Bone.

GUS FITS THE mouth of the gunny sack over the bottom of the filler and pulls the slide away from the wall and holds onto the sack and watches as the creases spread and disappear in the canvas. When it is full he closes the slide and pulls off the bag and sews it and stacks it in the corner with the others, then reaches for another sack.

His hands and face and hat are white with flour. The belt bucket elevators rattle through the shafts as they carry the grain from the holding bins to the grinding area. The ground flour and cornmeal to the sifter and bagger. All around him the walls and the floor vibrate from the torque and roar of the turbine, and above the clatter of it he can hear no sound save the millstones grinding.

He sews another sack and fits another one on the filler and pulls the slide out, and when the room darkens then comes into view again indicating someone has entered and passed under the light, he knows without turning around that that someone is Finest because he can smell him. Standing there behind him. He closes the slide then sews up the bag and stacks it and turns around and wipes off his face and looks at him awhile, then points toward the door and walks to it and reaches into his pocket and punches his time card and sticks it back.

Outside they scramble down the embankment and sit under the clouds. Legs swung over an indent in the dolomite cliffs, and they look down into the gorge at the river. The moon and the stars secreted from view.

Finest reaches inside his jacket and offers him a cigarette.

Gus shakes his head.

Finest smokes. Exhales and clears his throat.

"She ever talk to you?" he says.

"'Bout what?"

"Me?"

"You?"

Gus looks at him.

"Like what?"

Finest shrugs.

"Naw, man. She don't really talk to anyone anymore. 'Bout anything."

"What about Sojourner?"

"What about her?"

"She ever say who the father is?"

"Why? You think it might be you?"

Gus looks at him and laughs and shakes his head, then picks up a rock and lobs it into the gorge. It splashes when it hits the water.

"Just sayin'," says Finest. "Man got a right to know."

"Maybe the man already does," says Gus.

"Meanin'?"

"Maybe he washed his hands of it."

They sit there awhile. Listening to the river. Lobbing rocks and smoking. The turbine spinning and bucket elevators winding in the distance. Thinking about fathers and becoming fathers. Children. A barred owl calls from a tree on the other side of the canyon.

Finest brings his hand to his mouth and clears his throat.

"Was mine, I'd wanna know," he says.

Gus nods and looks at his wristwatch.

"You?" says Finest. He lights another cigarette.

"What? Wanna know?"

Gus throws another rock and thinks about it.

"Yeah. I'd wanna know."

Finest looks at him.

"You ever think about it?" he says.

"What?"

"Children. Family."

"Once," says Gus.

"Yeah? Who with?"

"Girl over at the college," he lies.

"What was her name?"

"Loraine."

Finest tosses his head back and says "Sweet Lo-raine," then twitches and smokes and exhales. "What happened?" he says.

Gus shrugs and stares into the gorge.

"Ain't in college no more," he says.

As they look at each other and laugh, the barred owl calls again and Finest cups his hands to his mouth and clears his throat and hollers back in a voice that grates on the air as if it were mined from the pockmarks of hell and hauled to the surface through a million miles of bedrock.

"Who cooks for you? Who cooks for you all?"

Gus looks at him. "Man, what the hell was that?"

"Call a the owl," says Finest.

"Not no owl I ever heard."

"Who cooks for you?" croaks Finest. "Who cooks for you all?"

They laugh and Gus shakes his head and stands and wipes his hands on his trousers.

Finest takes one last drag on his cigarette then stubs it out with his fingers and drops the unsmoked portion in his pocket.

They walk to the road.

"When you clock out?"

"When the sun comes up."

Gus reaches into his wallet and pulls out a couple of dollar bills and hands them to him.

Finest looks at the money and sticks it in his pocket.

"Schoolboy," he says to him. "Workin' man now."

They look at each other and Finest's eyes wrinkle up as he smiles at him and turns and walks toward The Bone.

"What about you?" Gus calls after him.

He turns around.

"You ever think about it?"

Finest walks backwards and cocks his head a little and grins at him awhile before he answers.

"All the time, Schoolboy," he says. "All the time."

# may 11, 2007

The air has thinned. Though it is no less hot. Outside the sun bakes the earth and the men. Clearing away the rubble still. The trucks beeping. A light reluctant breeze flows through the windows and cools the skin. The sky is clear and blue save a few white patches of cloud and the silhouettes of hawks soaring. Buzzards circling and rising on the currents.

Gus turns off the fire under the ham hocks and pours the water into the sink and cleans and strips the meat from the bones and stirs it in with the collard greens and kale. Onions and chicken broth simmering on the stove.

Sojourner is on her cell phone with Mr. Dixon's answering service.

"Sojourner Weesfree," she speaks into the receiver. "No… Weesfree."

Gus watches her.

She nods her head, then shakes it, then waits.

"No," she says and waits. "Wees-free… Yes! Four-one-five. Three-oh-eight. Five-five-eight-two… Yes… No."

She flips the phone closed and looks at it, then slides it back into her pocket and walks into the dining room where she sits at the end of the table and stares into the sitting room at the television set, at Finest. The handcuffs.

"I hate those damned automated operators," she says.

Gus puts the lid on the greens and checks on the coffee and brings it into the dining room and pours them each a cup and sits in the chair opposite and studies her.

Her hands are different. Larger. Her jaw stronger. The almond shape of her eyes a dead on match.

"He used to watch me," she says.

The voice as if she were calling to them from the other side of the grave.

"When I was older and Auntie Mabel would send me to town by myself or give me a dollar to go to the movies. He'd stand across the street and stare at me when I was coming out of Caleb's. Sit on the bench down from the movie theater and wait for me. At first I was horrified by him. My friends and I used to call him names and run the other direction whenever we saw him coming. Then after awhile I got used to seeing him there and he didn't bother me as much and I started watching him back. When I asked Auntie Mabel what happened to him, why he was so ugly, she ordered me to keep away from him and made me promise to tell her if he tried to talk to me. And if he touched me ever, she said I was to go straight to Sheriff Newsome."

She turns to Gus and smiles at him.

"Of course, that only made me more curious. So I started making up excuses. Reasons to go into town alone and seek him out."

She turns back to Finest and shakes her head a little.

"The first time he spoke to me I turned and ran all the way to the end of The Bone without once looking back over my shoulder, and weeks passed before I got up the nerve to go into town on my own again."

"What did he say to you?"

She looks across the table and stares at him. Startled as if she forgot that he was sitting there. Where she was.

"What? Oh... Sojourner," she says. "He said my name. Scared me so bad I had nightmares about it. That gnarled and grating voice. Churning my name over and over like a coffee grinder. Coming out of that face. Felt like somebody was dragging a rake over my skin. Over my whole body."

She looks at him, at Finest, and shivers.

"Then one day I went into the library to return some books I had borrowed. When I came out he was waiting for me across the street. There was nothing about that day different from any of the others. But for some reason on that one I wasn't scared. I don't know. Something about the way he was just standing there maybe with his hands in his pockets. He seemed safe to me. I have no idea why I thought that. He stood no less menacing than on those other days. Those other days I didn't even have to look at him. Just knowing he was there and that he was there for me made me run. But that day, instead of running away from him I crossed the street and went right up and talked to him. Surprised him almost as much as I surprised myself. How do you know my name? I asked him. He stood there and looked at me and his face scrunched up like he was squinting into the sun when he smiled down at me. He said Everybody knows the name of the most beautiful girl in the world. After that, whenever I came to town alone, he would walk me to wherever I was going, then wait for me and walk me back when I came out. He never said much of anything. Just walked. With his head down, and looked at me once in a while.

"After I left for school and moved to San Francisco and got caught up with life, I pretty much forgot about him. Then right before Auntie Mabel told me he died, I received a letter from an attorney in town with a cashier's check enclosed for several thousand dollars. Explaining that it was a gift from the estate of Mr. Finest Coon. Until I received that letter I hadn't even known his name was Finest. He was always just Old Man Coon to us.

"When I called the lawyer and told him I thought there had been a mistake, he assured me there had not. And when I called Auntie Mabel and asked if she knew how to get in touch with Mr. Coon, she told me that he had died. I'd always meant to return it. The check to the attorney. It was too much money. But then Auntie Mabel's legs started swelling up and she couldn't work anymore and I fell behind on the property tax payments and there was this check. And the man who gave it to me was dead." She stops and looks at the floor, then back at Finest. "That check kept us from losing this house."

At first the gunshots sound as if they are coming from the television. Like cars backfiring down an alley, and it is not until the explosion of the third shot that either of them registers the noise as coming from Mabel's bedroom. And when they move finally to investigate, it is in slow motion, as if they know what they heard. Have had what they heard confirmed and supported by corroborating witnesses, but there is just no way. No way in the world that what they are hearing could possibly be happening, and by the time they push through the door, she has fired a fourth shot and put a hole through the window to go along with the three in the walls and she sits there in the room in the bed. Eyes wild and sweat pouring from her face, and when they enter she looks at them as if she is frightened for her life and her hands tremble as she cocks the trigger and points the gun at Sojourner.

Gus stops inside the doorway and stares at her, at the gun barrel. Snubbed nosed. Jumping around in her hands.

Sojourner raises her arms in the air and glances around the room at the holes in the walls and ceiling as if she is in the movies and has been told to freeze, and the gun barrel is pointed at her back rather than threatening to go off in her face.

"Auntie Mabel," she says quietly. "Auntie Mabel. Put the gun down."

"Couldn't stay dead could you!?" Mabel yells at her.

The gun shakes and Gus closes his eyes as if he is dreaming and expects the room to return to normal when he opens them again.

"Auntie Mabel," whispers Sojourner.

"Couldn't stay gone! Couldn't stay dead!" says Mabel.

They stand there and look at her, at the gun.

"How many times you gotta get killed?" she says. "'Fore you stay in the ground?"

She aims the gun.

"She was better off without you. We all were. If you'd a just stayed gone."

Sojourner's voice is barely audible and like the gun barrel trembles when she speaks.

"Please, Auntie Mabel," she says. "Please put down the gun. It's just us," she says. "Sojourner and Uncle Gus here. Nobody else."

The doorbell is ringing.

"Please, Auntie Mabel."

A voice hollers from the porch.

"Mabel! Mr. Weesfree!"

It's Sheriff Newsome.

"Auntie Mabel."

"Everything alright in there, Mabel? Got a call some of the workers out here heard gun shots fired!"

Mabel juggles the gun and looks at them, at Gus, at the window. The bullet hole through the glass.

Sojourner looks at her and locks on to her eyes and takes a step toward her and reaches out her hand to her.

"Please, Auntie Mabel," she says and she takes another step and holds her hand out. "Let me have the gun and everything will be alright. No California, I promise. We'll all stay right here."

"If you don't open the door for me, Mabel, we're gonna have to bust it."

Gus watches and braces himself in the doorway as Sojourner closes her eyes and lowers her hand down and rests it on the barrel.

Mabel stares at her and draws back from her a little.

"It's okay, Auntie Mabel," says Sojourner. "It's okay," and when she eases the pistol away from her, though the sheriff still yells and the television blares in the other room, the world quiets around them as if releasing a long-held breath.

SHE DIDN'T EXPECT it to jump like that. Her body. When she grabbed the gun and asked Sister Tremble to sit with the baby and she saw the car parked on the side of The Bone headed back home and she found her there in the woods. When she pointed the gun at her and confronted her about the baby. About Finest being the father, and cocked and pulled the trigger, she didn't expect her arm to jerk up and her shoulder to pop and her feet to rock back on their heels the way they did from the force of it. Nor did she expect it to be so loud. To ring out and echo through the woods like that, nor for the second shot to ring out louder than the first. She didn't expect the bullet to travel so fast through the air and rip through and take out a chunk of her head the way it did, or for that look to freeze on her face. That smile as if she were thanking her for finally putting her out of her misery, and she did not expect her stomach to churn and turn on her that way that she would double over and retch when she crumbled to the ground and the life went out of her, nor for her legs to be so heavy and her feet to drag behind her like chains and shackles as she walked to the car and left her there. How difficult it would be to keep from turning around and looking back. To put the gun down on the seat and drive the car home. Walk into the house and stash it under the mattress. Thank Sister Tremble for sitting. Get supper on and feed the baby. And feed the baby! And look at her! Look at her! And straighten and turn down the house for slumber. How reluctant sleep would come. Eluding her for years before she got a hold on it. How the shots would keep ringing and echoing in her ears the rest of her life. That look on her face. Her body crumbling. That the only place she would find respite would be at the bottom of a bottle of creek water. That in all the world as the years wore on there would never be enough bottles.


FINEST WATCHED HER pass in the Model T and turn onto The Bone and followed behind her in case she stopped, and when he finally caught up to it, the car parked on the edge of the road, and heard the shots fired and saw Mabel coming out of the woods by herself and drive away alone in it, he hung back and waited until she was gone, then entered the woods where she emerged and followed the path. And when he found her there, crumpled and lifeless on the ground, a sound rose up from his lungs that he had never heard before. From human or any other animal, and he stood there and his legs chilled and numbed as he listened to it and his chest heaved and caved and ached as if someone had drilled a hole through it and all life at that moment shrank back and fled from the agony in it and the sky rumbled and darkened over his head and the wind kicked up and swirled and howled along with it, and when the feeling returned to his legs, he went to her and fell to his knees and held her there and rocked her, and after awhile he lay her back down and turned her on her side and he put his mouth to her ear and he whispered to her, to her soul. To calm it as she crossed.

GUS HEARD THE shots and came up from the millrace, from cleaning the grate over the turbine, and followed the sound into the woods and when he saw Finest a ways up ahead of him, bending over something in a thicket of walnut and tulip poplar, he quickened his pace, then slowed when he saw what it was he was bending over and his feet crunched over the earth under his feet. The brush and the twigs snapping and the sky rumbled as he pulled up short of the thicket and stared at him.

Finest heard something behind him and stood and faced him.

He was covered in blood as was the body at his feet.

"What happened?" said Gus when he found his voice and he stared at him, at the body on the ground. The brush beneath it saturated with blood.

Finest stood before him and tore up his face and tried to answer, but when he opened his mouth all that came out was the sound that he had never heard before and their skin goosed as they stood there together and listened to it, and when it stopped finally the wind swirled and howled in its place and Finest ran.

Gus went to Belle's body and saw the chunk missing from her head and the smile frozen on her face. The blood staining her dress, and he kneeled there and reached for her. The ropes of her hair. Wet and sticky with blood like sweat, and he wrapped the strands around his fingers and he looked at her, at her eyes open. Lips smiling, and he remembered the first time he saw that smile. In the kitchen at the table when he came in from seeing the blackbirds. And he kneeled there and he looked at her, fingering the ropes of her hair, and as he thought about birds and migrations and lay-ups and stopovers, he began to cry.

SIX DAYS LATER Sheriff Newsome came around to tell them they found the body and ask a few questions.

No, sir. They hadn't seen her in days.

Not particularly. She was always going and coming. Staying away for months sometimes.

Yes, sir.

No, sir.

They didn't see much of Finest Coon these days either. Not since he returned from the war.

When the neighbors confirmed her comings and goings and the absence in a long while of Finest Coon around the neighborhood, the sheriff apologized for their loss and for disturbing them and told them he would do everything he could to catch whoever did this to her. Nobody mentioned that on the day she left and took the car, Mabel was the one who drove it home. Alone. They didn't mention it because the sheriff never asked.

As they could find no family to notify or claim her effects, the clothing she was wearing was burned in the morgue incinerator. Her body buried in the county potter's field.

The case remained open for twenty-five years before it was closed, finally, unsolved.


THE DOCTOR INJECTS the sedative into Mabel's arm and tells her to rest, then walks into the kitchen with Sojourner and Gus and listens as the sheriff takes each of their statements. Luke sits in the sitting room on the sofa in front of the television with Finest.

"I think she's just been under so much strain lately," says Sojourner. "The fall and Uncle Gus coming back and not wanting to move to California. I think... you know and the medicine, it kind of all just got to her. I really don't think she's a threat to anybody. Certainly not to me." She nods to herself. "I think she was just overwhelmed by everything and now that she no longer has the gun…"

"Do you know where she got it?"

"I didn't even know she had it. And I certainly would never have let her keep it if I had."

When he finishes with his questions and closes his notebook, Doc Rawlins tells them the shot he gave her ought to keep her out awhile and hands Sojourner another prescription. He also hands her a business card and says he wants her to call the number on it and arrange for a psychiatric evaluation just to be on the safe side.

Sojourner takes the card and says she'll call first thing in the morning.

"You planning on sticking around awhile?" he asks her.

She nods. "Oh, yes," she says. "We're not going anywhere."

After they leave, when Luke offers to drive into town and fill the prescription, Sojourner thanks him and Gus rides along with him to get some air.

He sits in the passenger seat with the window down and watches the steering wheel spin back and forth as Luke navigates the turns around The Bone.

"Lot to come home to, I guess," says Luke.

Gus nods his head and thinks *you don't know the half of it.*

Luke drives.

"Finest seems like he's doin' alright," he says. "I see you shaved his beard off."

Gus nods.

"Probably a lot cooler for him. He sure does like that television, don't he?"

He nods again and tenses as they pass the old mill road and the overgrown lot where the mill used to be.

"He say anything yet?" says Luke.

Gus shakes his head.

"Thought maybe he might a told you where the money was. Sure you all could use it about now."

Gus looks out the window.

"Knowing Finest he probably burned it for firewood."

"There is no money."

Luke looks at him.

"He had a lawyer draw up a cashier's check awhile back and sent it all to Sojourner. She used it to pay the back taxes on the house."

Luke rolls to the stop sign at Oak and sits there a moment. Thinking. The engine idling. The sun high and shadowless. The wind calm.

He shakes his head. "Well, I guess that's that then," he says.

He steps on the accelerator and turns on to Oak Street. "I told Daniel it wasn't in the house. He wouldn't listen to me. Went through that place top to bottom and never found it. Ended up being the death of him. Even tore out the walls. Poor Finest was spooked something silly. Felt so bad for him, I took him in to live with me."

Gus looks at him.

"Wonder why he gave it to Sojourner," says Luke.

Gus stares through the window.

Luke pulls up in front of the drug store and presses a button on the armrest and unlocks the doors. "Maybe it was his way of tryin' to repay you all for takin' him in after... you know, help you all out. Her mother bein' your sister and all."

HE FEELS HIS way through the dark and reaches in the drawer under the silverware tray and stuffs the money into his pockets. In the distance coyotes yelp and howl down by the river as he places the handcuff keys on the table and the chimes ring muted from age as he leaves. He slides into the car and releases the emergency brake and lets the Edsel roll back a ways toward the deserted road before he starts the engine. But when he reaches the corner of Justice, instead of turning right toward The Bone he turns left toward what used to be Prosper. When they finish the construction the new street will be called Green Valley Parkway.

He turns onto Prosper and stops the car at the end of the street and sits there. The headlights shine on the foundation and framework of the new floor model Dix will use to attract prospective buyers. A field mouse scoots across the ground through the beams of the headlights.

Deep down, he guesses, he always knew Finest was So's father. Always knew Belle was his sister, too, if he's honest. Hard not to with all the rumors flying around. On both sides of town. Turns out they all knew, even Mabel. Though it never stopped them from falling in love with her.

He clenches his jaw and stares at the home under construction where the church used to be and thinks about the gunshots. He had come home hoping to give her peace. But the knowledge that Finest was Sojourner's father, that it was the Coon boy Belle chose instead of her was too much and he realizes now that peace was never his to give.

WHEN DAY BREAKS he is still in the car. The coyotes are back in their den for the day. He sits there and stares through the window and watches the sun come up. The sky awakening. And after awhile he opens the door and steps out.

Sojourner is on her cell phone when he enters. He smells coffee.

"They're charging her with a misdemeanor for having an unlicensed firearm," she says into the receiver. She has a pencil in her hand and waves it at him and points to the stove at the coffee pot. "I'm pretty sure the charges will be dropped. Once they see how old she is and understand the circumstances."

"I'm going to stay," she says into the phone. "At least for awhile. With Uncle Gus and Mr. Coon here now there's a lot to attend to and Sheriff Newsome gave me the number to a nonprofit that might be able to have this place listed on the National Register of Historic Places. Turns out this whole area was once Shawnee country. Might even be able to get a job there if I play my cards right."

He pours a cup of coffee and walks into the dining area and sits at the table.

Finest is on the sofa. Staring at him. The handcuffs are gone. The television silent.

"I know," says Sojourner into the phone. "I miss you, too. We'll figure it out."

Gus looks at him, at the hat on his head. The pajamas and shoes with no laces or socks. The cane. Stubble shadows darken his misshapen face.

Finest looks back at him and blinks.

"What's up, Superman?" says Gus and he takes a sip of his coffee. "No TV today? Guess it does get dull after awhile. Same ol' same ol', day-in and day-out."

Finest watches him and licks and chews his lips, then licks them again and swallows.

"Schoolboy," he whispers in that gnarled and grated voice, even scratchier now from so many years of disuse, and his face scrunches up and his scars twitch and jump and his head cocks back as he smiles.

# ACKNOWLEDGEMENTS

Special thanks to my family (biological and chosen). My agent, Amy Tipton. Lynn Vannucci, Charlotte Wyatt and the rest of the crew at Water Street Press. And the following individuals whose raining encouragement, belief and support helped to make this book possible: Harriet, Betty, Shelly, Jr., Shelly Kirk, Teri, Milton, Diana, Chissey, and Shereen.

# About the Author

Marci Blackman's first novel, *Po Man's Child*, was awarded the American Library Association's Stonewall prize for Best Fiction as well as the Firecracker Alternative Book Award for Best New Fiction. Blackman also edited the Lambda-nominated anthology, *Beyond Definition: New Writing from Gay and Lesbian San Francisco*, and, as an avid cyclist, was the author of the popular bicycling guide, *Bike NYC: The Cyclist's Guide to New York City*. *Tradition* is Blackman's second novel. Blackman lives and writes in Brooklyn, NY.

# READERS GUIDE

In her second novel, author Marci Blackman takes read-
ers back in time with the Weesfree family, in the rural
Ohio town of Tradition. The story travels backwards and
forwards in the lives of Gus and Mabel as they try to
reconcile themselves to the events of their past. Through
*Tradition*, Blackman expands on themes she explored in
her first novel, *Po Man's Child*, which won the American
Library Association's Stonewall prize for Best Fiction as
well as the Firecracker Alternative Book Award for Best
New Fiction.

# READING GROUP QUESTIONS AND TOPICS FOR DISCUSSION

1. THE ACTION of the story takes place in both the 1930s and '40s, as well as in present time (2007). Why do you think the author used this narrative device? Could the story have been told any other way?

2. THE NOVEL begins with an epigram, defining the word tradition. In what ways does the author use the concept of tradition—the force exerted by the past upon the present—to shape her characters and their relationships?

3. WHY DO you think *Tradition* is divided into three "Books"?

4. How DOES the relationship between Mabel and Finest change throughout the story? How did their childhoods compare?

5. AT THE beginning of the story, Gus returns to Tradition as an outsider, but each character has a reason to feel excluded, or "other", at least once in the narrative. How does this exploration of "otherness" contribute to the overall themes in Tradition?

6. WHERE DO the Simlers fit in this world of "otherness"? How is "otherness" impacted by race? Or is it?

7. Is THERE a difference in the racial and political climates of the 30s and 40s vs. today?

8. How DO animals and the natural world contribute to the themes of Tradition?

9. WHAT DO you think prompted Belle to seek out the Weesfrees? What prompted her to leave, and return?

10. WHAT ROLE does addictive behavior play in the story?

11. WHAT DO you make of the character of Sister Tremble? Her relationship with Mabel?

12. CONSIDER THE role of privilege in the story—from the ability to stay safe and fed, or go to school, to the ability to take a life. Who is the most powerful character? The least? How does this influence the fate of each character?

13. WHY DO you think the author chose to tear down most of Tradition in the present-day narrative?

14. How HAS Tradition changed the way you think about the relationship between the past and the present?

# Q&A WITH MARCI BLACKMAN

Marci Blackman lives and writes in Brooklyn, New York, but finished writing Tradition while living in a turn-of-the-century mansion on an Ohio nature preserve. Here she answers some questions about her process and the inspiration behind her second novel.

*Why did you choose this particular setting and time period to tell this story?*

Growing up I was fortunate enough to spend a lot of time with my grandmothers (both lived into their 90s), and their sisters and sister's husbands. These would have been my great aunts and uncles. Together with my parents and their siblings, they are the people who shaped me, or, rather, gave me the room and a safe place to shape myself. Their lives were hard, but they never complained about it. In fact, they often laughed, mostly at themselves. They came of age in the late 20s and 30s, just in time for the Depression and World War II. An awakening of sorts in our history, I think. I wanted to write about that time, about people who lived during that time.

As far as setting goes, I was born and raised in southern Ohio, and always knew that I would set a story there, both for the beauty of the landscape, and because of its close proximity to Kentucky, the South. Aside from quadrennial visits by presidential candidates, Ohio kind of ambles along without scrutiny. The landscape then, both natural and constructed, offers an abundance of grist from which to create.

*Why did you decide on this style of narrative in Tradition, both the "time travel," and the division into three books?*

I believe that nothing happens in a vacuum. Every moment of our lives is preceded and followed by other moments, which in turn are preceded and followed by others. This is not to suggest that we have no control, no choice nor the ability to change course or outcome (although some might argue as much), but every time we interact with someone, whether a stranger on the street, or close friend or family member, that interaction is influenced by the events and encounters that occurred in the moments leading up to it. Too often, I think, we lose sight of that fact, both in our daily stumblings upon one another, and in the larger continuing discourse on how we treat each other and go about creating a world that respects and embraces difference. The back and forth narrative in Tradition, or "time travel", as you say, is my attempt to capture the interdependent relationships between all the moments.

Breaking the novel into three books was more instinctual than anything else. Though after reading through the first draft I realized the story I was telling was a trinity of sorts, and the division into three books seemed to draw that to the surface.

*In general, your work focuses on the "Other" in society, but in Tradition you seem to create a cast of "others" in a community already deemed "other" itself. Can you talk a bit about this other inside the other, and why you are drawn to these types of characters?*

As an other-gendered, nonconformist queer person of color, I tend to occupy the "other-within-other" corner in nearly every room I enter. This is not a complaint, I actually enjoy this place; for the most part, it makes things a bit more interesting. Sometimes too interesting. Over the years, I have come to recognize that I am not alone here, that there are a lot of others-within-others moving about the world. For whatever reason, the mainstream dictates don't really work for us, and we are, as a result, forced to get creative in the mapping of our journeys through life. It is this creativity that attracts me, both in the people with whom I choose to surround myself, and the characters I opt to bring to life on the page. I have also observed, the more I explore this place and the people who reside here, that an intriguing pathology of human nature emerges: that even in disparate groups, there is always a mainstream, dominant way of thinking, and there is always a fringe.

*How has living in such disparate places as a nature preserve in Ohio and the middle of New York City influenced your writing?*

Ha! Actually, they are not so disparate. Both settings in their own way are jungles. When I packed up everything and moved to the woods, my cousin called and asked how I was adjusting to the quiet. "What quiet?" I responded. What I discovered living in the woods is that nature is anything but quiet. It is loud and boisterous and goes about its business like a bustling city. Instead of big towering buildings, there are big towering trees, with all different kinds of creatures scurrying about, creating, building things, and having sex below. And like a big city, nature does things on its own timetable, whether you adapt to it or not. As a writer, both remind me to "remember the room," or in this case, the world. That as much as we try to carve out our own private niches, it's not really possible to shut it out. Like it or not, our environment impacts us, influencing the choices we make, the way we do things.

*Do you believe literature has a social obligation?*

Yes, but more importantly, I believe that literature, whether fiction or nonfiction, has an obligation to tell the truth. If we succeed in that aim, the social debt will be met.

*Can you talk a bit about craft, and the way you like to work?*

I am asked about craft a lot, and my answer is always the same. I treat writing like a fulltime job. I am not one of those writers who can spit on a page and produce something gorgeous. I work at it by doing it, even when I don't feel like it, even when the thoughts and words aren't flowing so well. I took a workshop once where the instructor told us that in order to get to the meat, you have to cut through the fat. In other words, sometimes you have to write the bad stuff out of you in order to make room for the good. I have found that I do my best work alone, with no one else in the room. In fact, whenever I look for a new place to live, I am drawn to apartments and homes that are dark and quiet. My friends often comment that I live in a cave. It's true, the isolation makes it easier for me to dissolve into the worlds I'm creating.

*What prompted you to become a writer? Who are your influences?*

I am the youngest of four children. Often, as a kid, it was difficult to get a word in edgewise. Eventually, I discovered it was easier to gather and express my thoughts if I wrote them down. Officially, I wrote my first short story when I was eleven years old. We had just finished reading Hound of the Baskervilles, by Sir Arthur Conan Doyle, in my sixth-grade creative writing class—yes, I took creative writing in the sixth grade—and our homework assignment was to write our own detective story a la Sherlock Holmes. I took the assignment one step further and wrote what—in my sixth-grade mind—I thought would have been the sequel to Baskervilles, if Conan Doyle had lived to write it. In time, as my taste in literature matured, I discovered that the stories I really wanted to read weren't being written (or published, perhaps), so I decided to write them. Although I am constantly discovering new work and writers, the mainstays of my influences are in no particular order: Gabriel Garcia Marquez, Toni Morrison, William Faulkner, James Baldwin, Zora Neal Hurston, Ernest Hemingway, Alice Walker, Maya Angelou, and Junot Diaz to name a few. I am also continually inspired by my own contemporaries: Michelle Tea, Ali Liebegott, Mecca Jamilah Sullivan, G. Winston James, Sharon Bridgforth, Thomas Glave, and Randall Kenan, among others.

***How has the recognition for your first novel (the Stonewall Prize, and the Firecracker Best New Fiction Award) affected your career?***

Honestly, I'm not really sure. I believe it has opened some doors, and I know that Po is or has been taught in many curriculums, which is nice. But I think a number of people have been waiting to see what I write next. Hopefully, I haven't disappointed.

# OTHER BOOKS FROM WATER STREET PRESS

## *Virgins & Martyrs*
### A NOVEL

Hugh Mahoney

New Yorkers open their Sunday morning paper to find a photo of Virgil Quinn, teacher of history at St. Lucy's School for Boys, splashed all over the front page. How did he get there? Scandal, of course. Virgil has made enemies—the Cardinal of New York not the least among them. The Cardinal's research reveals that Virgil has lived many lives, all of them scandalous. Was he really a ranking nun in the Sisters of Mercy of Baton Rouge? Did he really walk the ramps of Seventh Avenue as the city's highest paid supermodel? Just how did he come to know all those men whose names appear in his notorious (and deadly convenient) Black Books? *Virgins & Martyrs* is shrewd and malicious fun, a wicked commentary on love, life, gender and the history of our nation, a work in which the peripatetic and intrepid—yet all-too-human—Virgil Quinn lets no one off the hook.

## *Stalking Carlos Castaneda*
NONFICTION

### Joan Wulfsohn

In 1972, professional dancer Joan Wulfsohn underwent a double mastectomy. And her soon-to-be-ex-husband abducted their three children and spirited them away to a foreign country. "I should have died," Joan writes. But she didn't. Stalking Carlos Castaneda chronicles her journey back to life by way of lessons learned from stunning transvestites and music hall dancers, teen porn stars, a brain-damaged boy, Eastern holy men, Western supermodels and a certain aging sorcerer. It is the story of how one woman learned to live a magical life—bound not by spells and hexes but rather filled with wonder and transcendence.

## The Happy Party of Honorable Women

FICTION

### Cate Quintara

Jill's daughter is getting married. The two women with whom Jill has been best friends since they were little girls—Deanie, a successful novelist, and Trick, who struggles with bipolar disorder—arrive to help celebrate the happy event. The bride, however, has a bigger role than "wedding guest" in mind for them all—she has decided she will make up her wedding party by honoring the women who raised and nurtured her.

Throughout the week of pre-nuptial parties, Jill and Deanie and Trick relive the events that have shaped their lifelong friendship—their marriages and relationships, the births and losses of their children, the tragedies and joys that have forged their bond. The women discover the true depths of this bond—and how the wish of one unconventional young bride has transformed them all.

Cate Quintara invites you to be a guest at a unique and wonderful wedding, and to celebrate a jubilant life milestone—one made possible only because of the lifetimes of ordinary, everyday love that have preceded it.

## *Creole Son*

FICTION

## Michael Llewellyn

In 1872, French painter Edgar Degas is disillusioned by a lackluster career and haunted by the Prussian siege of Paris and the bloodbath of the Commune. Seeking personal and professional rebirth, he journeys to New Orleans, birthplace of his Creole mother. He is horrified to learn he has exchanged one city in crisis for another—post-Civil War New Orleans is a corrupt town occupied by hostile Union troops and suffering under the heavy hand of Reconstruction. He is further shocked to find his family deeply involved in the violent struggle to reclaim political power at all costs.

Despite the chaos swirling around him, Degas sketches and paints with fervor and manages to reinvent himself and transition his style from neoclassical into the emerging world of Impressionism. He ultimately became one of the masters of the new movement, but how did New Orleans empower Degas to fulfill this destiny?

The answer may be found in the impeccably researched, richly imagined historical novel, Creole Son.

## *The Muffia*
### Ann Royal Nicholas

Madelyn Scott-Crane is a smart, 42-year-old professional mediator and single mom who's having the best
sex of her life—after twenty-two months of self-im-
posed abstinence—inspired by the ladies of her book
club, The Muffia, and the Muff's latest racy read. But
on their second date, as Maddie and her mysterious Is-
raeli heartthrob, Udi, come together in orgasmic splen-
dor that may or may not also be actual love, Udi collapses on top of her. Dead. When Udi's "friends"—who
resemble large appliances—arrive to claim his body, the
Muffs decide that Udi had secrets, and they need to
know what those secrets were. That's when these well-
read women put down their books and set out to expose the truth—whatever the dangerous truth might be.
International intrigue combines with literary pursuits,
lots of home-cooked food, and a little vibrator shopping.
One book club, seven women with seven stories, more
than seven fabulous meals and at least seven sex scenes
all wrapped up in one smart, sexy novel that's just this
side of scandalous.

Made in the USA
San Bernardino, CA
28 December 2015